SOHLBERG AND THE MISSING SCHOOLBOY:

AN INSPECTOR SOHLBERG MYSTERY

JENS AMUNDSEN

ISBN-13: 978-1477528099
ISBN-10: 1477528091

DEDICATION

This book is dedicated to Kyron Horman and all the other missing and exploited children who must be found and protected or given a full measure of justice.

A Vik Crime/Blue Salamander Edition 2012

New translation with added material by the author.

Although inspired by real events, this book is a work of fiction. Any resemblance to any living person is purely coincidental except that specific references to real institutions and people (such as Norway's serial predator *Lommemannen* The Pocket Man) are for historical purposes only.

Published in the United States by special arrangement of Nynorsk Forlag [Trondheim, Norway] with Nynorsk Forlag-USA/Blue Salamander [Seattle, WA]. Originally published as *Death on Pilot Hill* by Nynorsk Forlag in 2011.

FIRST U.S. EDITION

Author information:
www.deadlybooks.com
www.jensamundsen.blogspot.com

Book information:
www.deadlybooks.com
www.nynorskforlag.blogspot.com

Please send publisher and author inquiries to: nynorsk@ymail.com

Printed and Manufactured in the United States of America

Also by Jens Amundsen

[*Inspector Sohlberg series*]

White Death in Tromsø

Lost in Bergen

Skull Valley

The Trondheim Choir

CONTENTS

PART ONE: DEAD END 1

PART TWO: THE INVESTIGATION 91

PART THREE: DOORS OF PERCEPTION 173

PART ONE: DEAD END

A man can be destroyed but not defeated.

— Ernest Hemingway

Chapter 1/Én

MORNING OF THE DAY, FRIDAY, JUNE 4

The world promised much to Karl Haugen, a shy 7-year old. He knew a lot for his age. He knew from first-hand experience that the world promised good and evil and that the world delivered good and evil in unexpected and unequal amounts. Life despite its shortness taught him that nothing was what it appeared to be. That's why he liked to study icebergs.

In the school gymnasium he turned to his school friend Einar Lund and said:

"I wanted to do my project on icebergs . . . not on red-eye tree frogs."

Icebergs reminded him of the people in his life. They appeared to be one thing above the surface but deep below they were quite different if not dangerous. He knew all about icebergs and how one iceberg had ripped open the thick steel hull of the *Titanic* before sending it and more than 1500 passengers to a frigid and watery grave. He definitely wanted to do his science fair exhibit on icebergs. After all the floating blocks of ice have always been an important part of the north Atlantic Ocean that his Viking ancestors sailed on for centuries. But his father and stepmother Agnes stopped him.

"No . . . don't be silly," said his stepmother a month ago when he first proposed a science project on icebergs. "Do it on frogs. Everyone in Norway prefers a science fair exhibit on something warm and cute from the tropics."

"Icebergs?" said his father later that evening. "No. It's best to do it on the red-eye frogs that we have recently read about in the newspaper. They're real cute . . . like Agnes says. Don't forget my boy . . . people always like cute living things like frogs and not dead cold things like icebergs."

Karl hated switching from icebergs to frogs. But orders were orders at the Haugen household and now that his science project was done the thin little boy with glasses looked forward to spending most of the summer with his mother and her husband up in Namsos a small town north of Trondheim. Only three more weeks of school remained before school ended for eight weeks of heavenly summer vacations.

"Karl . . . you made a very good project," said Inga Lund the mother of his friend and classmate Einar.

"Thank you Mrs. Lund," he said pleased but not surprised that everyone seemed to like the science project that his father and stepmother had chosen for him.

Mrs. Lund smiled and pulled out her camera. She waved at them so that she could take a picture of him and Einar next to the pictures and drawings and written information that Karl and his stepmother had carefully glued to a tall poster. The poster and dozens of other exhibits rested precariously on a long table. Mrs. Lund aimed the camera and said:

"Move a little to the right Karl so we can see the mini-jungle you made in the shoe box . . . it looks so real with the trees and the river and the frog! Very good!"

Karl Haugen smiled confidently as the flash came on for his picture. He felt happy at how the adult guests (almost 200 of them) had stopped to look at his exhibit and comment favorably on his project. Teachers and fellow schoolmates also reacted well to his red-eye tree frog project at the annual science fair that Grindbakken Skole always held toward the end of each school year. The second-grader wondered how long his happiness would last.

"Thank you for coming," shouted the principal at exactly 8:40 AM. "Five more minutes! Parents . . . family . . . and friends . . . please say your goodbyes and get ready to leave in five minutes . . . we want to begin our first class at nine o'clock sharp."

Everyone smiled and laughed and hugged and took pictures that would soon be posted on Facebook and other websites on the Internet. Everyone looked so happy and healthy and prosperous and loved. But the little boy knew that no life is perfect even if it seems to be so.

Chapter 2/To

AFTER THE SCIENCE FAIR,
FRIDAY JUNE 4
AND SATURDAY JUNE 5

On Friday June 4th at nine in the morning the old man prepared his coffee. He looked out of his living room window and he noticed the white pickup parked for a third time in as many days where his street Orreveien curled into a dead end.

His family had lived for five generations on one of the many hills around Lake Bogstad. As an only child he inherited the large farm from his parents in 1952 when his widowed mother died. At the time the remote wooded hills northwest of Oslo felt like the end of the world.

Holmenkollen was the nearest village and it was as close as he got to a city when he was a child. He and his parents never ventured into Oslo. They only watched the distant city lights at night from their vantage point on the "roof of Oslo". The farms around Holmenkollen stand over Oslo at 500 meters (1640 feet) above sea level. Over the decades the farmers watched with jealousy and fear as the night lights of distant Oslo slowly came closer and closer to them. The forest-clad hills of Holmenkollen were now merely suburbs of Oslo and highly desirable locations in the wealthy Vestre Aker borough of the city as a result of being less than 10 miles from downtown Oslo.

The old man whispered to himself. "Why is that

strange car parking there? . . . Why do I have to be surrounded by all these professional people pretending to be rich people? Engineers . . . lawyers . . . strange people with too much money and time on their hands . . . up to no good."

He deeply regretted his decision to sell large chunks of land to developers who had built luxury homes and condominiums all around his farm. In hindsight his worst decision was selling 40 acres in 1980 to the Norway Medical Association which then built the Soria Moria Hotel and Conference Center in 1983 at the site of the old Voksenkollen Sanatorium for rich people.

The NMA's modern luxury hotel complex was less than a half-mile northeast from his home and hotel guests frequently trespassed on his land and they enraged him whenever they went "exploring" in the woods that surround his modest cottage. The old man did not like anyone parking on Orreveien because it reminded him that he had sold off most of his inheritance. He was now surrounded by noisy and nosy neighbors and way too much traffic.

Why had the mysterious driver parked the pickup truck for a third time that week on the circle of the dead end street? What was the driver doing there?

Two days ago the driver had stopped at the same spot and let the engine run on idle for more than an hour. Who would waste precious gasoline like that?

"What is that idiot doing?" he said loudly to himself. "Damn nuisance!"

Dag Svendsen yelled as if his strong manly voice could magically carry itself over the air to the nearest police station. He always shouted when he realized that he really should have a telephone.

But who could afford a telephone?

He had never owned a telephone or other such luxuries. Never. He did not even own a phone in the 1990s when he and his late wife made a bundle selling off most of the farm. The Svendsens did not even own a car until 1971 and then they only bought a dilapidated 1939 Mercedes Benz sedan.

Of course that was the old Norway. The Norway of Scrimp and Save. The Good Old Days when people sacrificed much to have little. When you worked hard and did not put on airs. But the new Norway was a whole other planet for him. Everything was different nowadays in Norway. And so expensive!

Since 1970 a flood of oil revenues from the North Sea had poured massive wealth into the nation and changed the people forever. Now everyone had too much money and good homes and clothes and vacations and cars and telephones and even the tiny new portable cell phones that supposedly took pictures and searched the Internet just like a computer.

Dag Svendsen took out his old Zeiss binoculars to get a good look at the frivolous person who drove such an ostentatious and enormous vehicle which certainly did *not* look like any European car. Although he could not determine if the driver was a man or a woman Herr Svendsen was certain that the driver was all alone this time.

Odd how the driver sometimes came with someone else who was much shorter.

Odd how the driver sometimes stayed in the truck for a long time or walked out into the woods for more than an hour.

The trees along his driveway blocked a good view of the driver. The Oslo police would later doubt his accuracy when he wrote down the license plate's last two numbers.

The police doubted such an old man was a credible witness and therefore they did not write down the two license plate numbers that he had observed.

"Herr Svendsen," said the young Police Constable who took his statement the following day on Saturday June 5th, "you are eighty-three years old. You seem confused as to exactly what day of the week you first saw the white pickup truck."

"Listen to me young man. I may not know the days of the week any more. But that's because I'm all alone . . . my wife died four years ago . . . I'm retired. Every day looks and feels like the other day. They all seem the same. It's different when you have to go to work or school. Then you are very aware of the days . . . you carefully count the days until Saturday or a holiday . . . or your next payday or vacation."

"So be it Herr Svendsen. But you cannot tell me the day of the week when you first saw the white pickup truck."

"No. But my neighbor can tell you. Go ask her. Herr and Fru Dahl and I have spoken about all the stupid people who park at our dead end. . . . Young people who drink and smoke marijuana . . . and others who come here to do you know what . . . they've even left their underwear on the street.

"Disgusting! . . .

"So why don't you ask her or her husband when that white vehicle first parked here. Her husband saw it when he came home early one afternoon from work. She . . . like me . . . got fed up with the driver coming here in the mornings and afternoons. She even let her dogs out to chase the driver away one or two days ago."

"We will talk with your neighbor. Now . . . did you see a boy in the car?"

"Boy? I don't know if it was a boy or girl . . . or an adult. I told you I sometimes saw the driver and a smaller or shorter passenger. Dark shadows . . . that's all I saw from here with my binoculars."

"That's it?"

"I could've walked down my driveway to see their faces but I thought they'd just drive away if I got close to them. You see I can't walk back up my steep driveway . . . . what with my knees and hips . . . the arthritis has ruined them."

"I see."

"Do you? I don't think so. Anyway . . . I told you that the driver parked down there almost every day right after school started and then at around one in the afternoon . . . and sometimes at odd hours of the night. The car was there yesterday at nine in the morning for about thirty minutes after school started . . . it came back and parked there for an hour later that afternoon . . . from about twelve thirty to one forty-five. "

"Herr Svendsen . . . what school are you talking about?"

"The elementary school . . . the only one nearby . . . Grindbakken skole . . . Pilot Hill School . . . on Måltrostveien."

"How did you know that the driver came here after school started?"

"Simple. I looked at my watch and wrote down the times on a piece of scrap paper. The driver usually came down here at nine in the morning and at one in the afternoon. You think I am senile . . . but I know when school starts and ends because my neighbors the Dahls have two children in that school . . . she drives to drop them off every morning at school and pick them up every afternoon. Of course it's not like in the old days when every rich and poor kid walked to school . . . even in winter. Now parents chauffeur the tykes. Ridiculous."

"Times have changed Herr Svendsen."

"Not for the better. Mark my words. Not for the better."

Chapter 3/Tre

SEPTEMBER 4, OR THREE MONTHS
AFTER THE DAY JUNE 4

Chief Inspector Trygve Nilsen looked forward to
spending the weekend with his wife and children at the
hytte that he had bought earlier that summer at a
foreclosure. He gave a five-minute presentation to his
superiors. Then he barely paid any attention to what the
other police chief inspectors discussed during their weekly
meeting with their boss the Police Commissioner for the
Oslo district.

The only words in Trygve Nilsen's ears during the
meeting with other chief inspectors that morning were
those of the realtor from the nearby town of Dovre:

"It's a steal I tell you! A steal! . . . The family put a
second and a third mortgage on their farm when Citibank
offered them a '*great way*' to cut down their debt on
Citibank credit cards.

"The poor fools believed them.

"Of course that was in the old days before the crash
in oh-eight. No way you'd get any Norwegian bankers
lending on a second or third mortgage up here in Oppland
County. Only real dumb American banks based in London
. . . or greedy banks from Spain. That's Euro-Union
craziness for you. Anyway . . . you're getting a real deal."

Nilsen looked forward to driving the 200 miles up
north to his hyyte and 12-acre farm in his brand new

Jaguar XJ. Life was very good after the 2008 financial crash if you had a government job. He had just gotten a huge pay raise and he spent a lot of time at work thinking about all of the additional perks and benefits and promotions that would keep coming his way as a Police Chief Inspector in the Oslo district.

"Nilsen," said his boss Ivar Thorsen at the end of the meeting while the conference room emptied out. "A word."

"Sir?"

Nilsen barely listened to his boss because all he could think about was the lovely traditional country cabin in the meadow and its rustic simplicity and how impressive it would look when he added a fresh coat of red paint that coming weekend.

"Nilsen did you hear me?"

"Sorry sir . . . I just have a lot on my plate . . . very difficult investigations sir."

"As I said . . . there's one you need to pay close attention to. . . ."

"Yes sir. Which one?"

"The one with the boy."

"The Karl Haugen boy? Any reason in particular sir?"

"Yes! I was playing bridge yesterday with Police Superintendent Brudelie. And he told me that. . . ."

"Oh yes . . . how interesting," said Nilsen from time to time while cringing inside. He hated the constant name-dropping that his boss used to show off about how close he was socially to the top brass in the Norwegian Police Service.

"So Nilsen . . . the long and short of it is that you need to call several press conferences . . . go for maximum coverage in television and radio and newspapers and magazines."

"Issue the usual press releases? Give the ususal interviews and exclusives and off the record background?"

"Yes. Make sure that you show in big graphs and charts how many officers and how many hours and how many resources we are dedicating to protect the little children at Grindbakken Skole. The school angle always gets parents interested and nervous. They always fall for it. Make big maps and then cross out in color markers all of the areas where your team has searched. You must make absolutely sure that it appears that you and your team are doing a lot of work on the case . . . and spending a lot of money . . . make sure that you put a lot of emphasis on how *budget* constraints are preventing you and your investigative team from doing *everything* possible."

"But why the boy? Any reason in particular sir?"

"The Minister of Justice wants the Prime Minister and the parliament to approve a nine percent increase to our budget for the coming fiscal year. A cute little boy is after all the perfect poster boy when lobbying for a budget increase for the police."

"I see."

"Nilsen . . . do you know those folks at the Ministry of the Environment?"

"No. What about them?"

"They got a twelve percent increase to their budget when they showed pictures and video of those cute seal puppies choking and dying in Russian solvents and pollutants in the Arctic."

"Don't worry boss. I know exactly what to do."

Chapter 4/Fire

MIDSUMMER'S EVE, OR
THE LONGEST DAY OF THE YEAR, OR
1 YEAR AND 19 DAYS AFTER THE DAY,
FRIDAY, JUNE 4

"Where's my Daddy?"

No one answered Karl Haugen.

The blinding sunshine fell on his eyes. He wondered where he was and why he could not see his father. So much time had passed and yet Karl Haugen felt as if he had last seen his father just a few minutes ago. He had lost track of time.

"Where's my Daddy?"

Silence.

"I want to see my father!"

~ ~ ~

The Norwegian Storting met in session. The ruling party confidently looked forward to a thorough grilling in parliament by the opposition parties on the danger to Norwegian banks from potential defaults on the government debt of poorly managed European Union countries like Spain and Greece.

After receiving recognition to speak Edvard Ruud stood up. He was the senior member of a small ultra right-wing opposition party that wanted to end immigration and other social engineering projects. Edvard Ruud stood silently for a long time before he said:

"Mister Speaker . . . although high finance and the well-being of international bankers seem to be the primary concern of the Prime Minister and his government . . . can the Prime Minister and his Minister of Justice explain why the government's police have gotten absolutely no results on finding a Norwegian child who's been missing now for twelve months. . . . The child is Karl Haugen age seven . . . an innocent boy who mysteriously disappeared from his school in the middle of the day."

The chamber erupted in shouts and catcalls which did not deter Edvard Ruud.

"Karl Haugen . . . an innocent child and Norwegian citizen is . . . in my opinion . . . far more important than the foreign deadbeat countries that are always seeking bailouts and handouts from Norway and other countries whose citizens work hard and spend wisely."

The Prime Minister stood up and said, "Does the right honorable member from Namsos actually have a question for me? . . . I lost track of his question in his long speech."

"I have three questions. Exactly when and how does your Minister of Justice plan on finding the little boy Karl Haugen and bringing him back home? . . . Are the school children of Norway really safe when the police cannot find a little boy after one entire year of looking for him? . . . Just what has been done to find Karl Haugen with all of the money and manpower that the Justice Minister asked for and got with his latest budget increase?"

~ ~ ~

Oslo Police Commissioner Ivar Thorsen could not

believe his luck in getting invited to the exclusive Oustøen Country Club on Ostøya Island about 15 miles southwest of downtown Oslo. His efforts had paid off. His mother had taught him well. She always said, "Hang around rich and powerful people. Then do what the rich and powerful people do."

"So," said his boss, "you really play golf?"

"Yes!"

"Really? Alright then. You're playing with me. Let's go."

They teed off and played in the glorious summer weather. His boss was driving the cart to the second hole when his boss suddenly stopped and said:

"We have a problem."

"I took care of it. No one will ever know."

"What? You did?"

"You know . . . our last mayor . . . his mistress getting a no-bid contract worth millions."

"I'm not talking about that. I'm talking about the missing boy."

"Karl Haugen?"

"The little shit is causing a lot of trouble."

"I did what you told me to do . . . to make it *appear* that we were doing *something*."

"That's no longer good enough. You see . . . unfortunately someone higher up has taken an interest in the case. He wants a final solution . . . he won't tolerate any longer for us to appear as if we're doing something."

The two men played and moved on to the third hole.

"Who is interested?"

"The Minister of Justice and Police," said his boss as he swung his four iron.

"Oh," he said somewhat in shock that the boss of his boss's boss had taken an interest in the boy. He had never heard of a member of cabinet taking an interest in such a matter. Powerful people surely had more important things to care about.

His wise mother had told him many many times, *"The powerful only care about what's good for them. Never forget that."* That's what his mother had taught him and she knew very well how the world worked.

Penniless his mother had come to Oslo to work at a bank executive's home as a maid. The poor but pretty peasant girl from a small village near the border with Sweden was no fool. She knew how the world worked and she became very good friends with the bank executive and his wife and their son and she soon got pregnant and very lucky as a single mother with permanent employment. She got lots of benefits and gifts from the bank executive including tuition for her son's university as well as a tidy retirement sum set aside for when she turned 55.

At the fourth hole his boss knocked the ball in at par and said:

"The Minister wants the situation with the boy resolved as soon as possible . . . no later than December."

"That's just six months from now."

"You have to do it. He's planning on becoming the next Prime Minister. And that bit of news is utterly and completely confidential. You must tell absolutely no one about it. Understand?"

"Of course."

The men played in silence and moved on to the fifth hole.

"What do *you* want me to do?"

His boss took out a seven iron. "Do whatever it takes."

"An arrest?"

"Whatever it takes."

"A confession?"

"Whatever it takes. It's your department. You're the Police Commissioner and Chief of the Oslo district!"

Ivar Thorsen was troubled and his game went from mediocre to horrible. His score reached pathetic levels for the next two holes. He felt sick over the situation that his boss had just put him into.

If he failed then he would have to take the blame as well as any unpleasant consequences such as a forced early retirement.

If he got results then someone else would take the credit.

After much thought Thorsen slowly realized that it was okay if he didn't get any of the credit before the public and the media and the government. This time he didn't mind someone else taking the credit because the Minister of Justice or his boss or his boss's boss would surely remember who had gotten things done.

After they teed off for the ninth hole Thorsen said, "I really appreciate you telling me that the Minister is interested."

"I told you because I want no doubts or timid half-measures from you. This way there's absolutely no doubt as to what *you* need to do . . . and what the rewards and consequences will be if you succeed or fail."

Shivers went up and down Thorsen's spine. "Any preferences on what I should do or how I should proceed?"

"It's your department! Just do it."

Ivar Thorsen couldn't play at all. He spent a lot of time hacking away in the rough and cursed when he dug himself in deeper at a bunker of yellowish sand. He finally reached the ninth hole that offered magnificent views of Oslofjord and the city of Oslo and the low mountains

His boss putted superbly. He motioned for Thorsen to come over and his boss said in the friendliest voice:

"I've noticed over the years that you have switched your hobbies many times."

"Why yes I have."

"Remind me. You started out on the Police Reserve . . . on probation. Right?"

"Oh yes."

"And then you became a Police Constable. Right?"

"Right."

"Interesting . . . that's also when you took up horseback riding as a hobby . . . because that was what your boss liked to do on weekends. Right?"

"Yes," said Thorsen uncomfortable and unsure where the conversation was going.

"Then you switched hobbies as you went up the ranks to become a Police Sergeant . . . and then to a Police Inspector. As I remember from way back then . . . you changed your hobbies to tennis and then to sailing each time that you got a new boss. Correct?"

"Yes. I took lessons for my hobbies. They were fun."

"Oh I bet they were. And then you got promoted to Chief Inspector and then to Superintendent. Right?"

"Yes."

"And if I remember correctly that's also when you again switched your hobbies to skiing and then to playing that board game . . . Scrabble. Right?"

"Yes. I love skiing and playing Scrabble."

"Just like your bosses."

"I. . . ."

"Then you switched to playing bridge before you became the Police Chief for the Oslo district."

"Why yes. I love playing bridge just like you do. As

you say . . . the cards exercise the brain."

"And now you have switched to golf . . . the hobby of *my* boss the National Police Commissioner . . . and his boss the Minister of Justice and Chief of Police."

"Yes . . . but only because the golf range offered me real cheap lessons thanks to a coupon I got in the mail."

"Do me a favor."

"Yes . . . of course."

"Stop taking golf lessons."

"Of course sir."

"You need to quit golf."

"Why not? . . .Yes. . . I will."

"In the first place golf is a whole other game in a totally different category than from what you've ever played. Don't you see? . . . Golf requires skills and talent that you simply do not have . . . no matter how many lessons you take or how much you practice. Understand?"

"I see what you mean."

"Do you? . . . Good. I'm also sure that you can now see why someone like you . . . with so little talent and practice . . . is playing so very badly today."

"Of course."

"What a shame that *my* boss the National Police Commissioner invited you to the golf course where he and his boss the Minister of Justice are members. I don't think that you see how you've embarrassed them with your atrocious playing and ridiculously vulgar polyester clothes and cheap clubs. I hope you will never again even think of accepting an invitation from any member of this club. Do you understand?

"Yes. Of course."

"Also . . . I understand that you got invited here today because you've been going to the same golf range as the National Police Commissioner."

"A coincidence I can assure you."

"One that will never be repeated since you are quitting golf. Correct?"

"Correct."

"Alright. I better hurry. I see that *my* bosses are almost at the eleventh hole."

Thorsen went to get his putter to finish playing the ninth.

"Oh no Thorsen. You're leaving right now. Go back to the office. I'll tell my bosses that you left because you just couldn't play well and realized that you're just not cut out for this game."

"Of course. Can you—"

"No. I won't be driving you back in the cart. You can walk yourself back to the club house."

"Thank you sir. Have a great game."

"I will especially now that we had our little talk."

Thorsen hid his shaking hands. He should have known that his boss was always watching his every move including his joining the golf range where the Minister happened to practice his golf swing. Thorsen had less than ten years to go before retirement. He could not afford to get demoted or even worse laterally transferred to Tromsø up north or some other frozen wasteland halfway up to the North Pole like Spitsbergen in the Svalbard archipelago where one Police Superintendent had committed suicide after being transferred there for the wrongful conviction of five innocent men.

At the club house Thorsen was directed to the private ferry terminal where Thorsen almost passed out when he realized that his boss had kept his round-trip ticket. Thorsen had almost no cash and as a non-member he had to pay 150 kroner or almost $ 30 U.S. dollars for the one-mile ferry trip to the Snarøya terminal on the mainland where he had left his car.

What would he do now that he had his marching orders?

He realized that he would have to move people around in his department and even worse bring in someone smart to get results.

"Never hire smart people to work for or around you," his mother had told him. "They don't take orders very well and they will always outshine you. Even worse they'll get promoted and sooner or later take your job. No! No! No! Make sure that you always employ people as dumb or dumber than you. And my son you are not smart so you be very careful. Only hang around smart people as long as they help you."

Thorsen smiled at the thought of his clever mother. She was absolutely right. As a puppet he too could play the part of the puppet master and start pulling strings and moving his own puppets around. He would rearrange the chess pieces so that he had a chance of success.

By the time the ferry got to the Snarøya terminal Thorsen knew exactly what he needed to do. First he would get flowers for his mother and go visit her in the afternoon and then he'd go have dinner with his good wife whom his mother had picked from the village. He remembered his mother always saying:

"Us simple country people are winners because we are survivors. Peasants are born to survive! Remember this Ivar and you will do well."

~ ~ ~

"Daddy! Daddy! I want my Daddy!"

The man looked at Karl Haugen and said, "Not now Karl."

"I want my Daddy!"

The man shook his head. Children never failed to amaze him.

~ ~ ~

"I'm going to take a nap as soon as we're done," she said.

"Good."

"Are you going to take a nap?"

"I doubt it." Harald Sohlberg dried the plates and silverware that his wife rinsed and handed him from the kitchen sink. "I'll read for a while . . . then maybe take a walk in the old neighborhood. I just can't sleep in the afternoon. Not even after my fifteen mile run this morning."

"If you don't take a nap then that means that you are not going to have any sleep over a twenty-four hour period. Don't forget . . . we have a party with the Otterstads that doesn't start until eight. They like to celebrate Saint Hans Aften . . . St. John's Eve . . . until very very late."

"I know. They don't even light their bål . . . bonfire by the beach . . . until after midnight."

"Then there's all that food. You'll get reflux if you eat late. . . ."

"I promise I won't eat so much that I feel like throwing up in bed."

"You always say that and then you go ahead anyways and overeat like crazy. There's going to be lots and lots of food. And that means lots of rømmegrøt . . . sour cream porridge. They'll probably be serving food until two or three in the morning. You know you always go crazy eating rømmegrøt. Remember when we went to my parents in Bergen after we met? . . . You had almost four liters . . . a gallon . . . of my mother's rømmegrøt."

He could almost smell and taste the pudding of sour cream with melted butter and brown sugar and cinnamon. "Yes! I still remember that. But I rarely have it any more . . . this will be my once-in-a-year feasting on my favorite food. Besides . . . it's been ages since we celebrated Sankthans . . . Midsummer's Eve. It's been what? . . . Maybe fifteen years since we spent a Sankthans in Norway? . . . It's been at least five years since we've been in Oslo during the summer for more than a few days."

"True. I'm so happy we came back. Three weeks of summer vacation!"

"Don't forget though. I must do a presentation at headquarters before we can leave. Then we'll be off to see your folks and enjoy lovely Bergen once again."

Fru Sohlberg handed him the last dish and noticed his eyes. "Won't it feel strange going back to the National Police Directorate? . . . Are you nervous?"

"Yes and no," he said fully aware that his wife could read his face and gestures like an open book. Not even the best lie detector and voice stress machine could surpass her skills at accurately and instantly detecting his real feelings and thoughts. Sometimes he wondered if she and not he should have been a Police Inspector. He had no doubts that Fru Sohlberg would probably have solved more crimes than Herr Sohlberg given her special talents.

She turned and looked at him. "It must be strange if not difficult to have so many reminders of the past . . . beginning with this house."

"Yes," he said. "A remembrance of things past. This house brings back my childhood . . . and so many memories . . . even those as a young adult."

During the past two days he had been embarrassed

when she had caught him lost in memories while he stared wistfully at different rooms of his old childhood home. He felt foolish at his sentimental longing for the good old days of his youth. And yet he yearned for the happy and carefree life that he had enjoyed at the lovely waterfront home of glass-and-cedar thanks to his generous and loving parents.

Emma Sohlberg read his face and said, "Well . . . you can't be blamed for feeling nostalgic over the great childhood you had here with your parents."

"True," said Sohlberg, "but it's all in the past."

She dried her hands on the towel that he held. She pulled him closer with the towel and kissed him gently on the lips. "Please take a nap if you can."

Sohlberg smiled and watched her walk down the hallway and up the stairs. He drank the last of the sparkling mineral water of the third Farris bottle that he had consumed after returning from his early morning run. He sauntered outside and headed past the towering pines down to the beach where his father had built a small guest cabin.

His father had built the cabin and used it as an office after his refurbished industrial machinery business took off in the early 1980s. Of course the cabin and the sailboat and the floating dock and other luxuries came only after many years of struggling and economizing. Sohlberg remembered many cold winters with little heat in the house and simple paper shades for curtains. Norway's oil boom greatly prospered his father's business in the 1980s and Sohlberg sometimes wondered if he should have gone into business with his father.

"Me the businessman," Sohlberg said to himself as he sat down before his father's desk.

The desk faced a panoramic wall-to-wall window

that extended from the floor all the way up to the ceiling. The sun-drenched Oslofjord's blue waters beckoned.

So . . . here I am . . . back home.

Intense melancholy overcame Sohlberg. He longed to live in his homeland. And yet he was doomed to permanent exile outside of Norway in an obscure paper-pushing bureaucratic job at Interpol. Sohlberg desired one thing above all: to investigate homicides and major crimes. But his "adviser" position at Interpol meant that he would never investigate any crime unless a local law enforcement agency authorized him to do so.

Satan has a better chance of working in Heaven.

Sohlberg's fancy title and decent salary as a Senior Adviser to the Secretary General of Interpol was no substitute for his ruined career as a homicide detective in Norway.

I got punished for doing my job. . . .

No way I was going to back down from arresting those two bribe-taking Supreme Court Justices.

Maybe I did go over the top when I dragged them out in handcuffs through the court's main doors on Høyesteretts plass . . . in front of so many newspaper and television reporters.

He watched a faraway sailboat skim the water so gracefully that it appeared to be floating in the air.

Time to do chores.

In less than an hour Sohlberg had carefully organized and added up the receipts and invoices that he needed to present to Interpol as soon as possible. He wanted to quickly get reimbursed for more than $ 12,932 U.S. dollars that he had spent on airlines and taxis and hotels and meals on his recent round of traveling to Norway from the USA. He decided that he would send the reimbursement request by fax later that night to Lyon in

France. But he had to make absolutely sure that he added and included every item correctly because he knew better than to submit a wrong reimbursement request to the accountants and bookkeepers at Interpol. The bean counters always made him and other Interpol advisers and field agents feel that they were somehow defrauding Interpol even when submitting the most accurate of expense reports.

Sohlberg had as ususal organized all the paperwork for the expense report on a day-by-day basis from the day that he and Fru Sohlberg had flown out of Seattle in the United States to the day that they arrived in Copenhagen Denmark for a four-day meeting of Interpol's National Central Bureau (NCB) for the European Region. He still needed to add the paperwork for the airfare from Copenhagen to Oslo and the car rental at the airport.

Representatives from all 49 member nations of the Regional European NCB had attended the Copenhagen meeting to review and discuss links between major organized crime groups that smuggled drugs and humans from Asia into the western shores of Canada and the United States.

Sohlberg spoke at the Copenhagen meeting in his official capacity as a full-time Interpol Adviser. During the past two years he had worked out of Seattle in the USA and directed a secret 12-country investigation into the smuggling of pure grade Number 4 heroin by criminal gangs from Russia and Canada and the USA.

He placed the Interpol forms for reimbursement on the desk and was focusing on not making any errors when his cell phone buzzed angrily. Sohlberg frowned when he saw the incoming phone number on the little screen.

"Hei," he said trying to sound as relaxed and casual as possible given the caller's identity.

"Are you free to talk?"

"Yes."

"Are you still on schedule to give a talk three days from now on heroin smuggling to all twenty-seven of our districts?"

"I am. Why do you ask?"

"We need to meet. Come by my office after you finish your talk."

The call from the Commissioner for the Oslo Police Regional District enraged Sohlberg. He hated Ivar Thorsen. Technically the man was still his boss and that made Sohlberg hate him even more. On days like this Sohlberg felt that he would explode and have a heart attack or a stroke over the cruel fact that he was still subject to taking orders from an incompetent fool like Ivar Thorsen.

To think that they had once been close friends all the way from kindergarten to high school!

Even as Sohlberg thought about their lost friendship from so long ago he remembered that he and other classmates could barely tolerate Ivar Thorsen after a couple of hours. Few could tolerate the man's hypocritical fawning. Thorsen's endless bootlicking disgusted all but the dumbest persons as grotesque and obvious attempts to ingratiate himself into a subservient but beneficial relationship. In other words Ivar Thorsen had inherited all of his mother's pushy and cunning social designs and schemes but none of her charms which included the ample bosom and other intimate delicacies that she first shared with her employer's son and then with the employer himself.

"Why?" shouted Sohlberg. "Why do we need to meet? What's this about?"

"I'll see you at noon sharp."

Sohlberg immediately hanged up without waiting to hear more. "What a piece of garbage that Thorsen! Just what does he want from me?"

His former friend Ivar Thorsen was now *the* enemy and 100% responsible in Sohlberg's mind for pushing him out of Norway and into Lyon in France for a job at Interpol. According to the press release at the time:

"The National Police Commissioner of the National Police Directorate is pleased to announce that the Commissioner is, effective immediately, assigning and loaning Police Chief Inspector Harald Sohlberg of the Oslo Police Regional District to Interpol at the request of the General Secretary of Interpol.

"Herr Sohlberg will serve as a senior Interpol Adviser for an indefinite period of time on critical international law enforcement matters that directly affect Norway and Europe. Furthermore, pursuant to long-standing arrangements with Interpol, Herr Sohlberg will continue in his capacity as a Police Chief Inspector for the Oslo Police Regional District and continue reporting to Commissioner Ivar Thorsen of the Oslo Police Regional District."

Of course the government's official press release failed to disclose that Thorsen moved Sohlberg to Interpol after Sohlberg exposed scandalous judicial corruption in Norway's Supreme Court. The humiliating exile still rankled Sohlberg even though it had taken place 15 years ago on the very day that Sohlberg was celebrating his fifth year as a highly respected Chief Inspector.

Sohlberg cursed. He left his father's cabin to take a long walk on Ulvøya Island before he got angry enough to punch a hole through his father's desk.

~ ~ ~

A few miles away another man was about to receive another troubling communication. The man turned on the laptop computer and waited. He was in for a long long night and it was not just because of the midsummer Sankthansaften celebrations. He did not look forward to the midnight sun which would serve as a constant reminder that his personal life was one of extremes. Oslo provided 18 hours of daylight in the summer and 6 hours of daylight in the winter and those unbalanced extremes were no different than those in his heart and soul. He felt that he was losing his grip on reality.

The spy software SILENT KEYLOGGER finally loaded and asked him for his password.

You are?

He typed in *******.

The man felt sick when he read the latest entries that the key logging software had picked up from the desktop computer in the small bedroom down the hallway. Waves of nausea rolled over him. And yet he was grateful for the keyboard monitoring software that he had bought at a computer store and covertly installed into a laptop at his home. The software accurately and secretly recorded every single keyboard stroke that anyone made on the computer that he wanted to spy on.

What does a man do when he is betrayed on every single possible level of a relationship?

The question disturbed him more than the answer or answers. The question inevitably raised the question of how he had allowed himself to be trapped in such a sick and false relationship. Twisted and putrid would not begin to describe the mess he had gotten himself into so stupidly and recklessly. The worst part of his troubles was that he still could not believe that someone as intelligent and educated as himself could be so thoroughly duped.

A door opened and closed somewhere in his house. Footsteps got closer. He quickly exited the spyware and clicked on his favorite game of solitaire.

"Hei," she said after opening the door, "what are you doing?"

"Nothing. Just my solitaire."

Lie upon lie.

~ ~ ~

Harald Sohlberg hurried away from his parent's home. He had been looking forward to his three week summer vacation until the phone call from Ivar Thorsen. He turned and looked fondly at his ancestral home.

The older Sohlbergs had insisted that he and his wife stay at their home on Fiskekroken or Fish Hook Drive in Ulvøya Island. His parents now spent most of the year living in the United States of America with his younger brother the petroleum engineer who lived in Houston Texas working for British Petroleum. His parent's generosity in providing free lodging at Fiskekroken meant that Interpol would save a fortune in hotel bills because Oslo was far more expensive than insanely overpriced cities like Tokyo and London and Moscow.

A block away Sohlberg walked past the grand old home where Thorsen had grown up while his mother worked as a maid for the bank executive. In the distance he saw a swimming pool through the trees and wondered if the banker or his wife or his son still lived there.

Sohlberg looked with suspicion at Ulvøya's attractive gardens and beaches. He knew how well the lovely yards and shores would temporarily trick residents into forgetting during the summer months that they lived in sub-Arctic Norway where six months from now they'd be in the dark in sub-freezing weather.

"And yet . . . so pretty," he said softly to himself.

The round island of Ulvøya—measuring just one mile across—is one of the many charming islands in the Oslofjord. The island is conveniently located five miles southeast of downtown Oslo and on that glorious summer day the sun-drenched views of the city and the Oslofjord reminded Sohlberg of the Pacific Northwest in the USA. Sohlberg and his wife lived in the Seattle suburb of Silverdale among the pines and waters of Puget Sound in the State of Washington.

"Hei!" he said warmly to joggers and pedestrians who threw him cold looks. He was no longer used to the curt and reserved nod that Norwegians traditionally give to strangers. Most Norwegians use the same greeting for neighbors and others whom they have know for decades without ever speaking one single word of acknowledgment or greeting.

He blushed at the thought of acting like a tourist in his own country.

Sohlberg wondered if he would ever fit in his homeland. He felt like an alien among his own people. Without a doubt he and Fru Sohlberg had changed a lot by living abroad for so long: four years at Lyon in France; four at New York City; two at Salt Lake City in Utah; and, ten at Vancouver in Canada and Seattle in the USA. Change had also arrived at Fiskekroken which was now packed with homes in what had once been farm fields and forests and fisherman's cabins.

He marveled at how Ulvøya Island had transformed itself since 1975 when his family had moved into their new home which was one of the first modern homes built on the island. Enchanting Ulvøya was now crammed with homes. Sohlberg fondly and sadly remembered the heavily-forested island from his childhood. He certainly did not expect to find the island so grossly overbuilt with homes.

He walked west on Fiskekroken and was shocked to see so many new homes on the narrow street without sidewalks. Sohlberg could see downtown Oslo between the homes although the larger northern islands of Malmøya and Ormøya sometimes blocked views of the city skyline. He turned into Måkeveien which circled the island.

At the corner with Vargveien he stopped. He looked up the gentle hill and stared at the house where his life had taken a turn for the worse when he was three years out of law school. The pretty blue house on Vargveien reminded him of the great painter Gauguin who had suffered so much in Tahiti in the *Maison du Jouir* or House of Pleasure. This Norwegian house of pleasure had also turned into a house of pain.

"Harald?"

A matronly woman stood by a hedge. She looked vaguely familiar. He thought a few seconds and said the first name that came to him:

"Fru Fredriksen."

"My . . . you've gotten very formal Harald."

He instantly realized his mistake but he did not let on to having confused the daughter for the mother. Instead he smiled and said:

"Margerete . . . one has to be formal in my line of work."

How she had changed! The sexy and thin high school vixen Margerete was now a thick-set grandmother with a square and solid body. He vaguely remembered that a few years ago his mother had told him that Margerete had gone through several unhappy marriages before moving back to live on Ulvøya Island with her parents. He wondered if he also looked as old and worn with his bald spot and thinning hair which he kept very short to hide his baldness and age.

"Come now Harald. Is that how you treat an old friend from high school?"

"Of course not Margerete. How are your parents . . . your mother?"

"Gone."

"Traveling?"

"No. Dead."

"I . . . I'm sorry to hear that. I really am." He wondered why his mother had not told him. After all his mother had been good friends with Fru Fredriksen who had been his math teacher in the 9th grade. Sohlberg had always suspected that the two women had conspired to act as matchmakers between him and the youngest of the four lovely Fredericksen daughters. But he had little in common with the extroverted Margerete.

"Harald. I've wanted to tell you in person after all these years that I'm sorry I did not come to Karoline's funeral. I should have. . . ."

Memories flooded and overwhelmed him. His first wife Karoline. Happy times. Three years married. Mountain climbing every summer in Romsdalen valley which is Norway's Yosemite valley.

Then Karoline suddenly gone.

The sickening *shisssh* of the rope going through the carabiner on her harness.

Falling.

Down down down.

Looking straight into his eyes without any surprise or any screaming.

Dead.

An accident.

For unknown reasons Karoline Sohlberg did not properly tie herself into the rope although she was an experienced climber who had summited Eiger and Mt. Blanc and the Matterhorn. She fell when they had almost reached the summit of the North Face Trollveggen (Troll Wall) of Trollryggen Peak—the tallest vertical cliff in Europe at 3600 feet.

"I . . . I have to go."

"Come inside with me Harald and talk. We'll have something to drink."

"No!" he said too loudly before lowering his voice. "No thanks. I have to go."

~ ~ ~

After 20 minutes of solitaire the man switched to play online poker. He quit a short time later when he realized he could not play well.

He whispered, "What shall I do?"

He weighed his options. They ranged from bad to worse. None attracted him. None promised an attractive outcome. He could always strangle her right then and there and dispose of her body in the wood chipper. Maybe he'd slice her lying tongue off before choking her to death. Perhaps before torturing her he would have to sneak up on her from behind and knock her sweet precious head into unconsciousness. He would have to surprise her and disable her because she had once been rather muscular and fit as a bodybuilder. He couldn't risk her using her athletic skills to somehow escape him.

Had she taken steroids to win competitions?

The drugs might still be in her body. They could endow her with extra-manly strength. So he might just have to shoot her in the head or bash in her skull from behind. On the other hand a stun gun would perfectly disable her with a jolt of 3 million volts. That would shut up her lying devious mouth.

The door opened. She said:

"Honey . . . it's time. Are you coming?"

He nodded.

"Honey," she said, "I really want to work out hard today. Get rid of the stress. You mind if we stay an extra hour at the gym?"

"Of course not," he lied. He was desperate if not dying inside. He wanted to be at home to hear any news on the television or radio about breaking developments in the case.

"You know something," she said with a bright smile, "I've been thinking that maybe I'll go back to competition."

That was another lie. He knew from eavesdropping on her phone calls that she had permanently quit bodybuilding after placing third in the "Women Over 35 Years Old" category in the Norge Austlandet (Eastern Norway) cup of bodybuilding. She always quit if she did not immediately succeed.

He forced himself to be pleasant and said:

"Have you really thought about that my sweet?"

"Honey you know as well as I do that I need to lose weight. I've even been thinking of going back to teach. I heard that a teacher position is opening up at Grindbakken Skole."

Grindbakken Skole . . . the scene of the crime.

No.

No way!

He could not let her work at the scene of the crime. He would not let her. Never.

Just what is she thinking when she talks about going

to teach at Grindbakken?

Or is she just taunting me . . . mocking me?

Her teaching! More lies and grand deceptions. For years she told anyone who'd listen that she planned on becoming a school principal and then a school district superintendent. He had fallen for that lie until it finally dawned on him that she had a bachelor's and a master's degree in education and yet she had never had a full-time teaching job other than working a couple of lowly part-time substitute teacher jobs. She couldn't even hold those jobs for more than a few months before pissing everyone off with her hyper-controlling nature and delusions of grandeur and competence.

He racked his mind trying to remember the type of full-time jobs that she had held after she lost the part-time substitute teacher gigs.

Where oh where did the crazy broad work at?

A one year gig at the McDonald's near Oslo University Hospital.

Yes. That was her job with a master's degree in education—Assistant Manager of the McDonald's hamburger-flipping outlet at Torgny Segerstedts Vei 11. She had even been named "Assistant Manager of the Month" for having the best sales for the drive-thru in the afternoon.

How special of the Little Frøken Genius.

"Honey," she screeched, "go get our bags and I'll see you in the driveway. Chop chop! We're running late. Don't forget to make sure that my deodorant is in my bag. Last time you forgot to check."

"Yes my sweet."

She flew down the stairs. He waited briefly for her to get out of the house because her cloud of cheap drugstore perfume gagged him. She blew the car horn twice to rush him.

"How stupid of me winding up with her in my bed and my house," he whispered to himself. "But Little Miss Genius is always one or two steps ahead of me."

In hindsight he should have known better than to sleep around with a McDonald's Assistant Manager of the Month especially when he was a highly-educated man with an enviable high-paying job that most Norwegians could only dream about. He should have known that she saw him as the ultimate meal ticket and that she would never stop pursuing him until she had a marriage ring on her hand and their baby in a crib.

"How very stupid of me," he said under his breath now that he had finally come to realize that he could not divorce her. Never. Otherwise she would tell the world about the molestation.

Little Frøken Blackmailer. Yes. . . the molestation would be an interesting topic for her to bring up with the courts and the media and the police.

Wouldn't it?

She has me cornered!

He wondered why he had told her about the molestation in the first place.

Why did I?

"Coming!" he yelled when she blew the car horn repeatedly.

He did not look forward to spending the endless light-filled summer nights under the midnattsol with her. He could not stand being near her or hearing her or seeing her or smelling her. And yet she had trapped him in a loveless marriage built on lies and discontent. A cage with no escape.

When will this torture end?

How will I end it?

He had absolutely no guarantee whatsoever that an end was in sight. There was no sunset in the horizon for his troubles. He probably would not even have the pleasure of torturing and killing her because she surely had her blackmailer's information conveniently tucked away somewhere—ready to be released by someone in case of her death or grievous injury to her person.

That's it.

I have to find out if she has any blackmail information on me hidden away somewhere . . . ready to be released if she croaks or winds up badly injured.

If she doesn't have that insurance then I'm going to literally rip her to pieces.

~ ~ ~

The Otterstads sent their oldest son Leif to pick up the Sohlbergs at exactly 8:00 P.M. in one of the Otterstad's motorboats. As usual the boat was a Bénéteau from France where the 120-year-old company kept Mathias Otterstad on a short waiting list for new powerboats like the *Antares 42* model.

"Wow," said Fru Sohlberg to her husband when the breathtaking 49-foot Bénéteau *Monte Carlo 47* model docked in front of the Sohlberg pier.

"She's a beaut . . . ain't she?" said 22-year-old Leif Otterstad while he helped Fru Sohlberg come on board. "So are you Fru Sohlberg!"

Both Sohlbergs laughed.

"I'm serious," said Leif. "Fru Sohlberg is a good-looking woman."

Harald Sohlberg nodded while his wife said:

"Well thank you Leif. This boat is incredible . . . it looks like an elegant torpedo on steroids."

Leif gave them a quick tour of the luxurious interior and then raced the boat south around Malmøya Island and then north across the Oslofjord. They drew gaping stares from everyone who saw them. The trip to the Otterstads took less than 20 minutes before they approached the northwest shores of Malmøya Island.

Although Malmøya and Ulvøya islands are separated by less than half a mile of water there's quite a big jump in net worth and income for those who live on the bigger island of Malmøya. Sohlberg spotted the Otterstad dock the minute he saw a massive Bénéteau *Swift Trawler 52* floating on the placid waters near his host's spectacular home on Skjellveien.

~ ~ ~

"I want to go home," said Karl Haugen.

The woman with kind eyes smiled. "This is your new home."

"No! I want my Daddy. I want to go home."

The woman tried to hug the little boy but he turned away from her and started crying.

~ ~ ~

A crowd of about 50 adults and children on the beach cheered when the Sohlbergs stepped out of the boat and onto the pier. Matthias and Nora Otterstad waved at them from a bench under a grove of cedars.

The two couples hugged.

"Welcome Emma and Harald!" said the always effusive Nora Otterstad. "I'm so glad you're here. Finally home. Will you stay this time and live here in Oslo?"

"Who knows," said Fru Sohlberg before Sohlberg

could say anything.

Matthias Otterstad interjected:

"Interpol must be somewhat like the French Foreign Legion . . . you never really know where you are going to posted . . . eh?"

"True," said Fru Sohlberg while Harald Sohlberg nodded.

Nora Otterstad pointed at two long tables. "Now come along Emma. Let's get something to drink and eat for us and our boys . . . I'll also introduce you to some folks you may not know."

The women left for the enormous koldtbord that offered amazing mountains of salmon—glazed and smoked and marinated and broiled. Slabs of crayfish and mountain trout towered over all sorts of cold cuts from Norway and Italy including prosciutto and mortadella along with salads and breads and pastries and desserts.

"It's been a long time," said Matthias Otterstad, "since we met in person . . . eh?"

"Too long."

"I saw your parents before they left for Texas. I invited them over for dinner."

"Thank you. I'm glad you did that. They rarely go out any more . . . even during those few weeks when they're here in Norway."

"I was surprised I found them here and not in Houston. . . . You're very lucky that they're still around. And in overall good shape for folks in their mid-eighties."

"I'd be glad to be in half as good health as they are when I get that age."

"I understand Emma joined a cult."

"What? . . . Did my mother . . . or father tell you that?"

"No. Absolutely not."

"Just what cult are you talking about?"

"You know . . . that cult from America. . . . Maybe I shouldn't have used that word. But it's something I've been very curious about."

"Matthias . . . I've also been very curious about something and yet I never asked you about it for years and years."

"Go ahead . . . ask me."

"As I remember . . . you faced nasty lawsuits from Goldman Sachs. They alleged that you had stolen some of their employees and clients. You prevailed in the lower courts . . . and won again at the Supreme Court until two justices mysteriously switched their votes and recalled their original opinions in your favor. . . . You lost a lot of money and swore you'd get even. . . . Right?"

"So far you're right Sohlberg."

"Well now . . . you can finally tell me . . . were you the anonymous tipster who led me to find those two corrupt justices in the court? . . . Did you do that to get even with those two crooked pieces of garbage?"

"Sohlberg! . . . Why would you think that?"

"Answering a question with a question. Interesting. . . ."

"You too answered my cult question with a question."

"So we're even . . . at a stalemate."

"A good old-fashioned deadlock. . . . Sometimes a deadlock is not a bad thing. It gives you time to think things over . . . figure things out."

Sohlberg nodded and observed the koldtbord carefully. He shook his head when Fru Sohlberg pointed at the fårikål which he could never digest—not even when he was a teenager. The heavily peppered cabbage-and-mutton stew left him bloated for hours.

Unlike most Norwegians he disliked meat including the ever-popular kjøttkaker meatballs. What Sohlberg most wanted—in addition to the grilled salmon—was a heaping plate of Norway's heavenly muiter or cloudberries. He also wanted a lump of mouth-watering lingonberries spooned on top of the Jarlsberg cheese that he had missed so badly when living abroad.

"Here," said Emma Sohlberg who arrived with two laden plates for her famished husband.

"Perfect!" Sohlberg grabbed the first plate which was packed full with flatbrød or paper-thin crisp rye bread topped with brunost or carmelized goat cheese. "Oh . . . this is good." The appetizer disappeared before the two women turned to go back to the buffet table. "Ah . . . heavenly." Sohlberg digged into the second plate topped with grilled salmon and his other favorite foods.

Matthias smiled at his friend's voracious appetite. "So . . . tell me . . . are you staying here in Norway for good this time?"

"No," said Sohlberg between bites. "Just for a conference. Then back to the United States."

"It's too bad." A downcast Matthias Otterstad did not hide his disappointment. "I wish you'd move back here."

"Why? . . . Are you getting sentimental?"

"Maybe. Besides . . . I don't like living off my investments. It's a comfortable but boring existence. Dividends and interest and capital gains aren't as exciting as running a business. I was hoping you'd stay and come work with me. You'd be a great business partner. We could easily build another company from scratch. As you know almost everyone with brains leaves Norway for better jobs and opportunities. Look at your brother . . . a top-notch petroleum engineer who should be helping his own country find more oil. Instead of staying at Statoil he's now helping British Petroleum find oil in America."

"Well . . . they need all the help they can get since a lot of their oil has spilled and polluted the Gulf of Mexico."

Matthias Otterstad laughed. "Yes. Those crazy British idiots. Unbelievable. And not one of those rats have been prosecuted. Interesting how the enviro-radical Obama people turn a blind eye when it comes to one of their biggest corporate campaign donors. I wish I could buy off politicians that easily and thoroughly in Norway."

"It would be too expensive."

Matthias Otterstad laughed. "As the old saying goes . . . politicians don't sell their integrity . . . they just rent it. It figures that the rent for a Norwegian politician would be much more expensive in good old Norway . . . as with everything else."

"How true. Norway has gotten way too expensive. Remember the good old days? . . . I still remember our law school days and going to your Nora's apartment so I could get some food when I was low on funds . . . which was almost always. Your Nora always had good food in her refrigerator. I think she earned more money in one month as a registered nurse than both of us made during all of our years in law school."

"Yes," said Matthias Otterstad with a chuckle. "I think we both married our wives because they made so much more money as nurses than we did back then as lawyers. By the way . . . I'm glad to see you and Emma are so happy together. That's getting to be a rarity nowadays."

"You name it . . . everything's getting to be a rarity nowadays."

"What you and Emma have is quite special . . .

which reminds me . . . that you owe me a lot . . . after all Nora and I introduced you to Emma."

"I'm so glad I married her."

"Nora and I were so worried about you those two years after Karoline died."

"Thank you my friend," said Sohlberg who quickly switched the topic. "But you owe me more for recommending you to your first clients when they asked for references."

The men laughed.

~ ~ ~

Karl Haugen did not understand why his father no longer looked for him. Several times his father had come so close to him but his father had not seen or heard him. He now felt so far away from his father.

"Daddy!" he yelled.

Silence. As always. The silence sometimes overwhelmed him. Other times he felt happy when he heard the pretty music. He wondered how long he would be kept away from his father.

~ ~ ~

Sohlberg finished eating. He discretely inspected Matthias Otterstad and his immense estate and he wondered how all this had happened to a law school graduate who had never practiced law. He only knew the basic details: that shortly before graduating from law school Matthias Otterstad had inherited $ 200,000 kroner or less than $ 40,000 U.S. dollars from an elderly aunt; and that within a year he had quadrupled his inheritance by investing in out-of-favor stocks and currencies from his home.

Matthias Otterstad caught Sohlberg giving him and his property the once-over. "My good friend . . . look at all this. . . . I owe you. And that's why I've asked you many many times to come work with me. Thanks to your references and recommendations I soon had wealthy investors in Norway and abroad begging me to manage their money."

Sohlberg nodded. He remembered the fawning newspaper and magazine articles about his friend. Within four years of starting his investment fund Matthias Otterstad was managing large amounts of Other People's Money for a hefty percentage of profits. Over a ten year period his take-home income added up to tens of millions of dollars and kroner and euros.

Matthias Otterstad moved closer to Sohlberg and said:

"Any regrets over not joining me in the business?"

"No. None."

"Really?"

"No. I truly love what I do."

"Why?"

"Because nothing excites me more than outsmarting the criminal mind. Nothing. I also love finding out how people really live their life in private . . . away from the public eye. Their choices fascinate me . . . how they make choices for the better or for the worse."

"But a policeman's pay is so little compared to what you could've earned in business."

"Material possessions never attracted me."

"How lucky. You know . . . it's always a fight to own things and not let them own you. My five children all know that they will get very little when I die . . . just as I got very little when my father died. See those fancy

Bénéteau boats floating out there?"

"They're hard to miss."

"Those boats are not a rich man's toys but rather the principal assets for three of my children who own small businesses that charter and rent the boats. No sir . . . my children will not to grow up to be weak degenerates like the royals of Europe or all those trust fund babies."

"Good for you. I've seen so many disasters when parents spoil their children. You have no idea how many of my worst criminals became just that thanks to a father or mother who coddled and spoiled them and encouraged them to do whatever they felt like doing."

"Yes! . . . That's why all of my children have to work if they want to eat."

"So they get nothing?"

"Practically nothing. Just seed money to start a business or get an education or learn a trade. Almost everything will go to foundations and charities and think-tanks and political causes when Nora and I kick the bucket. More than anything else we want to make sure that Norwegians stay Norwegians . . . that Norway stays out of the European Union racket and stops all this social engineering nonsense of immigration and other insanities."

"I'm surprised you haven't moved to Switzerland to avoid taxes."

"We did for a time after I sold the company to those idiots in New York. But we couldn't stand being in Switzerland . . . it's the money laundering capital of the world . . . after a while the stench of dirty money starts clinging to you. You know what I mean?"

"I think so."

"Sooner or later you start smelling like a filthy pig from all those dirty billions of euros and dollars parked in

Switzerland from drug bosses and corrupt Third World dictators. I'm sure most of Interpol's targets have all or most of their money in Switzerland."

Sohlberg smiled and switched the topic to avoid even the remotest chance of accidentally mentioning any Interpol investigation. "What luck of yours Matthias . . . or intelligence . . . in selling out your company before the market crashed."

"You wouldn't believe what I knew about. . . ."

Both men fell silent when other guests joined them. Fru Otterstad and Fru Sohlberg rejoined their spouses. The Otterstads sipped wine while the Sohlbergs drank an alcohol-free cider.

~ ~ ~

He lost track of his wife at the gym. She kept flitting about from machine to machine and then chit-chatting here and there with all of her dumb and superficial gym friends. Of course he now knew all about her flirting in the gym and picking up men for dalliances when he was at work.

"Faster! . . . Let's go people! . . . Faster!" yelled one of the cretins who posed as a fitness trainer and so-called Olympic cyclist.

He looked for his wife among the women who were panting after their leader in the stationary exercise bicycle group. The so-called Olympian was a bottle-blonde 20-something male who was often called *Gluts* behind his powerful backside by the more lecherous and hormonal-minded women and gay men at the gym.

There she is. Brazen as always. Look at her ogling him.

He caught his wife standing by a weight machine

and staring straight at the Olympian's bulging rump. He inspected his wife in her tight workout clothes and noticed that she was indeed no longer in as good physical condition as she had been when she was a body builder.

Although she was no longer a Miss Charles Atlas or Miss Arnold Schwarzenegger he knew that she would probably put up a good fight if he tried to strangle or stab her. He had to avoid any combat with her. The trick would be to disable her and maybe even drug her beforehand. Or get her really drunk. She liked smoking cannabis two or three times a week and that might do the job along with some beers and tranquilizers.

He took a break from the strenuous exercise that the Jacob's Ladder gave him. Of all the gym equipment the Jacob's Ladder was his absolute favorite because of the punishing nature of that exercise beast.

Who was the genius who designed the Jacob's Ladder exercise machine?

As he drank from a bottle of Farris mineral water he realized that the Jacob's Ladder exercise machine was nothing less than a perfect symbol for his life. In other words he was climbing a ladder and a marriage that went nowhere and the efforts were draining his energy and the ladder and the marriage would eventually exhaust and defeat him. He looked at other gym members on others ladders and the grueling workouts that they received as they climbed the endless procession of wood rails on the 40 degree slope.

Wasn't there a Bible story about a Jacob's ladder?
Or was it the story about Jacob wrestling with God?

He tried to remember the exact context of the Bible story.

Like almost all Norwegians he had grown up as a member of the government-sponsored Evangelical

Lutheran Church of Norway. Like most children he had taken the mandatory *Kristendomskunnskap* or Christian theology courses given in public elementary schools until 2007. Like almost all Norwegians he celebrated religious Christian holidays like Easter and Christmas as well as Lutheran ceremonies for births and confirmations and weddings and funerals. And like most Norwegians he never went to church except for those holidays and events.

Jacobs' ladder . . . what did the Bible say about that?

As soon as his wife joined the stationary bicycling group he went over to the weight lifting section and began a workout with dumbbells. He then switched to various hand grips in order to strengthen his hands and wrists in preparation for the happy day when he would kill her.

Strangling her with his bare hands would be such a pleasure.

First would come the sensual and exciting feel of squeezing the lovely flesh around her neck.

Second he would have the luxury of looking deep into her eyes and watch her life flicker away with the ultimate satisfaction that the last image ever to appear in her retina would be that of him snuffing the life out of her.

All that excitement would be the perfect climax following hours or days of torturing her.

This is his plan. This is his obsession.

A fetching and well-built woman in her 30s approached him and started working out with the dumbbells. She soon turned to him and said:

"Hei . . . don't those grips hurt your hands or wrists?"

He nodded and realized that he would have absolutely no problems in finding a suitable replacement for his wife within days or weeks of her death. He was perfectly sure that he would probably be able to hook up with some woman within hours of the funeral.

From what he's heard women immediately swoop in and start seducing the widower in a bid to quickly bed the grieving survivor. Men of course do the same on widows. The vultures circle and move in for their prey. They take advantage of the widow's or widower's grief and overwhelming desire and passion for their loved one.

He looked forward to the feeding frenzy over him—the grieving survivor. He knew that he would be no different than a piece of meat that sharks have smelled and tasted in the water. Without any doubts he believed that he could move some *Hot Babe* into his house to console him within days of his wife's tragic death.

Planning.

The key is in the planning.

He who plans well reaps the rewards.

Had not his entire life proved to him that he reaped great rewards *if* he planned thoroughly and well in advance?

His careful planning for his education and for his career had superbly rewarded him. Only when he got careless did he suffer the consequences as had happened with his wife. Therefore she must die not anytime soon but rather a year or so from now. And it must look like an accident

How can you torture and kill someone while making it look like an accident?

He could not afford to attract attention from the police. No sir.

His brain started working on all the calculations and permutations.

Then it hit him.

As a child he had read and heard about Jacob's ladder from the Old Testament Book of Genesis.

That's it.

Genesis. How fitting. I too will have a new beginning as soon as she's dead.

He scurried over to the locker room and got his Nokia cell phone out of his jacket. He had the latest smart phone from the giant Finnish telecom company. The phone could surf the web at lightning speeds and find anything on the Internet.

He ran the search for "Jacob's ladder" on Google. His eyes widened as he read the NASB translation of Genesis 28:10-17 which tells of:

Jacob traveling and sleeping outdoors at night with a rock for a pillow. He dreams "*and behold, a ladder was set on the earth with its top reaching to heaven; and behold, the angels of God were ascending and descending on it.*"

Then God tells Jacob that he will be rewarded with land and children and that "*Behold, I am with you and will keep you wherever you go, and will bring you back to this land; for I will not leave you until I have done what I have promised you.*"

His eyes filled with tears especially when he read further on that Jacob wakes up from the dream and says:

"*Surely the LORD is in this place, and I did not know it.*"

His hands shook when he read the last verse:

"*He was afraid and said, 'How awesome is this place! This is none other than the house of God, and this is the gate of heaven.'*"

If only he could see the gate of heaven. If only he could get to the gate of heaven. But he could not because it was far too late for that. The dirty deeds were done. Her deceptions had stolen that opportunity from him forever.

He would never be blessed like Jacob. She had taken that from him and to make matters worse she was without a doubt surely going to expose him with his little secret about the molestations. He had to kill her. She had blocked him from ever seeing and reaching the gate of heaven.

Did not the Old Testament law of "*an eye for an eye*" call for her death?

No amount of forgiveness would solve his problem.

Only her death would make things right and even and just.

The minutes slipped away while he was lost in thought. He wept silently and turned away so that no one could see him in the locker room.

Yes. I could be like Jacob and see the gate of heaven . . . except for her curse.

Right there before his very eyes was *his* life story. He turned off his phone. He looked forward to a future of planning every day and every minute on how to punish her as severely as she deserved and then how to get rid of her once and for all so that he could at least finish his life on earth in peace without her.

Scream . . . that's what I want to do. Can I scream?

His mind pulled images from old memories of his childhood and he remembered taking field trips during his high school years to the many excellent art museums in Oslo. One image in particular had stuck to his mind and the image terrified him for the deep truth contained in the image and he could not get the image or painting out of his mind.

The Scream by Edvard Munch.

How well he remembered the details of the swirling reddish-orange sky and swirling purple-blue waters and the skeletal and distorted face of the lonely and sick and terrorized person that he saw at the Munch-museet or Munch Museum.

He made his mind up at the gym to make sure that his scream would be the last thing that she ever heard while he killed her.

Yes.

His face and his scream would provide just the perfect ending for her. From the long window in the locker room he saw dozens of Sankthans bonfires blazing away.

In the pagan days the bonfires supposedly kept away witches or evil spirits from roaming the land during the endless daylight of midsummer. He remembered how his mother like many other old-fashioned and superstitious Norwegians used to throw straw dummies that looked like witches into the bonfires.

Should I burn her body in a Midsummer bonfire? Maybe even while she is still alive?

He had an evil witch to kill.

Yes.

The next June 23rd—one year from today—would be the day of her death. That would give him more than enough time to plan and execute. And execute he would.

~ ~ ~

One hour before midnight. The Otterstads and their guests sat by the beach in groups listening to jokes and music and playing games and it all seemed so festive and normal and happy to Sohlberg and yet the unnatural daylight filled him with dread. The pale midnattsol hung in the sky like an unwelcome guest of ill omen.

"Are you okay?" said Fru Sohlberg. She wondered if

he was falling again into a depression.

"I guess that I'm just not used to seeing the sun at night."

"I know. It's so odd to be back and see sun and daylight in the middle of the night."

"Maybe I should've taken a nap like you suggested. I feel a little lightheaded."

Nora Otterstad overheard the Sohlbergs' conversation. She immediately intervened and took both Sohlbergs to the main house. She lodged them in a small study near the main living room so that Sohlberg could take a nap on a very comfortable sofa while Fru Sohlberg watched over him.

A restless sleep brought little relief to Sohlberg. He dreamed that time itself was frozen and that the future was forever postponed. He felt trapped—in the past and the present. He was literally a man without a future.

At 11:45 PM Fru Sohlberg woke him up and said:

"The Otterstads are going to take us home as soon as they light the Sankthans bål . . . the Midsummer's Eve bonfire by the beach. Okay?"

"No. Let's stay. I'm okay."

"No. We're not staying outdoors on the longest day of the year . . . a day with no night. Imagine what that does to a man in your condition."

"What condition?"

"You know . . . you know what I mean. . . ."

"What do you mean by my *condition*? . . . Are you saying I'm depressed . . . in clinical depression?"

"Oh please . . . don't you see? . . . We never recovered from jet-lag since we arrived in Europe. We've had too much travel and too little sleep. You need to rest. And you've had so many memories to deal with after coming back to your parents' home and. . . . Look . . . I don't feel too good myself. We're just not used to these day-filled nights."

The Sohlbergs apologized and said their goodbyes to their hosts and everyone else at about thirty minutes after midnight. Leif Otterstad piloted them quickly back home through the placid waters.

Sohlberg turned one last time to watch the giant 30-foot bonfire on the Otterstad property. Bonfires dotted all of the beaches around the Oslofjord. The fires lent a wild and savage air reminiscent of the pagan Viking era and no one could escape the primal and visceral feeling that something imminent and far bigger than themselves was unfolding.

Chapter 5/Fem

1 YEAR AND 22 DAYS AFTER
THE DAY, FRIDAY, JUNE 4

"A new form of Number Four heroin is about to hit
the streets . . . it's cheap and extremely dangerous . . .
with purity rates of ninety-eight percent and higher. . . .
This deadly heroin is named Osama-H . . . because it was
developed and manufactured by Russian and Bulgarian
scientists hired by Osama bin Laden."

With that introduction Sohlberg had the undivided
attention of the department heads in charge of vice and
drugs in all 27 of Norway's police districts. They had
gathered in downtown Oslo to hear Sohlberg's 40-minute
talk on international heroin smuggling. They met in a
small auditorium at 12 Hammersborggata where the sleek
and modern 7-floor building of the Politidirektoratet. The
National Police Directorate occupied most of the city
block on the southeast corner of Hammersborggata and
Torggata.

After his talk Solhlberg took the elevator to Ivar
Thorsen's office on the top floor.

They shook hands and sat down. On Thorsen's desk
Sohlberg observed a pair of elegant water glasses made by
the specialty glass firm of Kosta Boda from Sweden. Two
fancy bottles of Voss artesian water sat ostentatiously next
to the expensive glassware. Of course Ivar Thorsen no
longer drank Farris mineral water out of the bottle. He

was now a big man in the police. Sohlberg smiled at the pretensions which included elegant Swedish furniture and modern art paintings.

How the Oslo district police commissioner's office had changed!

Who would have thought that Ivar Thorsen would ever sit in a lavish corner office?

In his wildest imaginations Sohlberg would never have *dreamed* of the dumb and plodding and unimaginative Ivar Thorsen ever sitting in a commissioner's office decorated by an interior decorator and probably a Swedish one at that. Back when Sohlberg was a rookie police constable the most a district commissioner could hope for was Ikea furniture that was allotted on a very tight budget to only the most senior of commissioners. Now the police budgets were lavish if not extravagant.

"Do the taxpayers know how their money is being spent up here?"

"Don't be obnoxious Sohlberg. Try to be pleasant for a change."

"I am being pleasant. I didn't say what was really on my mind."

"Well . . . I myself will tell you exactly what is on my mind."

A long and uncomfortable pause followed.

Sohlberg's mouth almost dropped open when he heard Ivar Thorsen's next words:

"I need your help Sohlberg. I have a cold case. Perhaps you've already heard of it . . . the missing seven-year-old boy who vanished one morning in school and has never been seen again."

"The Karl Haugen boy?. . . I saw it on the news a few days ago on N.R.K. One and Two."

Sohlberg also remembered his wife showing him a special anniversary section on the case in the Sunday edition of *Aftenposten*.

"Yes," said Thorsen. "You can't miss the case."

"Just this morning . . . as I was coming in . . . I saw huge headlines plastered on *Verdens Gang* when I passed a newsstand."

"That's the case Sohlberg. The media is all over us because the one year anniversary came and went without us getting any closer to solving the disappearance."

"One year . . . that's almost beyond solving."

"But—"

"Thorsen . . . you know the rule . . . less than half of all missing cases and homicides are ever solved at all unless they are solved within the first forty-eight hours. And you now have a missing case that's twelve months old?"

"We did our best. We put tons of people and man-hours into it."

"That's why my rule is to work smart not hard."

"Obviously we are not as intelligent as you are. That's why a few months ago I shut down the investigation . . . it was obvious we were getting nowhere. But now the higher-ups want the investigation reactivated . . . they're getting a lot of flak over it."

"Who was in charge?"

"Trygve Nilsen."

"Are you kidding me?"

"He's a Chief Inspector . . . just like you."

"Why am I not surprised that you promoted him?"

"He's a hard worker. And loyal."

Sohlberg almost shouted a vulgarity. Instead he shrugged.

"Listen here Sohlberg . . . I'm reassigning him . . .

he'll be investigating recent death threats over the Nobel Peace Prize . . . seems some Islamic terrorists are pissed off over some of the recent candidates that our parliament picked for the Nobel Peace prize. These crazy punks put out a video in Pakistan saying that they're going to blow up the Storting."

"How nice for Nilsen. Instead of getting fired he gets a plum job for a botched investigation into the unsolved disappearance of a little boy. I see nothing has changed here."

"Actually it has . . . Sohlberg."

"Don't make me laugh."

"Effective immediately I am appointing you to lead the investigation into the disappearance of Karl Haugen. Sit down! . . . Don't even think of walking out of this office to call your pals at Interpol. The Politidirektør . . . yes the National Police Commissioner himself . . . already called the General Secretary of Interpol. He gladly released you to solve this apparent kidnaping."

"What?"

"Interpol is assigning you here indefinitely until you solve the case."

"What?"

"Check your e-mail. You'll find official Interpol notification. You will also find the Politidirektør's written assignment officially naming you as the lead on the Karl Haugen case."

Sohlberg said nothing but felt lightheaded enough to pass out.

"Ain't it great Sohlberg? You're back working for *me* . . . just like in the good old days. The good news is that you can leave Norway as soon as you solve the case. I suggest you work fast and solve the case soon. I've heard through the grapevine how much you and your wife love living in Seattle."

At first Sohlberg thought that he was the target of a prank. Then he thought that Thorsen was testing him to see if he wanted to come back to Norway. Sohlberg felt like vomiting when the reality sank in that this was no joke.

"Come with me Sohlberg and I'll show you your cubicle down the hallway. I've assigned you a recent graduate from the academy . . . Constable Wenke Wangelin. She participated in the investigation from the very beginning."

Sohlberg expected Wangelin to be nothing less than a dumb mediocrity chosen by the dumb mediocrity of Ivar Thorsen. He was surprised when a muscular and good-looking 30-something blonde walked up to him and introduced herself with a very strong handshake.

"Chief Inspector Sohlberg . . . it's an honor to meet you. I've read a lot about you . . . I wrote a term paper in law school on how you solved the Wassenaar murders through new forensic techniques."

Sohlberg nodded. He rarely came across good-looking people who had intelligence. He liked the fact that she did not call him by his first name. Having lived abroad for so long he had come to intensely dislike how Norwegians used first names at work and overall went too far at work with a fake equality that bordered on the insolent.

After a few questions Sohlberg knew that Constable Wangelin was intelligent and dedicated. That meant one thing: Ivar Thorsen and his bosses definitely wanted the case solved. In other words Sohlberg was *apparently* not being set up to fail nor did it appear that he and Wangelin were being thrown together as window-dressing to trick the media and the public into believing that the government was finally serious about solving the case.

"Chief Inspector Sohlberg," said Wangelin, "I suggest we go down the hallway to the Karl Haugen room . . . as we call it."

"You two go ahead," said Ivar Thorsen. "I have other chores to look after. Let me make it perfectly clear Sohlberg . . . you are authorized to do whatever it takes to solve the case. Take any and all action. I will sign any requisition form you present me for manpower or equipment or any other resources."

Sohlberg walked away in a daze and still somewhat incredulous at the unexpected turn of events. He could not quit or resign. He still had ten more years to go before he could collect a full pension. He and Fru Sohlberg had made many sacrifices and plans around that pension.

Constable Wangelin pointed at the combination door lock and whispered, "The code is one-one-seven . . . that was Karl Haugen's height . . . one point seventeen meters. . . . The code to get in the computer files is 'kh at twenty-two-point-seven' . . . his initials and weight in kilometers. He is a cute little boy. Imagine him so slight . . . just fifty pounds and three-feet eight-inches tall."

"I notice that you said 'He *is* a cute little boy'."

"I'm sorry . . . am I being too optimistic?"

"I don't know. One also has to be realistic no?"

She walked him through four rows of tall metal shelves that held 68 binders filled with 4500 leads among thousands and thousands of pages of police reports. Each binder was at least four inches thick.

"Hhhmmm . . . interesting," said Sohlberg. "But we'll never be able to read this ourselves. It would take twenty or thirty investigators many weeks to go through this stuff."

"That's not going to happen anytime soon . . .

Commissioner Thorsen dismantled the Karl Haugen Task Force . . . fifty-two investigators at one point. I think that's why he brought you in."

"To do the work that fifty-two people couldn't do right the first time?"

"We worked hard Chief Inspector. The problem was that no one coordinated our work. We had no direction or leadership. It was more like . . . *'Just go out there and do something.'*"

"Ah yes . . . the idiot's solution of throwing people and money at a problem and hoping it gets magically solved."

Constable Wangelin smiled and pointed at three secure laptops on a conference table. "These computers connect directly to a mainframe at KRIPOS."

Sohlberg was not impressed. KRIPOS was supposed to be all about crime scene investigation. That's how the agency had started out after its humble beginnings as a national crime lab in 1959. Then in 1967 the National Crime Investigation Service morphed into a sophisticated crime scene investigation unit that was meant to help small police districts which faced complicated and expensive cases—murders or organized crime or other major crimes. But ever since the 1990s the new management at KRIPOS liked to squeeze out the local police from investigations while seeking maximum publicity. Even worse from Sohlberg's point of view was the fact that KRIPOS wasted enormous amounts of time and effort on dumb but politically correct investigations such as those involving "racist remarks on the Internet".

"KRIPOS isn't what it used to be," said Sohlberg. "It used to be much more effective in the old days with Rolf Harry Jahrmann . . . the father of KRIPOS."

"I've heard of him," added Wangelin.

"I met him . . . quite the character. I think he's still alive . . . in his eighties. I also met several of the people who worked for him . . . the old E-Group . . . the Homicide Commission. But enough of old memories."

"This laptop . . . Chief Inspector . . . is dedicated to a special software on the KRIPOS mainframe that has helped us catalog and sort through more than four thousand two hundred fifty-seven tips that investigators have received over the past year."

"I'm sure that the proverbial needle is in that haystack Constable Wangelin. But how are we going to find it? Let's not get mesmerized by fancy technology . . . these computers are really toys. I prefer good old fashion questioning . . . as if we just started the case fresh . . . new."

"A fresh approach will be best."

"Obviously . . . one year later no one can explain how a seven-year-old boy vanished in the middle of his school in the middle of the morning while he was surrounded by hundreds of adults and children and teachers attending a kiddie science fair."

She blushed and showed him stacks of maps with various colors that plotted the 155 square miles searched for Karl Haugen.

"Interesting graphics. But those maps won't help us."

"I know. But Thorsen wanted me to show them to you. As you can imagine Chief Inspector . . . a big reason for these maps was to show the media and the public that we were working hard."

"That seems to be the problem here . . . working hard but not smart. Or should I say . . . *appearing* to work hard."

"Do you want to see more?"

"No. I'd like you to prepare a one page summary of what is actually known . . . as facts . . . to have happened to the boy on the day that he disappeared. Just stick to the facts and do not include any theories. Write up a second summary on the boy's circle of family and friends that he hanged around with."

"That's it Chief Inspector?"

"Trust me . . . it's hard work. Summarizing all pertinent facts into two pages will take a lot of thought. I suggest you take the rest of the afternoon today . . . and all day tomorrow to write the summaries. Please make sure that you write or talk to every single investigator involved in the case. Get their input on what needs to be in the summary. All of the information that you get from all of the investigators will now be stored in your brain . . . far better than any computer."

"Chief Inspector . . . will you be here if I have questions?"

"No. But feel free to call me any time on my cell phone. I'm going home. I have a lot to explain to my wife about this unexpected assignment. She thought we'd be leaving for Bergen to visit her parents."

"Oh. I'm sorry."

"So am I. But isn't it interesting . . . when my wife saw the news on television about the one year anniversary of Karl Haugen's disappearance . . . she said she hoped that somehow I'd be able to help the investigation."

"I'm glad you're here Chief Inspector. It was about time. You see . . . some of us do take the case very seriously . . . we feel bad for the boy. We're worried about him."

"Everyone should think like that. I certainly do."

Sohlberg left the building. His mind worked better in the fresh air and under sunny skies. A thought hit him. He immediately called Ivar Thorsen on his cell phone and said:

"Do not tell the press that I'm working on the Haugen case. Make sure that no one leaks anything to the media about me working on the case!"

"Alright. Alright. Calm down Sohlberg."

"I'm serious about this. The person or persons who took the boy must not be warned that we're reactivating the investigation. We must have the element of surprise. Understand?"

"Well—"

"No! The most you can tell anyone on the outside is that you have assigned the case for review. Understand? You say anything more to your buddies in the press and I will tell everyone that you sabotaged the investigation from the start."

"Alright!"

"Also . . . I'm not going to wear a uniform at all . . . nor will Constable Wangelin. And we're not coming to work at the office from eight to four like everyone else. Is that understood?"

"Yes."

"Also . . . I need an unmarked car that doesn't yell police to everyone who looks at the car. Yes?"

"Sohlberg! . . . Here we go again with your demands and conditions."

"Just like the good old days that you seem to remember so fondly."

Feeling calmer Sohlberg decided to walk all the way to the Oslo Central Station to take advantage of the pleasant sunny weather. He had more than enough time to get to his tram. The walk also gave him time to think about how he would break the news to Fru Sohlberg.

Would she be pleased or angry?

Just how disruptive and difficult would this new assignment become?

~ ~ ~

Fru Sohlberg was already waiting for him in his parent's Volvo at the Kastellet station of the Oslotrikken tram line Number 18. His parents had begged them to use their car to prevent the battery from dying.

"How did the conference go?"

He explained and included all the details.

"Unbelievable!" she exclaimed. "What a turn of events."

"Are you angry? . . . I doubt if I'll be able to go with you to Bergen to see your parents."

"That's alright. Maybe they'll come and stay with us for a week."

"That's a great idea . . . it would be very good. We have more than enough room."

"I'll call them tonight and see if and when they can come."

"So you're not angry or disappointed?"

"Not at all. Why should I be? I knew this would be our life with you in the police."

"Thank you Emma."

"No need to thank me."

"But I do."

"Actually . . . I'm glad you took the assignment. I've thought a lot about that little boy."

"It doesn't look good . . . he's been missing for more than a year and there's no sign of him. I have to warn you so you don't get your hopes crushed . . . he's probably dead."

Fru Sohlberg shook her head. Her eyes welled up.

"How sad . . . if that turns out to be the case then at least he's in a far better place . . . that little eternal soul of his."

Sohlberg's throat hardened.

Did Ivar Thorsen know that they had lost their two-year-old son to leukemia shortly after moving to Lyon in France?

Was that another reason for putting him on the Karl Haugen case?

Did Ivar Thorsen or the higher-ups know that a child abduction was likely to bring back painful memories of the death of their own son?

Harald Junior's death almost destroyed Sohlberg and his wife. He could not help wondering whether Thorsen had dragged him into the case as the result of a diabolical plan to cause him and his wife severe if not permanent emotional distress.

Was the Karl Haugen assignment another form of payback for Sohlberg exposing corruption by the Supreme Court justices?

Chapter 6/Seks

1 YEAR AND 23 DAYS AFTER
THE DAY, FRIDAY, JUNE 4

Sohlberg reached into the shelf and took out Wagner's *Tristan und Isolde*—the doomed lovers.

"Well . . . well."

He's amazed that his parents still have all of the compact discs that he bought them over the decades for their birthdays and for Christmas and for Mother's Day and for Father's Day. He opened the case and studied the libretto for the divine and unsurpassed 1953 classic EMI recording with Kirsten Flagstad (Soprano) and Blanche Thebom (Mezzo Soprano) and Ludwig Suthaus (Tenor) and Dietrich Fischer-Dieskau (Baritone) and the Royal Opera House Covent Garden Orchestra directed by Wilhelm Furtwängler.

The prelude overwhelmed Sohlberg with its intensity.

He pressed the STOP button and slipped Wagner's masterpiece off the CD player because Wagner's music hits too close to home. The music reminded Sohlberg of the overpowering nature of love and death and how those two mixed together can easily lead to insanity itself.

The music evoked remembrances of the past. Memories crashed into Sohlberg's mind like the winter storms that hurl overwhelming waves into Norway's fjords.

Sohlberg remembered the details of the death of loved ones.

He remembered the sickening *shisssh* of the rope going through the carabiner on Karoline's harness. He remembered her eyes wide open and filled with love and acceptance of her fate.

He remembered the last soft breath of Harald Junior before the leukemia killed him.

He remembered the boy's dreamy eyes slowly dimming away until the light was extinguished and gone.

Grief.

Insanity.

He remembers how—a month after Karoline's death—he took a trip to a country house at Åsgårdstrand. A partner at Sohlberg's law firm offered him indefinite use of the house for Sohlberg to have all the time and space to decompress. Sohlberg had always wanted to visit the popular summer vacation spot and pretty fishing village in Vestfold County about 65 miles south of Oslo. He spent days just watching the sailboats and the fishing boats from the lovely southwest side of the mouth of the Oslofjord. At night he watched panoramic lightning from immense thunderstorms that roll in from the North Sea over the Strait of Skagerrak.

His grief worsened. A guilty conscience consumed him for not having asked Karoline to check her ropes and knots. On the third night he grabbed his uncle's double-barrel shotgun out of the car trunk and loaded the shells.

His plan: walk down to the dock with the loaded shotgun when no one is around and end his pain and reunite with Karoline.

Unfortunately a knock on the door at midnight. Then more loud pounding.

"Hello," yelled Matthias Otterstad. "Wake up

Sohlberg . . . I know you're in there. I'm here to keep you company. Open up will you! . . . I brought a ton of food with me."

Sohlberg's plans remained inactive until his son died.

A guilty conscience hounded him again. This time for not having spent enough time with his son or for that matter with his wife. Again a loaded gun and again plans interrupted by an unexpected visitor—Chief Homicide Detective Alec Mikesell of the combined Salt Lake City Police and Salt Lake County Sheriff Task Force in Utah.

Sohlberg's memories fled when he heard Fru Sohlberg call him out of his painful reverie:

"Sohlberg where are you?"

Sohlberg bounded up the stairs to his wife and said, "Just checking out stuff."

"What stuff?"

"Oh . . . just looking at some of the operas that I bought my parents many years ago."

"Anything interesting?"

"Actually yes. Wagner. Tristan and Isolde."

"Why that one?"

"I don't know . . . I picked it at random but it seems appropriate."

"How so?"

"How love sometimes leads to insanity."

"Are you thinking of the missing boy . . . Karl Haugen?"

"Of course . . . what else?"

"You need to rest for this investigation. Please come to sleep."

"I can't with this midnight sun. I have a lot to think about."

~ ~ ~

Nothing. Absolutely nothing surprised him any more. After eight years she had exhausted any surprise left in him. He knew that he certainly wouldn't be surprised if she did *not* break down in a torture session and tell him what he wants and needs to hear. The only surprise will be how she reacts to the torture and how she reacts when she realizes that he will exterminate her.

Will she scream?

Will she cry?

Will she beg for mercy?

If she begs for mercy he will remind her that she gave him none. Therefore all that she can expect is justice.

Yes. That's all she can expect. And that's all she deserves.

"She deserves a long and horrible death," he said softly to himself as he mowed the lawn with a manual grass mower that she forced him to use because she's very worried about climate change and carbon emissions.

The grass clippings flew off the sharp blades just like the many illusions that he had had about her and their love and their marriage. Together eight years and married half that time. And the mystery of her true nature only kept getting stronger.

She is unfathomable.

She is unknowable.

He almost laughed when he thought of how much he will enjoy shoving her lifeless body into a special barrel that he brought from his workplace a few months ago. The barrel was specially designed to hold acids and it is marked 'CORROSIVE" and he shivered with ecstasy at the thought of how greatly he will enjoy pouring acid on her lifeless body and how after 6 hours in an acid bath she will become nothing but a pink fluid to be taken to a chemical recycling plant. He giggled when he thought of her tombstone—a barrel marked CORROSIVE.

He started laughing and laughing when he realized that finally *something* in her miserable and toxic life of lies was true: CORROSIVE.

Yes . . . that's her!

His shoulders shook as he laughed and thought of her winding up as an acidic gob of pink nothingness. Yes. She will be truly unfathomable *and* unknowable at the chemical waste management plant that will receive the barrel with her remains.

The barrel. He's glad to have snuck one out of his employer's factory during a long holiday weekend when no one was looking or paying close attention. He's already begun stealing two bottles of acid at the time from the factory's nearby warehouse. No one noticed because they literally use thousands of gallons of acid every week.

When a man plans the end of a project then everything else falls into place all the way back to the beginning of the project.

Is her acid grave a case of the end justifying the means?

He laughed at his hilarious observation.

An hour later he began to rake the dead grass clippings off the lawn and she watched him from the deck in their backyard. She tanned topless—as usual. He waved at her and blew her a kiss. She barely smiled as if she's a stunning celebrity bored by her beauty and the fawning idiots who worship her.

How did she first trick me?
What was her hook and bait?
What lies did she use to catch me?

His mind searched the earliest memories that he has of her. He went over these memories and he's sickened by the realization that he's been played like a violin by a virtuoso.

He decided that when he tortures her he will cut off one of her fingers for every big lie she ever told him. That means he'll have to start lopping off her toes soon after he finishes the ten amputations on her hands.

He realized that with all of her many many lies he'll quickly run out of fingers and toes to chop and slice off.

Should I instead cut each finger and toe one little piece at a time?

That would certainly increase my quality time with her.

~ ~ ~

The first big lie. For that whopper he has to cut off her right thumb.

"You're adopted? So am I."

Was that her first hook into me?

"I was born in the Østlandet the East Country. My mother came from a wealthy family. She was forced by her family to give me up for adoption."

Her coming from a wealthy family background lowered his natural resistance to sleeping with someone who was vulgar and tacky and worked as an assistant manager at the McDonald's where he went once a week for a milkshake. Everyone at his company especially the senior managers and their wives would have been embarrassed to see him with a woman who wore garish makeup that startled and gaudy-colored polyester clothes that revealed too much of her spectacular breasts. She chewed bubble gum loudly and all day long even while eating a meal or making love or sitting on the toilet.

Her mother later corrected her daughter's misinformation:

"Born to a wealthy family? No. The social worker told us her mother turned tricks just to get a bottle of vodka. Sometimes just for a smoke and a beer. Wealthy family? Nonsense. She's making things up . . . as always. Oh well. I should've put a stop to that when I caught her telling her teachers and friends that she was one of the King's illegitimate children."

"Why didn't you stop her from lying?"

"I just didn't want to affect her self-esteem. You know what psychologists say about parents ruining a child's self-esteem. . . ."

He said nothing although he wanted to say, "What do these dumb psychologists say about you pathologically spoiling a child and letting them get away with bald-faced lies?"

The two university professors had gone overboard in spoiling her as their only child. She always got whatever she wanted from them as a child and it was just as bad after she turned 20.

There was *one* thing that she had not lied to him about and that was when she told him:

"My parents are idiots. They'll do anything and everything for me. I snap my fingers and they ask me how high they need to jump."

Her parents always believed whatever she told them at face value even when they should have suspected some of her behavior as an adult. For example: after she got a drunk driving conviction they believed her lie that she had not been drunk but rather driving impaired because she was sleepy and exhausted from taking care of him and their children.

"Our poor daughter. She works so hard. That judge was so mean. He simply wouldn't listen!"

Of course she never told her parents that she had also received a suspended conviction for child endangerment because her son had been in the car with her when she crashed into a tree while driving plastered with *double* the legal blood alcohol limit. But to her credit she did milk the drunk driving crash for all it was worth. She stopped doing chores at home and never cared for her son because she had "migraines" and "back pain" from the "accident".

~ ~ ~

The second big lie. For that lie her right index finger comes flying off the chopping block.

"Did you know I came from old money on my mother's side?"

"No," he said without realizing that she used this lie to make her vulgarity and failed career as a teacher more palatable. He would never have brought a McDonald's worker into his home as a sex partner let alone a live-in companion. The lie about old money tricked him.

"My poor mother . . . she was forced to give me up because her family and my father's family opposed their union. His family is blue blood if you know what I mean and they couldn't tolerate her being a commoner even if her family had money."

He wondered if her endless lying perhaps came from an adopted child never getting over feelings of abandonment. He never had. Nor his brother. He and his brother were grateful for the love and care of their adoptive parents. But deep down he always wondered *why* his mother had tossed him and his brother aside to another set of parents.

Constant feelings of abandonment always left him torn between having to commit to a permanent relationship with a woman versus the convenience of a temporary disposable relationship. Somehow he always wound up with the convenient and disposable relationships because that was after all the relationship that his precious birth mother had inflicted on him and his brother. He also noticed that he always became enraged whenever he thought about his birth mother and her decision which had enormous consequences—including the molestation.

Do unto others as you have had done unto you the abandoned.

Does she think the same thoughts I have?

In hindsight he realized that she did indeed feel abandoned. She later admitted that much one day when a few drinks loosened her tongue. And yet she would never admit that she had an unsatiable need to be accepted by someone who would love her and want her and only her. Nor would she admit that she was angry or bitter over the abandonment. Unlike him she never said anything about her anger and bitterness over being abandoned. Not even when he plied her with alcohol to get her talking. She always fell into a silent dark brooding that at first charmed him and later scared him.

When I torture her will she feel abandoned?

When I snuff the life out of her will she feel abandoned?

He couldn't wait to see her reaction to her torture and her own death. Finally she'd get a taste of her own medicine.

~ ~ ~

The third big lie. For that lie he slowly saws off her middle finger.

"I love teaching elementary school. I've always wanted to be an elementary school teacher since I was nine years old."

Was that her third hook into him?

Did she know that this statement would win me over as a single father?

Of course she did. An elementary school teacher is the ultimate example of a kind and nurturing role model who exercises a positive influence over children especially those living in a single parent household. He's angry and disgusted by how easily he fell for that lie.

After they got married her mother dropped another bombshell on him when she said:

"Did my daughter really tell you that she wanted to be an elementary school teacher since she was nine years old? Oh no. Absolutely not. She always wanted to be a beauty queen . . . and an actress when she got older . . . oh yes she definitely wanted to be a movie star when she got older. But she really didn't have the looks did she?"

He almost told the mother: "But she does have a talent for acting!"

Her talent for acting never failed to impress him. The problem was that almost no one ever saw it was acting until long after the performance was delivered and the desired outcome was accomplished and her gullible audience left ready for more after having swallowed her lies—hook—line—and sinker.

He once met her former mother-in-law (per husband Number Two) who said:

"She always put on a big production. *Everything* she did was only to impress people. I mean . . . goodness me

. . . well her productions were extravagant. She was after my son and trying to get him to marry her and so she used to bring me and my husband all these flowers and candy and gifts and poems and cards and that all stopped after she got married to my son. She had what she wanted and didn't need us no more.

"Then she started again with the gifts and cards and phony friendship when she tried to get us to loan her money. She used to make these pretty cards with top ten lists of why we were good parents or friends or whatever and it was incredible how totally accurate she was about us. That was surprising. She knew us very well . . . a lot more than we ever knew her."

"Did she get the loan from you?"

"No and you can imagine what happened when she did not get the loan . . . no more gifts or telephone calls or cards or visits for us."

~ ~ ~

The fourth big lie. Her finger comes off after he beats it to a pulp with a hammer.

"I was good at swimming. My parents were swimming champions in high school and the university. I even got to national finals in my senior year of high school. I love swimming and competing in sports."

She told him the lie about her loving swimming after he made the mistake of showing her *his* high school swimming trophies and medals. That's when she instantly became Little Miss Swimming Champion who loved swimming and competing.

At a high school reunion the swim coach quickly corrected the false information:

"Loved swimming? No. She hated swimming. Her

father forced her to do it. She lost her first competition on purpose. She never made it to national finals. That's a big fat lie! She wouldn't even jump into the water at the starting line of her first competition. After that she dropped out of the team and never swam or competed again. I never understood how even after she did that her parents kept showering her with money and clothes. They even bought her a brand new Volvo while she was in high school. Can you believe that?"

~ ~ ~

The fifth big lie. For that he makes her eat her own right pinkie finger which he severs with a cleaver.

"I'm kind of a shy bookworm . . . a homebody really."

Was that another hook into him the introvert who preferred reading for hours in silence at home?

He was soon dissuaded of this wrong impression at a booze-fueled party by one of her friends who was a teacher at the school where the monster briefly taught part-time:

"Book worm? Other than being forced to read books at school for homework I don't think she's even read one comic book or magazine in her life. No books. Just partying and spending money. She's a party girl alright. Did you know that she always dated two or more boys at the same time in high school and college?"

"No."

"Oh yeah. Done the same thing when she was married those three times. I guess I've told you too much. But you guys ain't married . . . are you?"

"No. But we've talked about it."

"Keep it at the talk level honey."

"Why?"

"She once told me she couldn't wait to get married so she could start dating again."

"That's funny."

"It sure wasn't funny for her first or second or third husband. See . . . she married Husband Number One because he was a Rich Daddy's Boy who partied hard and could get her away from her parent's control without her having to leave home and get a job. The problem was that his parents absolutely hated her. They had to pay her off when her husband decided to get a divorce after his parents showed him that she had lied about having to get married to him because she was pregnant when it of course turned out that she wasn't knocked up.

"Then before she's divorced from Husband Number One she jumps into bed with future Husband Number Two who's as smart as a drunk donkey. She gets him started in business with her parents' money in a business that eventually failed. She soon gets pregnant and after she has their baby Thor she goes nuts and starts dating other high school flames and generally sleeping with anything in pants. I remember one week when she bragged about sleeping with nine men during a long weekend in addition to her future Husband Number Two."

"She told me she was divorced when she met her second husband."

"No. No. She was still married to the Rich Daddy's Boy. Later on she was dating several men while that dumb donkey of Husband Number Two was out busy busting his tail trying to make her parents' business work."

"And the baby?"

"She couldn't stand the baby after a couple of weeks. Couldn't stand being tied down to a kid. The Mommy thing got boring for her real fast. She dumped the baby with her parents since she wasn't working. When they got tired she dumped the kid on her husband's parents."

He now realizes he was blind blind blind to her pattern of getting bored and frustrated with a child. He's angry and disgusted at how he never caught on to how she always abandoned anything and anyone after she got bored and frustrated with anything or anyone she could not perfectly control. Like her first swimming competition. Like her teaching career. Like her bodybuilding. Like her husbands. Like her son.

~ ~ ~

The sixth big lie. That means he burns off her left thumb with a blowtorch.

"I've always worked. No welfare for me. I always worked to put food on the table for me and my son. When I couldn't get permanent full-time employment at any of the schools I swallowed my pride and went to work in restaurants."

Was that another hook into him who always feared getting stuck with a parasitic woman who'd latch unto him just for his incredible income?

Of course it was. One summer she had a bad cold and asked him to take her son Thor to spend the weekend visiting Husband Number Three—the boy's *adoptive* father. By that time he was wise-ing up to her. He decided to have a talk with Husband Number Three because one of his friends—a twice-divorced manager at Genentech—gave him what turned out to be priceless advice:

"The best way to get a handle on your wife is to talk to and be friendly with your wife's ex-husband or ex-husbands."

At the drop-off point he invited Husband Number Three for lunch while the boy played at a park next to the restaurant. It didn't take long for the truth to come out even before the waitress served them traditional open-faced sandwiches.

Thor's adoptive father looked straight at him as if reading his mind and said, "Ah. The joys of fatherhood."

"Yes. That is true."

"Problem is that sometimes the joy gets forced on you."

"That's true too."

"Look at me. Three years after we got married I finally fell for the daddy trap that she had carefully prepared and laid out for me months if not years before. I should've seen it coming from the first year of our marriage when she released her second husband from financial maintenance for their son.

"My mother warned me over and over to be careful. She told me over and over that it was a trap . . . a set-up.

"I stupidly thought she had released her second husband from his financial obligations because the man was a deadbeat who spent most of his time unemployed and drinking after she left him. I should have seen it coming when she got the ex-husband to release all of his parental rights to the boy in exchange for being released from the child support."

"What could you do?"

"Leave her. Kick her lazy lying cheating butt out of the house. Instead I stayed and she worked up a big production for me every day about the boy growing up all alone in the world without a father. Then at night she would love my brains out. She knows how to work a man. I stupidly caved in and adopted the boy. The loving stopped of course.

"I adopted the boy despite the fact that my parents warned me a million times not to do it. They begged me. They showed me how much of my income would disappear into child support if she was to ever divorce me down the road."

"What did you tell them?"

"That she'd never divorce me. Yes. . . I knew that she loved me working and bringing her money while she did nothing at home other than sleeping with other men and partying with her girlfriends. Two months after I adopt the boy she divorces me and tells the court that I'm '*controlling and abusive*'. Ain't that something?"

"The pot calling the kettle black."

"Yes. Ain't that something? She dumps the kid on me during the divorce . . . I think that's when she started dating you. Then after she moves in with you she takes the kid back . . . which means that I had to start paying her child support again."

"I'm sorry. This is all so much to think about. I didn't know about this situation with her. We should talk more from now on."

"Yes. By the way . . . it kills me that she always brings him back here to me with no change of clothes. I now have to buy him clothes for the weekend. Just what the heck do you guys do with all the money that I have to pay every month now that she has custody and I only have visitation."

"What do you mean?"

"I mean the big fat check I send your wife every month for my son's support!"

"That's her department. I don't see any of it," he said. "How much do you pay her?"

When he heard the enormous sum his rage almost exploded that day at the restaurant and the drive back home. But to his credit he did not say anything at all to her about how he had discovered that she was hiding and secretly pocketing all that child support money while she made *him* buy *all* of the boy's clothes and toys and food and you name it.

"So," said the ex-husband, "do you see why I'm angry that she sent the boy here today with no extra clothes for the weekend? Not even pyjamas . . . now I have to buy him more clothes."

"I see your point."

"Do you? You know . . . I once went to see her . . . and begged her to *please* lower the child support payments because I had to help my widowed sister in New York City who had cancer. My sick sister had five children to care for . . . and I desperately needed to send her and the five children money.

"What does your wife do?

"She smiles and says yes . . .that she'll gladly go to her lawyer and ask him to lower the monthly payment . . . then . . . an hour later the police are at my office asking about me '*harassing and threatening*' her."

"Not good."

"There's more. Much more. A year after we got married she went back to school to get her undergraduate degree. She had me pay her tuition. I never got to go to the university and get *my* degree because I paid for her schooling. She always told me she'd pay me back once she got to teach but the crazy broad could never get full-time work at teaching because all of the teachers and principals and staff soon got to hate the Bossy Queen Bee."

"She told me that getting a full-time teaching job at an elementary school is not easy . . . but rather difficult."

"Oh really? I don't think it's *that* difficult since I

later found out that she finally got a full-time job offer to teach."

"She never told me."

"Why should she? That's when you proposed to her. She turned down the job offer as soon as you slipped that big fat engagement ring on her finger. The meal-ticket of her newest Prince Charming had arrived to rescue her from working at McDonald's and at a school . . . and so . . . she traded me the old beat-up model for the higher income model you offered and now provide her."

~ ~ ~

The seventh big lie. For that he slowly electrocutes and burns off her left thumb with a live electric wire wrapped like a ring around the base of her thumb.

"I'm not big into material things. I don't like showing off. Hate it. My family is my life. That's all I care about."

Was that another well-placed hook into him who was so careful with his hard-earned money?

She said she wasn't big into material things and yet she made it abundantly clear that she wanted a big fat diamond from him for the engagement ring and the wedding ring. He remembered how she had spent a small fortune on clothes at H & M shortly after claiming that she had '*lost*' the engagement ring. Of course he had to buy her a second engagement ring.

She doesn't like showing off but she forced him into an expensive wedding on a private island in Greece. She then pushed him into buying her the red Audi TT sports car as a wedding gift with the car title in her name only.

She says she hates showing off and loves family above *everything* else and yet she abandoned him and everyone else so she could spend 8 to 10 hours a day every day of the week at the gym training for bodybuilding championships. During that time he had to cook and care for her son from another marriage *and* for his son from a previous marriage because she simply refused to do any other work other than working on the sculpting of her body.

Is that when her anger started getting out of control?

Did she take steroids?

After all they are well-known for causing uncontrollable rage as a side-effect.

So . . . did she take steroids?

Probably.

For sure she took those fat-burning pills that acted like amphetamines and left her paranoid and wide awake night after night. That's also when she started hanging around all these female muscle-building freaks at the gym. They were such disgusting repulsive freaks. The sight of women ogling each other was sickening to him especially when the women lathered themselves in oil and then slowly flexed different muscle groups such as their stomach muscles or butts. Their rippling muscles looked like oiled snakes moving under their skin.

She hates showing off but she made him pay for her giant breast implants after she quit bodybuilding.

Her family is her life but she dumped their children at the gym's daycare so she could spend most of the day doing whatever she wanted with whomever she wanted.

~ ~ ~

The eighth big lie. For that he chews off her left index finger.

Or should he buy a pet rat to chew her finger off by putting the rat into a tube and then lighting a blowtorch behind the rat and letting the rat chew through her bone and flesh?

Or should he use the rat to chew through her nose and cheeks or through her ribs or stomach?

The eighth lie was one of her worst and most damaging lies. She trapped him forever with that lie. She would have her hand inside his pockets for the next twenty years paying child support if they divorced.

The eighth lie had been so so clever.

"I can't have more children. The doctor said my tubes and uterus are scarred beyond repair from a bad infection I got from my IUD . . . my intrauterine device almost killed me. Anyway I take the pill just to make sure."

Her pregnancy almost two years ago left him stunned and in a daze for weeks. He was beyond surprised because she made him think that there was absolutely no way that they were going to have children. She often left the circular birth control pill dispenser on the bathroom counter so that he was sure to see it.

When he no longer saw the pill dispenser on the bathroom she told him:

"Oh honey . . . I forgot to tell you . . . I switched to Implanon . . . it's even more effective than the pill . . . the nurse put the little plastic rod in my arm a week ago . . . just under my skin . . . kind of hurt a little . . . the slow and steady drug release lasts three years. We won't have to worry anymore about my forgetting to take the pill. Now you take your clothes off and come into bed right now so we can celebrate my little rod with your big rod!"

The baby.

She changed even more after the baby than she did

with the bodybuilding. After the baby she had no patience and lots of explosive temper with my son and her son. The baby turned her world upside down. She was no longer in control. The baby controlled her and everyone else.

Why was she so angry about the baby?

Aren't babies supposed to change you from selfish to altruistic?

Aren't babies supposed to make you grow into a better adult?

No. Not with her. Her moods only got worse and worse.

Was it postpartum depression as she claimed or was that just another lie to avoid responsibility?

Right after having the baby is when she started getting on the Internet for hours and hooking up with all of her old boyfriends. The worst was finding out with his key logging software that she put herself out on many websites for singles and for people looking for *relationships*. Trolling for men hour after hour. Sending them lewd disgusting messages and nude pictures.

Why have a baby if you start acting like you hate the baby?

Her moods. They left no room for error. She got nasty even with her son and of course with my son.

Should I have let her be so strict with the two boys especially with my son?

Who wouldn't have let her have her way if they had heard her arguing *all* the time about disciplining the boys especially my son?

He decided then and there that the torture sessions will include him forcing caustic lye down her throat to let her feel what it was like hearing her rant on and on every day about how she was an *educator*—a trained professional who knew how to *handle* children.

~ ~ ~

He finished mowing the yard and planning her torture and he walked into the kitchen exhausted and dripping in sweat.

"Are you going to feed the baby?" she said in her surly bad-mood voice.

"Sure . . . but I was going to clean the deck and then prune the driveway bushes. Why can't you—"

She walked out of the room in a huff. "I'm going to the gym. I need a break!"

She's too far away to hear him say:

"Yeah bitch . . . I'll give you a break . . . break your neck!"

He realizes that there's no way he's going to wait a full year before exterminating her. He's got to do it sooner. If not he'll go absolutely stark raving mad. He called his parents.

"Hiya . . . good . . . I wanted to see if I can use Grandpa's old barn for a painting project. Yes . . . I've got several things I need to spray-paint."

He hung up and closed his eyes.

The old barn.

The pervert.

The molestations.

The violations.

Bad bad memories.

Can a building attract bad people doing bad things?

He's gonna do bad bad things. Just like in the old days.

PART TWO: THE INVESTIGATION

It is better to go to a house of mourning
Than to go to a house of feasting,
Because that is the end of every man,
And the living takes it to heart.

. . .

The heart of the wise is in the house of mourning;
but the heart of fools is in the house of mirth.

— Ecclesiastes 7:1, 4
   [1-New American Standard Bible,
     4-King James Bible]

Chapter 7/Syv

MORNING OF 1 YEAR AND 24 DAYS
AFTER THE DAY, FRIDAY, JUNE 4

Sohlberg and Wangelin met at 9:00 AM in his cubicle on the seventh floor. To Sohlberg's surprise the cubicle had window views of the city and it was large enough to accommodate a small sofa and a round table for six. The cubicle's wall panels did not have the cheap and depressing gray fabric that Sohlberg hated as a rookie cop. Instead this new form of cubicle offered pleasing and tasteful walls of wood and glass. Sohlberg wondered how much the new cubicles cost the taxpayer.

"Good morning Chief Inspector."

"Good morning Constable Wangelin. Let's sit at the table and go over your executive summary. Were you able to talk with all members of the team?"

"I'm still waiting for a few call-backs . . . lots of people are on summer vacation."

"Find them . . . call them at home if necessary. Get everyone's feedback two days from now at the latest. Who hasn't called you back?"

"A couple of constables who interviewed witnesses . . . and two KRIPOS experts . . . one on cellphones and computers and the other one on D.N.A."

"Did you ask everyone to tell you about anything unusual . . . or anything that they wish that they or someone else had done differently?"

"Yes. I did as you told me."

"Good . . . proceed."

She gave copies of the two pages to Sohlberg.

"Friday June the Fourth was not a regular school day but a special day for Karl Haugen and all the children at Grindbakken Skole. He and his classmates had a science fair in the morning before class began. The regular first period class was moved back by one hour to nine o'clock so that the principal could look at the exhibits and rank them. He was to award prizes later that day."

"So . . . it was an unusual day."

"Right. And there's more on how unusual the day actually turned out to be. The media is wrong when they paint Karl Haugen as simply having vanished from school during a regular school day when the children are carefully looked after and accounted for."

"Excellent. Proceed."

"The science fair meant that the children and their parents or guardians had to arrive early at school to set up each child's science project or exhibit. Therefore instead of taking the school bus as usual Karl Haugen came to school with his stepmother Agnes Haugen in the family car . . . a Toyota Hilux."

"A what?"

"It's a monstrous four-door pickup . . . I looked it up . . . in America it's the Toyota Tundra."

"I see . . . I just can't believe that Norwegians now drive those types of cars."

"Everyone likes the big cars that Americans drive . . . even if they're made by the Japanese."

"They cost a small fortune to fill up at the gas station. Go on . . . what else?"

"This white pickup is also unusual."

"How so?"

"It's not the stepmother's regular car. Her car is an Audi sports car . . . a red T.T. coupe."

"Why did she drive the pickup?"

"She said that she drove the pickup because Karl Haugen's science project would not fit in her sports car. Those Audi sports cars are very small . . . they really have no space in the back."

"Hhhmm . . . interesting," said Sohlberg. He took out his favorite pen—a Waterman *Phileas* fountain pen filled with green ink. He pulled the cap off and drew a rectangle around the words 'science project' and 'Audi sports car' in the summary. He drew the same rectangle around the words 'white pickup' before putting the cap back on the fat pen from France.

"Who's the owner of the pickup?"

"Her husband. The boy's father."

"How did he get to work? What does he use the pickup for . . . does he own a business that requires a van or a pickup?"

"No. He's a highly-paid engineer at Nokia . . . the cell phone company from Finland. He's in charge of a team that designs some of their computer chips."

"Nokia? . . . I've heard of them. They're in the U.S.A. too. Does she work?"

"No. She's a stay-at-home mother. She and Karl Haugen's father have a nineteen-month-old baby daughter."

"And this business with the school bus. In my day we all walked to school . . . are children in Norway now taking school buses?"

"In the suburbs . . . yes . . . because of the distances."

"Huh! When he was a kid my father walked almost two miles to school. Alright. Keep reading. . . ."

"On a normal day the school opens at eight thirty-five in the morning and the final bell to start classes rings ten minutes later. That Friday however because of the science fair the school opened early at eight o'clock. Karl Haugen and his stepmother and most of the students and their parents or family members showed up a little before eight to set up the children's exhibits and walk around looking at everyone else's exhibits at the fair. Dozens of children and parents and teachers saw the boy and the stepmother arrive at the fair at eight o'clock and stay there until quarter to nine."

"So they were seen for a total of forty-five minutes inside the school?"

"Yes."

"Continue."

"Karl and his stepmother arrived at the school two or three minutes after the school opened at eight in the morning. They first went to his classroom where they dropped off his backpack. Then they went to set up his exhibit . . . on the red-eye tree frog . . . in the auditorium with the other exhibits."

"His backpack," said Sohlberg. "Where is it?"

"Good question. I'm not sure. It may be in the evidence room. I'm pretty sure we still have custody."

"Good. Please find it as soon as you can. I'd like to take a look at it."

"Or . . . we may've returned it and left it at his home with his parents."

"Not good." He took the cap off his Waterman fountain pen and drew a rectangle around the words 'backpack' in the summary. "Alright. What else?"

"The stepmother took a picture of Karl Haugen and his science project. They had worked a lot of hours together on the project. When she got home later that day she posted the picture on her Facebook page."

Somewhat amused Constable Wangelin studied Sohlberg and his routine with the Waterman pen as he drew another rectangle around the words 'science project' in the summary. She noticed that he had also drawn a small star on the left margin by each of his green ink rectangles.

"Keep on. What happened next?"

"After taking the photograph she and the boy looked at other projects in the auditorium. That day exactly three hundred-and-two students attended school and all of them contributed exhibits to the science fair. After checking carefully it appears that a total of two hundred thirty-five adults visited the science fair as parents or relatives or guardians of the children. No one observed any strangers inside the school building that day."

"Not even during the science fair?"

"No."

"Any vendors or people delivering supplies or picking something up . . . anything like that?'

"Not that day."

"Did any teachers or staff or administrators or volunteers call in sick that day?"

"No."

"Did any school employee have any periods of time that day when they should have been somewhere but were not?"

"No."

"Do any of those people have criminal records?"

"No convictions other than . . . three drunk driving guilty pleas . . . and five convictions for marijuana possession. Karl Haugen's mother was one of the drunk driving convictions."

"I want everything on those convictions. And I mean everything."

"Yes. But why—"

"Because I know how very sloppy and extremely careless Nilsen and Thorsen have always been when conducting investigations. Constable Wangelin . . . did anyone in the team take a close look at each of the drunk driving and marijuana possession case files?"

"No."

"Did the team call every witness and judge and lawyer in the convictions for drunk driving and marijuana possession?"

"No."

"That's your number one job this week."

"I'll do it as soon as possible. Definitely it should've been done. Also . . . you should know that three years ago a man in his late twenties early thirties molested five girls at Grindbakken Skole."

"What?"

"He just walked into the playground . . . posing as a volunteer . . . before anyone knew or had time to react he took three girls one by one into the bushes and forest around the school and fondled them. He did the same to twelve little girls at other Oslo elementary schools in Ullevål and Huseby."

"Where is he now?"

"We don't know."

"What? . . . No arrest?"

"No."

"How can that be?"

"I don't know. I was not here then. You'd have to check with Commissioner Thorsen."

"I can't believe this."

"It's . . . well . . . between you and me. . . ."

"Yes?"

"The talk I heard among the older investigators was

that Commissioner Thorsen got orders from the higher-ups to *not* investigate too thoroughly . . . or make an arrest."

"What? . . . Why not?"

"The suspect was a dark-skinned man. That was the summer when anti-immigrant feelings started running high and boiling over." Wangelin noticed a blank look on Sohlberg's face so she filled him in on the details. "That was the summer when two Pakistani drug gangs had a shoot-out in Aker Brygge . . . in the cross-fire they killed a tourist from Sweden and a grandmother from Trondheim."

"Are you kidding me? A shoot-out in Aker Brygge? . . . Where they have a Prada boutique and an Ermenegildo Zegna store?"

"Used to . . . Chief Inspector. Prada closed the store and the men's clothing store with Zegna products moved to Bogstadveien . . . where it splits into Valkyriegata . . . a very exclusive neighborhood as I remember."

"Criminal gangs shooting away at Aker Brygge? . . . That's like a gang shooting in Rodeo Drive in Beverly Hills . . . or Fifth Avenue in New York. Hard to believe. Norway certainly isn't the cozy little isolated spot of paradise it once was . . . eh?"

Sohlberg could not accept that a shootout was possible in Aker Brygge which is an elegant and pricey urban redevelopment zone in what used to be the derelict eyesore of the old and abandoned shipyards of downtown Oslo.

"Alright. What else do you have for me Constable Wangelin?"

"Agnes Haugen the stepmother . . . she's a volunteer at the school . . . she went back with Karl Haugen to the boy's classroom at about eight forty-five. The mother and the boy's teacher agree on that fact. However the teacher says that a few minutes later something or someone in the hallway caught the boy's attention and that he then walked out of the classroom as if someone was waiting for him or wanting to talk to him. Another teacher declared that she saw Karl Haugen leave his classroom and walk down the hallway more or less at the same time."

"With his stepmother or alone?"

"Alone."

Sohlberg took the cap off his Waterman fountain pen and drew a rectangle around the words 'volunteer' in the summary. "What is the relationship between the stepmother and the teacher?"

"Not good. The stepmother Agnes Haugen often volunteers at the school and works closely with the boy's teacher Lisbeth Bøe . . . a little too closely according to the teacher."

"Oh? . . . What does that mean?"

"The stepmother is a frustrated teacher. She has a bachelor and master's degree in education and a teaching license but no longer works as a teacher. The school has three more volunteers just like her. The teachers appreciate the help from the volunteers . . . but the teachers don't like the second-guessing that goes on from fellow professionals who make impossible demands because their own children attend the school."

"I see."

"There's more. At the end of each week the school sends the children home with a colored paper slip that has their name on it. Green means that they behaved and learned well. Yellow means they have some issues with behavior or learning. And red means they had problems with behavior or learning."

"I see," said Sohlberg. After living abroad for a long

time Sohlberg now found it bizarre as to how the Japanese and Norwegians teach school children to conform socially and always act and think as part of a closely cooperating team working for the common good. "I see the old Norwegian principal of *Dugnad* is alive and well."

"I think the Americans call it barn-rising? . . . Like the Amish people?"

"Barn *raising*. . . . Yes. . . the Mormons in Utah also practice that . . . their state symbol is the beehive . . . everyone working together."

"That's where you investigated and solved the case of some murders tied to a lot of missing nerve gas at a military base . . . right?"

"No," he said surprised at her knowledge of his career—including his time in Utah solving the Dugway Proving Ground murders.

"No?"

"I only *helped* others investigate and solve the case of the missing nerve gas. How very *dugnad* of me . . . aye?"

She nodded and continued reading the executive summary. "Anyway . . . the stepmother demanded daily not weekly color slips. That meant much more work for the teacher because Agnes Haugen would then call her every Monday and have long conversations to find out exactly why the boy had been tagged with a yellow or red slip."

"So there's no love lost between teacher and stepmother."

"None."

"But Constable Wangelin . . . it seems to me that at least the stepmother involved herself in the boy's life and education. I see so many mothers and fathers nowadays . . . they have zero interest on what goes on in the lives of their children."

"True."

"Keep on."

"According to the stepmother the bell rang at quarter to nine and she then walked with her stepson down a hallway toward his classroom and the boy told her '*I'm going back to the classroom Mom*' and he took off in the direction of the classroom while she waved at him and she left the school through another hallway thinking that he was safe at school just like he is everyday."

"But it wasn't just any day . . . was it? . . . This science fair . . . it was the perfect cover for the boy's disappearance unless the boy left on his own . . . and then something or someone happened to him. I know about this Hasidic boy who got lost in New York on his first day walking home alone from school without his mother and a predator found him and took him."

"Horrible. What happened?"

"A lucky break in the case led to the suspect a day later . . . but it was too late. They found the boy cut up in garbage bags . . . in the man's refrigerator."

"Awful!"

"Can you imagine? . . . What are the chances of that . . . one in a million? On the one day of the year when the little eight-year-old boy asks to be allowed to walk home alone from school without his mother he meets a murdering predator. What a disaster."

"Yes."

"Anything pointing to that happening here?"

"Not really. In this case Chief Inspector Sohlberg it's not likely at all that Karl Haugen took off on his own. The father and everyone we've talked to insists that he was afraid of the woods and being alone. He was shy and afraid of strangers."

"What does the stepmother say?"

"Only that he had been acting oddly a few weeks before he vanished . . . he'd stare off into space like a zombie . . . was very distracted at times."

"True?"

"Apparently. The father attributes it to the baby crying at night and keeping them awake. I guess that babies cry a lot when they're nineteen months old."

"Hhhmm. Wouldn't you think Karl Haugen had his own room in the house since his father's a well-to-do Nokia engineer?"

"Yes."

"And wouldn't you think that Karl's parents would close the door to his room if and when the baby cried?"

"That crossed my mind."

"By the way . . . have you ever come across a seven- or eight-year-old who was not able to sleep because of background noise? . . . I've seen some children sleep in the noisiest of trains or airports with no problem at all. I saw some kids sleeping right in the middle of a loud party that my wife and I attended for St. John's Eve."

"I saw my own little nephews and nieces in that age group at Sankthans . . . they slept soundly through all the loud music and talking."

"Continue please."

"At nine o'clock the children were supposed to report to their classes where they'd be divided into small groups . . . of a couple of students each. A volunteer was to chaperone each group during a tour of the science fair in the auditorium. Of course all of the teachers made sure that all of their little groups stayed together from the minute they left the classrooms to the minute that they came back to the classrooms. A half hour later they all returned to their classes for roll call and Karl Haugen wasn't at his class with Frøken Bøe. She marks him absent."

"So we have a half-hour window for him to walk out or be taken out of the school?"

"Actually less than a half-hour. No one remembers seeing him go on the tour of the science fair with the chaperones and teachers."

"Really?"

"We're highly confident that he never went to the auditorium with a chaperoned group of classmates because more than twenty of us spent two weeks interviewing and re-interviewing *all* the teachers and chaperones and students and administrators . . . . And no one remembers seeing him at the auditorium from nine to nine-thirty . . . or anywhere else in the school after nine in the morning."

"So Karl Haugen disappeared in that fifteen minute time frame . . . from eight forty-five to nine o'clock . . . when his mother let him walk to his classroom?"

"Yes."

Sohlberg closed his eyes as he tried to comprehend the mind-boggling implications of the place and time of the little boy's disappearance. He rubbed his eyes with his fists as if he could squeeze an image into his eyes that would explain the mystery.

"Fifteen minutes?"

"Yes Chief Inspector."

"And no one remembers seeing any stranger or anyone who did not belong at the school that day?"

"That's correct. No strangers. Everyone recognized everyone else. Also . . . extensive fingerprinting of all bathrooms and door-handles and rooms and desks and playground equipment etcetera . . . revealed no prints for anyone who should not have been there that day. We also questioned and verified the whereabouts of all known sex offenders in a ten mile radius and none were near the school that day."

"Thank God the team *at least* did the fingerprint dusting . . . *and* they rounded up and ruled out the usual suspects. Well . . . the case is half-solved."

"How so Chief Inspector?"

"First of all . . . remember to always work smart and not hard."

"That sounds good . . . in theory . . . does it work in practice?"

"Yes. You see we could waste time and resources and exhaust our mental energies by going the hard route and calling in half the Oslo police force to look for someone who hid inside the school or slipped into the school to take Karl Haugen. But at this point there's only one logical path to follow based on the evidence . . . and only two people . . . you and me . . . are needed to crack this case."

"How can just the two of us solve a year-old case that more than forty investigators could not?"

"It's simple . . . we already know the kidnaper . . . he or she is right under our noses. Don't you see? We know the person who took Karl Haugen . . . we just don't know their exact name."

Constable Wanglein frowned. "I . . . I guess that no one ever wanted the investigation to come to this point . . . where a parent or someone else at the school took Karl Haugen. . . ."

"But all the evidence points to a parent."

"I . . . I hate saying this Chief Inspector . . . but I guess that we didn't really want to admit that we had a predator among the teachers or the staff or the administrators or the parents at Grindbakken skole or any other elementary school in Norway."

"Exactly Constable Wangelin. We also know that the kidnaper probably won't be a teacher or a staffer or an administrator since all of their whereabouts have been accounted for that day . . . and evening . . . right?"

"Yep. None were missing in school and all of their times and activities during and after school were checked and re-checked."

"So I doubt if any of them would have had the time and opportunity during a fifteen minute period to overpower Karl Haugen and stuff him in a suitcase or bag and keep him there all day long and then take him away from the school when school ended in the afternoon."

"True."

"Now as for the school building and grounds . . . I hope they were thoroughly searched. There's a case from the nineteen-sixties where children disappeared from school . . . it turned out that a camp of homeless bums raped and killed the school children who went to play in the schools' basement where the bums lived."

"Uhhh."

"I imagine the team carefully searched the school?"

"Yes."

"Every nook and cranny from roof to foundation and wall to wall . . . right?"

"Yes," said Constable Wangelin who nodded slowly as she came to understand the implications of what Sohlberg was saying. "This means Chief Inspector that . . . all of our suspects are the normal and lovely and well-dressed and well-educated and law-abiding citizens of the well-to-do suburb of Holmenkollen . . . home of the Holmenkollen Ski Festival and the Ski Museum."

"Exactly Constable Wangelin. The banality of evil."

"And . . . the person who took Karl Haugen is most

likely found in his circle of family or friends . . . or less likely . . . it's someone else . . . a parent . . . who went to the school that day and left with him."

"Bingo."

"But we all thought the culprit would be a known sex offender. We thought—"

"That's the problem Constable Wangelin. All of you *thought*. A detective should never *ever* think at the beginning of an investigation. He or she should only investigate and collect all the facts . . . the good investigator must not *think* . . . but rather keep an open mind as the evidence starts coming in. Once the evidence collection phase of the investigation is over then the good investigator starts thinking and following hunches or intuition or logic."

"I see that now. I'm glad I'm training with you."

"Thinking in the initial phases derails an investigation . . . bias creeps in . . . groupthink takes over . . . I've seen huge and horribly botched investigations eventually collapse because investigators made a few small but very wrong assumptions from the start."

"Rule Number One . . . work smart not hard."

"Right."

"Rule Number Two . . . don't think at the start of an investigation. Collect all the facts. Keep an open mind."

"That's it."

"Anything else?"

"Get ready for some difficult interviews because it's going to be nasty and difficult finding this most depraved of criminal minds among the suburban parents who live in pretty homes and drive nice cars and dress in Ralph Lauren and . . . smell and look nice and are polite. . . ."

"A monster," said Constable Wangelin.

"Which leads us to Rule Number Three. Never

judge. That prevents you from understanding the criminal. Judging throws bias into the picture. No . . . it's best to just sympathize with the criminal . . . understand what makes them tick."

"Disgusting . . . but I can see how effective your strategy is—"

"Not mine! I learned it from my mentor . . . Lars Eliassen . . . an old police officer in the Romsdal valley. Now I'm passing it on to you . . . and one day you will pass it on to another generation."

"Thank you."

"Anyway . . . we're dealing in this case with an upper middle class parent who has the audacity to boldly launch his or her criminal enterprise in Pilot Hill Elementary School between quarter to nine and nine in the morning on the Fourth of June."

"This is stunning . . . hard to believe."

"That . . . Constable Wangelin . . . is the audacity of evil."

~ ~ ~

Karl Haugen woke up. He wasn't sure if he had slept for hours or just dozed off for minutes. Nothing seemed real. Sadness rose in him as he realized that his father had not looked for him for a long long time. His father felt so far away. They had been so close.

"Daddy! Where are you?"

He wondered why no one heard him. It had been a long time since anyone had looked for him.

"Daddy! Where are you?"

He missed sitting with his father on the sofa after his father came home from work and telling him everything that had happened to him at school. He had so much he wanted to tell his father.

"Mom! Mom . . . can you hear me?"

He missed his mother as badly as he missed his father. She had kept looking for him unlike his father. He wished that she was not living so far away. Namsos was too far away.

Why didn't she ask Daddy to let him live with her throughout the year?

If she had asked then he would not be where he was.

~ ~ ~

Wangelin and Sohlberg took a short break. She went to re-fill her enormous coffee mug following the Norwegian tradition of consuming huge amounts of coffee at work. Meanwhile Sohlberg called his wife.

"Are your parents able to come?"

"Yes! . . . My Dad said they'd need a day or so to pack up."

"I won't be home for dinner."

"Case speeding up?"

"Drastically. . . ."

"I'll leave your dinner in the frig . . . top shelf . . . if you're coming in after midnight."

"I doubt it," said Sohlberg. "I should be in by eleven. I have to go see someone at Halden Fengsel."

"Wake me up when you get home."

"But—"

"No *buts*. You wake me up so I know you're home safe and sound."

"Alright."

"Love you."

"For time and for *all* eternity."

The Sohlbergs always said goodnight to each other

with a little routine of one saying '*Love you*' and the other one replying '*For time and for all eternity*' or '*Forever and ever always*'. They had kept that routine during their more than 25 years of marriage because Sohlberg was permanently traumatized over the fact that he had never had the opportunity to say 'Goodbye' or 'I love you' to his first wife Karoline before and while she fell to her death. The sudden unexpected death of Sohlberg's first wife had left him terrified of not being able to saying 'I love you' to those dear ones whom death steals without a warning.

Commissioner Thorsen walked into the cubicle just as Sholberg ended the call with Fru Sohlberg. Thorsen plopped down on the chair in front of Sohlberg. "So . . . did you solve it?"

Sohlberg stared at Thorsen with undisguised contempt. "No. Not yet . . . but we're getting there. At least a few things were done right."

"Imagine that. The great detective from Interpol approves of what us bumpkins do in Norway. Well now! . . . How marvelous that you approve. . . . So tell me . . . what did we do right?"

"Dusting everywhere possible for fingerprints in the school . . . checking out the whereabouts of known sex offenders."

"I pushed hard for a deep look into the S.O. population . . . I'm sure you know by now that a young pervert had previously trespassed in that same school and molested some girls."

"Wangelin told me. But that's not who did it."

"Oh?"

"I'm not telling you more."

"Oh?"

"I know you're here fishing for information that you can pass on to the higher-ups . . . who will then interfere with the investigation . . . or screw it up. But that won't happen on my watch."

"Oh?"

"I already instructed Wangelin not to leak or disclose any information on the investigation to anyone . . . including you . . . unless I tell her to do so."

"Breaking the chain of command so early in the investigation?"

"Quite the opposite Thorsen. I'm following it. She reports to me and I report to you."

"Make sure you do a lot of that. I need to hear from you twice a day. In the morning just before noon and in the afternoon no later than three-thirty."

"Of course. Heaven forbid that you . . . like everyone else in Norway . . . be one minute late getting out of the office after four o'clock."

"Sohlberg you've forgotten your own country . . . haven't you? We're efficient here in Norway. There's no need for overtime."

"I'm sure you need to get out at four so you can hit the links during the summer."

"Who told you I play golf?"

"Word gets around."

"Well . . . it's outdated gossip. I no longer play golf."

"Oh?" said Sohlberg who enjoyed his turn to act coy.

"I bowl."

"Bowling?"

"I'm sure you've heard of it Mister International Traveler."

"Oh?"

"I'm taking lessons and getting quite good at it."

"I'm sure you are. I wonder . . . who else bowls in the department . . . or in the Ministry of Justice?"

"None of your bee's wax!" Ivar Thorsen jumped up

and left. He almost slammed into Constable Wangelin and her giant coffee mug which offered third degree burns in any spill.

"What's bothering him Chief Inspector?"

"His new hobby."

"Hhhmm. Weird. Shall we continue with the summary?"

"Read on."

"Agnes Haugen left the school no later than nine and went about her regular day doing errands and household chores."

"What errands? What chores?"

"She went back home to pick up the baby and post pictures that she took of Karl Haugen at the science fair . . . she uploaded the pictures into Facebook and other social network websites on the Internet."

"Wait a minute . . . did she leave the baby alone at home?"

"No. Her husband stayed in that day."

"What? Wasn't he at work?"

"No. He called in sick. We confirmed this from Nokia. We also found out that he was logged into his company's computers from eight in the morning to three in the afternoon. There's no doubt it was him because the work involved is highly specialized design engineering on computer chips. According to his boss at Nokia only someone with his expertise and experience could have made the entries found that day in Nokia's design systems."

"But why was he working on his work computer if he called in sick that day?"

"Nokia told us that he called in sick for himself and not because his kids or wife were sick. He was very vague when we pressed him for details on his sickness and whether he had gone to a doctor or told anyone else that he was sick."

"What did the team finally find out?" said Sohlberg who grew increasingly curious as to the little boy's father.

"Gunnar Haugen admitted that he should not have called in sick but rather . . . should've taken family leave because his daughter was sick and crying all night long and keeping him awake."

"And yet he was wide-awake enough to work for hours on complicated engineering and computer chip design."

"Now that you mention it . . . his statement is nonsense if he worked all day on his computer and yet claimed to be kept up the previous night."

"Did Nokia ever give you a minute-by-minute record on what he was doing on the computer? Is there a chance he could've just logged on and then walked away?"

"Oh boy . . . we sure didn't get any information like that from Nokia."

"Get it. Also . . . did he or his wife take the baby to the doctor or call a doctor?"

"No. They did *not* take the baby to a doctor . . . or call a doctor for the baby."

Sohlberg rubbed his chin. "Strange."

"You'll see just how strange Chief Inspector. The boy's father is an odd duck. Very intelligent and yet seems oddly detached . . . almost absent-minded . . . even dumb and naive on some things."

"Can you be more specific?"

"Yes. I always remember how strange it was to hear him repeat things that his wife had previously mentioned to us . . . his eyes always got a glassy look whenever she was around . . . it was like he was a zombie robot repeating verbatim whatever his wife wanted him to say to us."

"Like what?"

"I just can't put my finger on it. He was . . . an echo chamber of his wife."

"And he's a scientist type?"

"Oh yes Chief Inspector . . . he's definitely Mister Cold Logic . . . a science and math guy."

"People like that think the world is just about plugging numbers into some magical formula here or there. . . . Or is he a business type? . . . They think everything in life is profit or loss or that life is all about good *management* or good *marketing*."

"He's an egghead *and* a businessman . . . a Pointdexter."

"A what?"

"A nerd. You know . . . book smart but not street smart."

"Yes! This is a man whose naive or stupid enough to lie to his employer about being sick. Then he lies to us about being kept up all night by a sick baby and yet he puts in a day's work the following day at his home computer *and* does not call or visit a doctor for his sick baby."

"Like I said Chief Inspector . . . he's an odd duck."

"Did the baby's mother Agnes call or visit a doctor for her sick baby daughter?"

"No. She took the baby and left her husband alone for a couple of hours . . . from eleven in the morning to two o'clock in the afternoon . . . she drove around with the baby to get the baby's medicine at a pharmacy. She then went to her workout at the gym . . . with the baby."

"She took the baby and left him all alone?"

"Yes."

"Why would you take a sick baby in your car to go

buy the baby's medicines when one parent is already staying at home and not going to work? . . . Why would anyone take a sick baby to a gym . . . and drop off the sick baby at the gym's daycare?"

"I . . . well at the time no one thought it strange. Both parents made it sound so natural. Now that you mention it . . . it does sound strange indeed."

"This doesn't make sense."

"True. We found that she did indeed drive around with the baby looking for medicines."

"What's the proof?"

"At nine-twelve in the morning we have a credit card purchase by her for candy at a SPAR neighborhood supermarket that is three miles from the school. She claims that the Apotek One pharmacy next door did not have the baby's medicines. She says that she then drove another four miles and at ten-fifteen we have her credit card purchase for baby diapers at one of the EUROSPAR mega-supermarkets. Fifteen minutes later at ten-thirty she buys the baby's medicine at a nearby Apotek One with the same credit card."

"This sounds to me like proof that she was busy establishing an alibi for herself."

"Exactly. There's too much time that's unaccounted for her and him. Except for the three credit card purchases at nine-twelve and ten-fifteen and ten-thirty we really have no idea where the stepmother was at . . . especially from noon to one-thirty. The father is even worse since we're still unsure if he really was on his computer."

"So neither the father or the stepmother can really prove *exactly* where they were from nine in the morning to three in the afternoon expect for some scattered drugstore purchases she made that morning . . . and whatever occasional computer entries he may have made on his computer throughout the day."

"Unfortunately that is the situation Chief Inspector."

"Nilsen should have called a press conference and asked for the public's help that very same day and the next day . . . he or some official spokesperson from headquarters should have asked the public whether they had seen the parents anywhere that Friday or whether they had seen the white pickup or the red sports car at the stores or the school or elsewhere that Friday."

"We did ask the public for help . . . but that was three months later . . . when the investigation was stalling."

"Nilsen is such a moron! That delay made the request for the public's help practically worthless. How stupid. People would forget such things three months after the fact . . . and their memories would be suspect even if they said they remember seeing so and so at a certain day and time."

"That was a problem throughout the case. Nilsen always took the parents at their word. He thought that they were as perfect and pure as the first snowflake of winter. He never wanted us to verify or check their statements because 'They're good people' according to him. He called them 'solid simple folk'."

"That was rather incompetent of Nilsen."

"I know. But he was in charge and that was his decision. Of course. . . if Karl's parents been very poor . . . or blue collar types . . . Nilsen probably would've arrested them or at least suspected of them of lying."

"What a clown. How could he take what these people said at face value just because the father makes a lot of money as a Nokia engineer?"

"Well . . . Inspector Magnus Matningsdal was part of the team for a couple of weeks and he thought that

Chief Inspector Nilsen was taking the stepmother too much at her word. As the investigation progressed all of us noticed that Nilsen began to believe everything that she said as true while suspecting everything the father said as a lie."

"Really?"

"Well . . . I think Nilsen. . . ."

"What? C'mon . . . say it."

Constable Wangelin looked away from Sohlberg. Her averted gaze alerted him to the fact that she was very embarrassed. Since arriving in Oslo he had come to appreciate all over again how Norwegians as a rule always look the other person straight in the eye when speaking to them. He was happy that the old Viking tradition still prevailed because the Vikings knew that the eye was not only the window to the soul but also the ultimate lie detector. Sohlberg fondly remembered unnerving his law enforcement colleagues in other countries and all the people he interviewed with his dead-on stare.

"I'm sorry Chief Inspector . . . I meant no disrespect," said Constable Wangelin who gathered her composure and looked Sohlberg again straight in the eye.

"I understand. Go ahead . . . tell me about Nilsen."

"He liked her . . . Nilsen *really* liked the stepmother . . . lusted after her. He stared at her chest all the time."

"Why?"

Steeling herself Wangelin said, "The stepmother has enormous breasts. Nilsen stared at her every time he saw her. You could see his eyes undressing her."

"He's fifty-two . . . a little old to get distracted by such teenage boy nonsense."

"Ah . . . it was repulsive . . . her breasts are obvious fakes. Even Nilsen knew it . . . he took down bets as to whether she had silicone or saline implants."

"Ridiculous. I can see why this investigation went nowhere. Anyway . . . keep reading me your summary."

"After buying the baby's medicine the stepmother said the baby was irritable and crying and so she drove around for 'a few minutes' to get the baby to sleep with the rocking motion of the car."

"Wait a minute . . . what car? . . . The white pickup or the red sports car?"

"She took her husband's white pickup. She says that driving around always calmed the baby into sleeping. The father says that was news to him. I think that's the first and only time that the father contradicted the stepmother."

"Interesting," said Sohlberg. "Proceed."

"The stepmother then drove to the gym where she arrived at eleven-twenty. That's when the main desk has her signing in. She leaves the gym an hour later at twelve-twenty. She then—"

"Stop. So her baby is sick and she goes to the gym with the baby."

"Yes. She dropped the baby off in the gym's daycare room."

"Unbelievable." Sohlberg shook his head in amazement at the selfishness of Norway's newest generation of parents. "Then what does she do after the gym?"

"She says that she drove around with the baby . . . to calm her down . . . and finally arrived home at about one forty-five . . . almost two o'clock. Says her husband was not there and that he left her a note saying he went to pick up some takeout food for lunch. He arrives back in her red Audi sports car at around two in the afternoon. But she's not sure exactly when he arrived because she took a shower and a nap."

"So basically he's all alone on the day that his son disappears . . . six hours . . . from nine to three."

"Yes. It's almost as if he used the need to buy the baby's medicine as an excuse to get rid off his wife and the baby."

"Call the pharmacy and see if it's true that they were out of the baby's medicine when Agnes Haugen went to buy the medicines."

"Actually we did that a few months ago."

"And?"

"They had the medicine in stock."

"What did she say to that?"

"That the pharmacy must've been confused and thought she asked for another medicine."

"How convenient for the father and stepmother . . . to have her driving around looking for the baby's medicines while he's all alone. Keep on. . . ."

"Karl Haugen was to have taken the school bus home. But he was not on the bus at three-thirty when the stepmother walked to the bus stop near their driveway. The bus arrived and another child from next door got off but not Karl. That's when the driver told her that Karl had never gotten on the bus.

"She ran back home and called the school to tell them that the driver had just told her that the boy had never gotten on the bus. The school informed her that her stepson had been marked absent for the day by his teacher as soon as roll call was completed at about nine-fifteen. The stepmother dialed one-one-two and we immediately got involved. Nilsen ordered an inch-by-inch search of the school and the school grounds and the parent's home and their one-acre property."

"Who else was called in to help?"

"Of course Nilsen got KRIPOS involved . . . they

sent a crime scene investigator squad that arrived at eight-thirty in the evening."

"But that was almost twelve hours after the boy disappeared."

"True but Nilsen thought the boy had just wandered off or left with another family and that we'd find him before nine at night. Commissioner Thorsen got extra help for us from nearby districts that sent officers and two dog-sniffing teams . . . we carefully searched the school and the hilly wooded area immediately around the school. We even searched the school's roof."

"Any videos . . . close circuit cameras at the school?"

"Not in this school. Only in the newer schools."

"Explain something to me."

"Go on Chief Inspector. Ask me."

"What's the school's procedure for visitors? . . . What did the school do that day to accommodate all the visitors for the science fair?"

"The standard procedure is for all adult visitors to check in at the main office and receive a badge. But not everyone got a badge the day of the science fair."

"Why?"

"Because of the huge crowds . . . the science fair had to start before the official school hour of eight in the morning since a lot of parents came to help their children set up the exhibits before the parents rushed off to work. The school's principal called the science fair a 'semi-public' event. She said the building was packed with more than two hundred adult visitors who went from classroom to classroom with their children and to and from the auditorium."

"Fascinating," said Sohlberg as he massaged his increasingly tense neck muscles. Joint pain and muscular spasms plagued his neck whenever he was confronted with a complex case.

"What's fascinating Chief Inspector?"

"The father and stepmother. They have six hours that are . . . for the most part . . . unaccounted for. . . . And the father seems to have a lot more unaccounted for time than the stepmother. He literally has a lot of explaining to do. At least the stepmother has some proof to establish some of her whereabouts when she went out on that medicine-buying trip. He on the other hand has little or nothing to show as to exactly *where* he was that day and exactly *what* he was doing those six hours."

"Keep in mind Chief Inspector that her medicine-buying trip itself is a mystery. Why would she go to a second store when the first store had the medicine?"

"Another contradiction . . . maybe even a lie. By the way . . . what type of baby medicine are we talking about here?"

"I . . . well . . . here's another strange thing that this couple made sound so natural when we first interviewed them."

"Together or separate?"

"Both . . . together and separate."

"Not good. Interviews must always be separate."

"True . . . but in the rush to get basic information Nilsen and the first responding constables took statements from them in each other's presence."

"A huge mistake in this investigation."

"Sorry. But as I was saying . . . the Haugens took their sweet time to finally reveal . . . four months *after* Karl disappeared . . . that the baby's prescription medicine was for colic and that any over-the-counter remedy would've been easy to find and a far cheaper substitute."

"What did they say when confronted with this

information?"

"That they do not buy cheap things . . . least of all generic drugs. That they buy only the very best for their children. She even made the very arrogant statement that they don't eat leftovers."

"Interesting. Unfortunately I know people like that."

"Wait till you hear this . . . we calculated her total mileage that Friday for her shopping expedition for the baby's medicine . . . almost forty-five miles for a medicine that she could've bought for less than five dollars had she gone for the less expensive over-the-counter substitute."

"Whose idea was it for her to go on that crazy shopping trip?"

"The father and stepmother both take responsibility for it."

"Not his idea?"

"No Chief Inspector. She's adamant about going through all the motions to establish to the world that they have money to spend. Of course the weird thing is that the father and stepmother dress like high school kids . . . they mostly wear t-shirts and blue jeans and tennis shoes . . . every time I saw him he was in long baggy shorts and sandals."

"By the way . . . what role did they take in the search for Karl that Friday and in the weeks that followed?"

"Again Chief Inspector . . . they are strange people . . . an odd family. Everyone on the force made comments about how the Haugens are the first family that did *not* participate in the search for their missing child."

"That is unusual . . . the father or the mother or both or other relatives always get involved in the search . . . they go on television and ask for the public's help. They walk the streets and they hand out flyers with pictures. Matter of fact . . . I've always looked carefully to see who in the circle of family and friends was not participating in the search for a missing person."

Constable Wangelin nodded. "People don't look if they think . . . or know . . . that the missing person is dead."

"What about the biological mother?"

"Maya Engen . . . she lives in Namsos . . . north of Trondheim . . . married to Police Inspector Arvid Engen of the Sør-Trøndelag district."

"Really?"

"Do you know him Chief Inspector?"

"No. But that's another interesting twist in this case. Did Karl's biological mother . . . this Maya Engen . . . look for her missing son?"

"No. Physically and mentally she could not. She was devastated. . . . She fainted at the news of his disappearance. She collapsed several times after she and her husband came down here the night of June fourth. Maya Engen suffered a great deal . . . unlike the father and the stepmother who seemed rather cool if not lackadaisical about the whole thing."

"You've personally seen the father and the stepmother after Karl disappeared . . . right?"

"Yes."

"Which one of them would you say was angry or in mourning . . . or grieving over Karl?"

"Hard to tell."

"What?" said a surprised Sohlberg. "I don't understand. What do you mean?"

"I . . . I can't describe it . . . when you're with them you feel everything is normal but when you leave them you realize something's not quite right in that family."

"That's why I'm very interested in focusing on Karl Haugen's family and friends. Are we done with the first page of your summary?"

"I'm ready to start going over the second page."

"Good. But we'll have to do that in the car."

"Where are we going?"

"Halden Fengsel. I understand Norway's newest prison is something to behold."

"I've seen it on television . . . quite luxurious . . . but I've never been there."

"Let's go."

"Are we taking the train or a car?"

"Thorsen is lending us a marked car for today. He already made arrangements for our visit."

"Who are we seeing?'

"The Smiley Face Killer."

Chapter 8/Åtte

AFTERNOON OF 1 YEAR AND 24 DAYS
AFTER THE DAY, FRIDAY, JUNE 4

Traffic was relatively light before the lunch hour. Normally Sohlberg would have taken the super-fast NSB train down to Halden. The trip would have been a quick one hour forty-five minute ride in pure comfort and a local police constable would have picked them up at the station and taken them to the fengsel. But Sohlberg needed to be free from nosy eavesdropping passengers and more important he needed to spend as much time as possible discussing the investigation and the second page of the summary with Constable Wangelin. Sohlberg had to be fully prepared before he interviewed the family and friends of Karl Haugen.

"At least we got out before the rush hour traffic," said Wangelin.

She put the large Volvo crossover SUV on cruise control at 90 mph as soon as they left the Oslo suburbs behind. They shot down the E-6 highway out of Oslo which runs 352 miles south all the way down towards the lovely twin cities of Malmö in Sweden and Copenhagen in Denmark. Less than ten miles separate Halden Prison from the border with Sweden.

Sohlberg sipped his favorite Farris mineral water. He had an entire case in the backseat. "Ever hear about the Smiley Face Killer?"

"Vaguely. . . . No. Not really Chief Inspector."

"He was active in the seventies and eighties . . . he began killing when he was real young . . . in the late sixties . . . kept right up until captured in eighty-nine. He was Norway's worst. Then came the Lommemannen . . . the Pocket Man. Heard of him?"

"Oh him? Yes. I've heard about the Pocket Man . . . molested an estimated four hundred boys . . . raped dozens over a thirty year period before his capture in two thousand eight. But the Smiley Face Killer . . . he doesn't sound familiar at all. That was *so* long ago. I wasn't even born in the seventies."

"Well . . . I wasn't in the force until April of eighty-nine . . . the Smiley Face Killer was captured in October of that year. But I still knew about the Smiley Face Killer."

"Sorry Chief Inspector but that's ancient history."

Sohlberg grew depressed over Constable Wangelin's blank look and comments. He suddenly felt old and tired. He was only 20 years older than Wangelin but she made him feel like an outdated relic of the past. Sohlberg had a hard time being told that his frame of reference belonged to ancient history.

"Are you alright Chief Inspector?"

"Just thinking. . . . Interesting how time fades the public's memory as well as that of the police force . . . at one time the Smiley Face Killer was big news . . . as big as Ted Bundy and the Green River Killer in America or the Butcher of Rostov in Russia."

"Who?"

"Andrei Chikatilo . . . the Smiley Face Killer's counterpart in Russia from seventy-eight to ninety. . . both killers would move their rape-and-kill frenzies to different and faraway locations whenever they sensed that they had stirred up a hornet's nest of investigators with their spectacular murders. . . . They both got very good at switching back and forth from local murders to faraway atrocities. Even at the height of the repressive and all-controlling Soviet police state Chikatilo would find clever ways to travel to Moscow and distant Russian Republics on his state factory job to kill dozens of women and children whenever he got the police and public riled up in Rostov over his killing sprees."

"He was able to move around so freely . . . to kill in a dictatorship like the old communist Russia?"

"Yes. . . ."

"Where there's a will there's a way," said Constable Wangelin while shaking her head.

"Chikatilo raped . . . killed . . . and cannibalized at least fifty-eight women and children . . . and not always in that order. He'd torture them and cut out the women's uteruses and the boy's parts and eat them. He always blamed his depraved conduct for what he and his family suffered as ethnic Ukrainians thanks to Stalin and the genocidal communists in the Thirties. I imagine you've heard about the famine that Stalin intentionally created in the Ukraine."

"No. Not really."

Sohlberg shrugged. He wasn't surprised. Norway's government and school system always turned a blind eye to communist atrocities or socialist failures. "Anyway . . . good old Stalin made the famine worse because he refused to let food get shipped into Ukraine after his crazy socialist collectivized farms couldn't produce enough food."

"How awful. I'm sorry but I never studied or read or heard about that."

"Stalin made sure that hundreds of thousands of

Ukrainians died like fleas . . . many people started taking children off the streets and eating them to survive. Chikatilo was traumatized by his mother's obsession over the possibility that he'd get kidnaped and then killed and eaten."

"Unbelievable what men do."

"Men *and* governments."

"True."

Sohlberg put a Ricola lozenge in his mouth. "I mentioned Chikatilo because I've always thought that criminals reflect their families and country and society and the times. It's too bad that they don't teach more at the Academy about the criminal mind."

"It's all about forensic science nowadays."

"The Academy doesn't train officers properly. They just don't want to invest the time and effort. You see Constable Wangelin . . . to know the criminal mind you have to study real-life cases. Only by truly knowing the criminal mind can you be truly effective as an investigator."

"I believe you."

"Take the Smiley Face Killer . . . Anton Rønning. We had no evidence other than some circumstantial evidence that Rønning was the killer. Of course this is before D.N.A. analysis. Anyway . . . it took one man . . . Inspector Lars Eliassen . . . nine days of interrogation to break the Smiley Face Killer."

"Nine days?"

"Inspector Eliassen was able to do that because he knew how to get inside the criminal mind thanks to his superb interview and interrogation skills. That and he was a darn good profiler."

"Chief Inspector . . . do you believe in profilers?"

"Yes and no. Sometimes they're helpful in an

investigation if the police are stumped or have little or no creative thinking. Otherwise profilers are best used to help detectives prepare for interrogations that break down the suspect."

"I've not heard that before . . . the Academy instructors promised we'd be taught the best and most modern techniques."

"I guess I'm old-fashioned after all . . . I mean . . . if the police are not good profilers then they're incompetent idiots no? . . . If you have a violent rape . . . do you stop and question the twenty-year-old man who's a violent ex-con? . . . Or do you question the ninety-year-old woman who's barely walking with a cane?"

"I see what you mean."

"Suspect profiling and interrogation techniques are what Inspector Eliassen taught me. . . . He always said that every good police officer must be a good profiler *and* excellent at interrogation . . . two sides of the same coin so to speak."

"Who's this Eliassen?"

"A small town police officer. He spent years and years on the trail of Anton Rønning . . . who by the way had twice been caught early in his career of crime and named as a prime suspect but released by incompetent police officers in Oslo and Trondheim."

"Where's this Inspector Eliassen now?"

"He died a few years ago. I miss him . . . he taught me a lot. Anyway he was a genius at interrogating."

"How did he catch Rønning?"

"For quite some time Eliassen had Anton Rønning on his short list of suspects for sex crimes in Eliassen's district. Then he got a lucky break. Rønning crashed into a light pole when he hurriedly left the scene of one of his molestation victims. Eliassen seized the opportunity and locked Anton Rønning up on a minor traffic charge for destruction of public property. . . . Eliassen then just kept interrogating Anton Rønning until he caught him in all these lies and inconsistencies."

"That's impressive!"

"Inspector Eliassen was known for solving impossible-to-solve cases just by interrogating and breaking the suspect down without torture or physical pressure. This Eliassen . . . he was a master at interrogation . . . out of one hundred interrogations he had only three suspects who refused to confess."

"That's pretty good. Too bad the Academy doesn't teach his techniques."

"Last time I looked at their curriculum I saw that the Academy . . . and the force . . . are playing around with this silly stuff about community policing . . . detectives eating ethnic food at Asian restaurants or listening to rap or hip-hop music with African teenagers. Seems that policing in Norway is now all about touchy-feely political correctness and feel-good public relations."

"Perhaps Chief Inspector. But maybe it's because effective policing is now based on all the advances in DNA and forensic crime investigation. . . . Don't forget those advances Chief Inspector."

"Forensics are important and sometimes the only thing to go on . . . but nothing beats good profiling and interrogation techniques. Too bad the Academy believes all that junk about hiring psychologists and psychiatrists as profilers when the cop on the beat or the detective on the case should be the profiler. Of course I can see the love affair with profilers . . . they are very useful in making excellent American movies and television series."

Wangelin chortled. "So what happened with Eliassen and the serial killer?"

"Anton Rønning would not break down and confess . . . despite a lot of psychological pressure put on him during the nine days. But Eliassen broke him by the end of day nine. He does this by questioning and talking to Rønning every day at the little local jailhouse . . . until Rønning breaks down. Eliassen makes the pedophile killer realize that by confessing he has a chance to avoid the death penalty overseas in death penalty countries where he raped and killed children. The killer also sees that he can stay in Norway and probably not get extradited if he's deemed insane. That way he can spend the rest of his life explaining his story to psychiatrists who might eventually cure and release him to enjoy his life and wife and adult children and grandchildren."

"Chief Inspector. It's always a shock to me how even the most hardened criminals at one point or another in their life of crime always expect or demand or beg for mercy."

"Ninety-nine percent always ask for the mercy and compassion they refused their victims. One of my colleagues in America . . . Alec Mikesell the Chief Homicide Detective in Salt Lake City Utah . . . once shared with me this bit of wisdom:

"*Justice must always be satisfied and yet mercy is needed to balance the scales because sometimes justice blindly delivered is an injustice by itself.*'

"That's pretty good. . . . So what exactly made the Smiley Face Killer confess?"

"Eliassen knows that his suspect is a physical coward and terrified of winding up in any prison here or overseas with inmates who might not be as tolerant as many judges are about child molesters or child rapists or child killers. Rønning fears the rape and the torture and the death that he so freely imparted."

"Typical."

"Anton Rønning finally confesses when Inspector Eliassen offers him a chance to explain himself and therefore perhaps avoid prison here and the death penalty overseas if Rønning can show that he's sick enough and in need of psychiatric treatment.

"Eliassen tells Rønning that a full confession with all the grisly details of all his crimes will help prove Rønning's insanity. Rønning sees that he might even get out of the all-too-lenient sentence of a maximum twenty-one years in prison that he'd receive here in Norway for *all* the molestations and rapes and killings."

"Yes. I can see his motivation in confessing."

"Of course the ultimate motivation is that the Smiley Face Killer knows for sure that he will get the traditional Russian method of execution with a Makarov pistol shot behind the right ear if he's ever extradited to any of the Russian Republics where he committed dozens of crimes. Anton Rønning confesses that he is the serial killer but still does not offer details.

"The weekend comes and when it's time on Monday to provide the details Rønning instead gets a lawyer and tries to limit his confession to children that he molested while he worked as a tax collector for a few years as a young man. Of course that's long before he started killing."

"Again . . . that's typical . . . offering a partial confession to throw off the investigator."

"Well a partial confession won't do for Eliassen . . . . so he shows Rønning how he's caught Rønning in all these lies during the interrogation. Eliassen tells Rønning that he now knows the exact details of Rønning's work-and-travel schedules and how these match up perfectly with all of the times and places of the horrible crimes.

Eliassen shows Rønning how all of these facts and circumstances will be enough to convict him in any country with the death penalty.

"Eliassen reminds Rønning about the knives and ropes that Eliassen found in Rønning's briefcase . . . and he also reminds Rønning about the numerous eyewitnesses who saw Rønning at the crime scenes trolling for victims.

"For example, one woman in the United States . . . in Miami Florida even took a picture of Rønning at the beach where he was trolling for children . . . of course two boys were later found dead near his hotel. Rønning's stupid lawyer says they'll go to trial and the idiot leaves the room. Eliassen decides to again toss Rønning a lifesaver by making the offhand comment, '*It's too bad you want to do it this way when you could've gotten off with insanity.*'"

"Does it work?"

"Like a charm. It works perfectly well because Inspector Eliassen knows the killer's mind . . . and in Rønning's mind Rønning knows that he's doing totally insane and repulsive crimes and yet he's using his sanity and logic to prevent capture by leading a so-called normal life with his wife and children and grandchildren. . . .

"You see . . . Rønning used his sanity to avoid capture by never leaving evidence at the crime scenes . . . and he used his sanity to evade the nationwide manhunt by not killing at all for long periods of time . . . or by killing in distant locations when he has to do that to throw off investigators.

"So . . . Inspector Eliassen gets Rønning to use the sane part of his mind to logically chose to confess . . . and to convince or force the insane part of himself into accepting a confession that allows Rønning to eventually use an insanity defense that will let him avoid going to prison here and eventually getting extradited to some nasty foreign prison where he could get life or the death penalty. . . . Basically Rønning's again been offered the chance to get off scot-free by having psychiatrists treat him for a few years and later declare him sane."

"That's awful Chief Inspector."

"The ugly truth is that it's a great deal for the killer . . . no? After all . . . if some shrink could ever come up with a treatment to cure Rønning from his insane compulsions then it's all real good for the killer. He's finally free of his insane half. And if they can't treat him then he gets a second proverbial bite at the apple when he's released after his maximum twenty-one-year sentence here in Norway."

"Uuughh!"

"That's the way of the world unfortunately."

"So what happens to the Smiley Face Killer?"

"Anton Rønning breaks down completely and confesses. Inspector Eliassen even gets him talking about his childhood . . . Rønning breaks down in tears . . . literally trembling and shaking when he talks about the horrible childhood he had with a mother and grandmother who beat him mercilessly. The two women starved him for days while he was locked up in a small dark closet. He also talks about how he had been molested and raped as a child by his mother's boyfriend. The confession lasts almost two weeks."

"Wow! That's something else."

"Do you see Constable Wangelin? . . . You *must* get inside their heads. You must find their passions and fears . . . find out their true thoughts however irrational or illogical or disgusting. . . .You *must* see the world from their point-of-view."

"How will this Smiley Face Killer help us?"

"A craftsman always recognizes similar handiwork. Rønning will tell us if a stranger took Karl Haugen. Rønning knows all about taking little boys."

"What an animal." Wangelin shook her head in disgust.

"Rønning is an animal . . . a predator. . . . By the early seventies Anton Rønning had already killed at least twelve children here in Norway and Sweden and many many more in Germany and Russia and the United States. And Hungary. Bulgaria. Spain. Portugal. Greece.

"During a two-week summer vacation he killed three boys in Iceland alone and four in Greenland. He was a master at luring and taking the children without anyone seeing him in broad daylight . . . much like Chikatilo in Russia. I've always suspected that Anton Rønning killed many more innocents in Canada and the U.S.A."

"What was his M.O.?"

"He'd lure them with a story about him or his pet being lost. He'd molest them and then kill them . . . all under twenty minutes . . . because he didn't want them to live with the nightmare of the molestation . . . the same nightmare that had haunted and tortured him since he was molested as a six-year-old. Or as he told me . . . '*I needed to break the chain*' . . . and he did. Whenever possible he used a heavy gold chain to strangle them. He then left a Smiley Face painted in lipstick or red crayon or red ink marker on their bodies."

"Smiley Face . . . what's that?"

"The sixties and seventies had two symbols . . . the peace symbol with the three branches and the smiling face with two dots for eyes and a crescent-shaped smile. Anton Rønning picked the well-known Smiley Face because it symbolized the fake *happy* face that molestation victims are forced to put on for the world . . . a generic smiley face that reinforces the anonymity and secrets of the victims of molestation. Eliassen even got Rønning to tell him about several children whose bodies have never been found."

"Wait. Just who is this Inspector Eliassen? I've never heard of him."

"A genius."

"The name doesn't sound familiar."

"Shouldn't be. Lars Eliassen spent his entire life as a small town policeman from the Romsdal valley . . . never cared for promotions. . . . He put in fifteen years as a constable . . . then ten as an inspector and five as chief inspector in the Møre og Romsdal district. He never sought the spotlight . . . he avoided it . . . let his bosses do all the talking and get all the credit especially when he got a full confession from the Smiley Face Killer. Afterwards Eliassen refused to be promoted above chief inspector."

"How did you know him?"

"I . . . I mean he . . . he investigated. . . ." Sohlberg decided to go for the half-truth instead of a lie. He could not tell her the whole truth. One Norwegian tradition that he decide to observe was that co-workers never made friendships at work or otherwise discussed in detail their personal lives at work.

"He investigated what Chief Inspector?"

"Eliassen investigated a fatal climbing accident that I witnessed . . . you see I used to climb back then. Someone fell and Eliassen had to investigate and confirm it was an accident."

"How sad!"

"It was. . . . Something like that makes you think about life and whether you're doing what you really love and want to be doing . . . less than a year after the accident I gave up my law practice and became a police officer just like Eliassen.

"We later became friends . . . he had impressed me so much with his questions . . . and how can I phrase it? His compassion. His understanding. I'll never forget how he got inside my mind and immediately saw that the climber's fall was an accident."

"Did he think it was murder . . . or suicide?"

"For a time. Inspector Eliassen had to investigate all the possibilities. That's what a good cop does."

"I would've liked meeting him."

"I saw him on and off for a long time. He died two years ago. I came to his funeral. Too bad he's not here or we'd go get his advice."

Sohlberg closed his eyes. He wanted to tell Wangelin that the dead are still with us long after the grief fades away and that even if you are an atheist who does not believe in the afterlife the fact remains that the dead are still with us even if just by leaving that empty place behind in our hearts or memories. Karoline gone. Harald Junior gone. Lars Eliassen gone. Soon others would be gone. His parents and then he himself and Emma Sohlberg would be gone. Death and grieving.

He had to find out who in Karl Haugen's family mourned the empty spot left behind by Karl Haugen.

Who was in grief over Karl Haugen?

Who was *not* grieving over the missing boy?

The one who was *not* grieving over the missing boy is the kidnaper and maybe even the killer of Karl Haugen.

Was the Haugen home a house of mourning?

~ ~ ~

The car's rocking motion lulled Sohlberg into a deep

sleep.

He dreamed that he was locked inside a dank underground prison. Spiders skittered over him while he read a letter in a cell that he shared with Anton Rønning. The Smiley Face Killer began chasing him with a butcher knife. Sohlberg ran down the frigid and pitch-black corridors where other prisoners tried to pull him into their cells.

The depraved inmates reached out to him with their clawing hands and their angry recriminations:

"Hey cop . . . you put me in here. Now you die in here."

Sohlberg moaned loudly and woke up.

"You okay Chief Inspector?"

"Just a nightmare."

"I have those too."

"Sorry to hear that Constable Wangelin."

"I was warned before I joined the force. Some of us will sleep perfectly and peacefully. Some of us will have nasty dreams about all the toxic people and crimes that we come across."

Sohlberg nodded. "And for some of us . . . our dreams will get worse as we see more and more awful people and crimes as time goes by."

"A career hazard," said Wangelin with a grim smile.

"Yes. Few people understand what it's like to have a first-hand look at evil."

"How true Chief Inspector. That's why . . . in the short time that I've been in the force . . . I've come to one conclusion . . . there's no God. None."

"I'm sorry that you feel that way Constable Wangelin."

"It's not just that I *feel* that way . . . it's a logical and very rational conclusion when you see the suffering and the evil that's in the world."

"Like why do innocent children die . . . from accidents or from disease or from crime?"

"Exactly."

"Why do bad things happen to good people?"

"You got it . . . . And if there *is* a God then I'm very angry at Him for letting horrible things happen to us down here."

"I don't blame you for the anger . . . I also used to think that way until one of my Utah friends . . . Alec Mikesell . . . asked me a question that changed my thinking."

"What was the question?"

"Have you ever considered the fact that human beings are not robots who are forced to do good and be good all the time? . . . We have free choice . . . free will . . . isn't *that* God's great gift to mankind?"

"Well . . . but that means we have to suffer the evil and mean and dumb decisions of other people."

"Yes. Even our own bad decisions. We have to suffer wars and crimes and earthquakes and all the other good and bad things that mortal existence throws our way. . . . Otherwise how would we learn? . . . How would we progress beyond an innocent carefree childhood? . . .

"We're here to experience good and evil.

"Happiness and grief.

"Life and death.

"Health and disease.

"Without those polar opposites we'd know nothing. We'd appreciate nothing.

"We would live and die as undeveloped or underdeveloped human beings. It would be like being stuck in kindergarten or the first grade the rest of your life. You'd never progress."

"I . . . I . . . well . . . I have to say there's a strong logic in what you're saying *if* there's a God."

"Even if God does not exist you have to admit that life has a much greater meaning once you understand that human beings *need* to experience good and evil . . . joy and grief. . . health and illness . . . life and death."

Wangelin shrugged and fell into a moody silence. An overpowering slumber soon caught up with Sohlberg.

~ ~ ~

The car stopped. Sohlberg opened his eyes and he was surprised that he had fallen deeply asleep.

For how long?

They had pulled into a Statoil gas station. His eyes popped wide open when he saw the $ 12 a gallon price on the digital display. That was 400% more than what he paid in the USA. He wondered why Norwegians put up with outrageous prices at home when their government-owned Statoil exported billions of dollars of oil to other countries where gasoline was far cheaper than in Norway.

As soon as they got back on the road Sohlberg said:

"Sorry I fell asleep. You must think I'm getting old. . . ."

"No. I stopped back there at the gas station because I too was getting sleepy with the afternoon heat and that big sandwich I ate a couple of miles ago. Do you want some coffee? My thermos holds almost a gallon."

"No thanks. I no longer drink coffee . . . haven't in years."

"I'm surprised you don't drink coffee. All good Norwegians drink plenty of it. Why did you stop?"

"We were living in the United States . . . in Utah where it was impossible to find good coffee."

"Why? Don't the Americans have good coffee?"

"They do but most of Utah is Mormon and they don't drink coffee or black tea . . . or alcohol for religious and health reasons. Anyway . . . feel free to drink whatever you want from my case of Farris water."

A few minutes later they both stretched to shake off their grogginess. Wangelin drove expertly at high speeds on the highway.

"Constable Wangelin . . . tell me about the Haugen family. Tell me everything. I'm meeting the father and stepmother tomorrow."

"I'm looking forward to that. We interviewed them five times each but they gave jumbled confusing explanations that only made sense when you heard them and no sense at all after you left the parents and had time to think about their statements. In hindsight . . . they bamboozled us."

"Let's start with the biological mother."

"I feel sorry for her and what she's going through but she's a bit of a flake."

"How so?"

"She's not crazy but somewhat slightly unbalanced."

"How so?"

"You'll notice that her hair style and hair color change radically and constantly. One day it's straight black-hair . . . the next day frizzy blond-ish hair . . . a week later she has dreadlocks and a month later she has bleached spiky hair. . . ."

"Come now Constable Wangelin. Surely her hairstyle is not that important."

"Maybe yes. Maybe no. Why does she do it? I can't even imagine the amount of time she puts into fixing her hair."

"You should've asked her. . . . Why do you change

your hair style and hair color so frequently? . . . How much time does it take? . . . Her answers truthful or not would've been revealing."

"I should've asked."

"You'll see as you get more experienced how those little open-ended questions add up . . . the innocent little questions about so-called meaningless or trivial or irrelevant matters almost always bring you tremendous insights into the person's mind . . . that's what you have to do . . . ask ask ask . . . dig the truth out."

"You're right Chief. We tend to quit too early. We're too busy. We want to move on to the next witness or the next to-do chore."

"Constable Wangelin . . . you *have* to ask questions even when it feels very uncomfortable. Sometimes the stress in awkward personal interactions will break down the walls and let you take a peak inside."

"But it feels so awkward to ask personal questions of a stranger."

"I know it goes against our famous Norwegian *reserve*. But you have to do it to be an effective police officer. You have to put aside our Viking tradition of living in extreme isolation because of the steep mountains between each fjord . . . you have to get past the ingrained mind-set where everyone from the next isolated fjord is a total stranger who speaks a totally different dialect."

"I never saw it that way but it's so true."

"Tell me about Maya Engen. Start with her reaction to Karl's disappearance."

"In a nutshell . . . she's a woman with a guilty conscience . . . for abandoning Karl Haugen when he needed her the most."

"How so?"

"In her mind she brought Karl into the broken home

of a failed marriage . . . she separated from Karl's father less than two years after marrying him. The marriage went bad shortly after the first year anniversary . . . if not beforehand."

"What caused the breakup?"

"She says he cheated on her. The father refuses to admit this . . . he's vague on the reasons but he insists that he and his wife led separate lives while living together as husband and wife."

"Interesting . . . a man who insists that things are one way under his roof when things are in fact another before the eyes of the law. In other words he was married in the eyes of the law to Maya Engen but in his eyes he's not married to her under his own roof. The man seems to live in his own universe . . . his own version of reality no? He is married but insists he is not. Interesting. A man who denies reality . . . or creates his own reality."

"He says that their separate lives were the reason for why he started dating Agnes Haugen then known as Agnes Sørensen . . . her maiden name."

"What's his first wife's version of the breakup?"

"According to Maya Engen their marriage ended because of his adultery with Agnes. Of course he continues insisting that by the time he met Agnes the marriage was on the rocks and that they were already separated. I checked and found out that really was *not* true . . . he was still living with his wife in the same house when he began a relationship with Agnes."

"That was gutsy of him."

"Or cowardly. Anyway . . . they got a divorce when Maya Engen was eight months pregnant with Karl. And by the time Karl was born the father had his new woman Agnes living in the house with him."

"How convenient."

"It gets more convenient for him as you'll see in a few minutes. Gunnar and Maya have Karl on April . . . they file for divorce in May . . . and the divorce is final five months later in October . . . just two years after they got married."

"He's a fickle man," said Sohlberg who detested uncertain men. "The wishy-washy sort who change wives like they change shirts or shoes. A fickle man would explain why Karl's mother is always changing her hairstyle and colors."

"How so Chief Inspector?"

"She does that to keep a fickle man happy . . . the constant hairstyle and hair color changes mean that he has a *new* wife to look at every day."

"Very good Chief Inspector. That fits perfectly with her behavior. Also she was briefly married before she met and married Karl's father."

"So the Haugen marriage was her *second* marriage by age thirty?"

"Yes Chief Inspector. She had a son with her first husband and that boy has always lived full-time with the father."

"Huh! So she too changes husbands as frequently as her hair style and color. Think of it. She's now on husband number *three* by the age of thirty-eight. Or an average of one husband and one child per decade. . . ."

"That's how it is nowadays . . . not unusual," said Constable Wangelin. She gave Sohlberg a look that made him feel like some old-fashioned prude.

"What else?"

"After the divorce Maya Engen the mother has primary custody of Karl and the father Gunnar has visitation rights. He always pays the child support on time and in full. Gunnar and his live-in woman Agnes pressure

Maya Engen to let Karl spend more time with them.

"Maya Engen doesn't want Karl to have an absentee father and she has to work and needs someone to watch the baby in the afternoons after daycare. So Maya and Gunnar reach an agreement. Karl stays nights with his mother Maya after he spends two to three hours every afternoon with Gunnar and Agnes . . . and Thor who is Agnes's nine-year-old son by another marriage."

"What a cozy family. The father . . . the mistress . . . and the son of the mistress. I don't see Karl fitting easily into that cozy family."

"Karl had to fit in because a year later his mother Maya gets very sick with liver disease . . . hepatitis B . . . she is forced to go to Sweden for life-saving treatment."

"What? I've seen her on television and the newspapers and she looks like a picture of perfect health!"

"The fact *is* that she had to go to Sweden for treatment."

"Sweden? . . . Don't we have good doctors in Norway?"

"I—"

"What's wrong with Norwegian medical care?" shouted Sohlberg. He was extremely sensitive about Norway's humiliating subjugation until 1905 to Denmark and Sweden which had respectively conquered Norway in 1536 and 1814.

"Chief Inspector . . . we checked and her doctors confirm that only Sweden offered her an innovative drug treatment that attacked the virus."

"I don't see why she couldn't have gotten just as good care in Norway."

"Maybe it's because Norway sometimes doesn't have everything we need."

"Norway has everything Norwegians need."

From her pitying looks Sohlberg could tell that Wanglein found his patriotism touching if not quaint and old-fashioned.

In high school Sohlberg had joined *Ny Norge*. The nationalist group advocated eliminating Norway's monarchy because the king came from a line of Danish royalty that had served as puppets for Denmark. Sohlberg like most other Norwegians felt that Denmark had ruthlessly ruled Norway as a colony to be exploited. *Ny Norge* also advocated moving the capital out of Oslo and back north to Trondheim the old Viking capital. And Sohlberg like most other Norwegians was perfectly aware of the fact that Denmark and then Sweden had kept Oslo as the capital in southern Norway in order to control and keep tabs on Norwegians. The *Ny Norge* group also pushed hard for nynorsk or "New Norwegian" to be the only official Norwegian language to the exclusion of bokmål or "book language" which is a Danish bastardization of the Norwegian language.

"Chief Inspector . . . regardless of how you feel about Sweden . . . the fact remains that Karl's mother went to Sweden . . . where she got the medical treatment that successfully controlled her hepatitis. She was forced to let Karl live with his father and Agnes the stepmother when her Swedish doctors informed her that she would not be able to care for the child while she got the debilitating treatments."

"So just like that she left Karl with the father and stepmother?"

"Yes. . . . Maya Engen came back a year later and she was still too weak to care for Karl. The father made it clear that Maya should spend her time and energies on recovering and not on Karl since he and Agnes were already raising him. Because of her illness Maya reluctantly agreed."

"I can see why Maya Engen has a guilty conscience. First she brings her son into a broken marriage. Then she dropped the boy off with those two odd ducks because she was sick . . . and then she was maybe too lazy to care for the boy during her recovery."

"Could be . . . but who knows what she was really going through during her recovery period. Regardless . . . time passes and the father and stepmother kept finding excuses to keep Karl away from Maya. Three years later they flat out refused to return Karl to her because . . . according to them . . . Karl had already bonded with Agnes the stepmother . . . apparently Karl was already calling her '*Mommy*' or '*Mama*'.

"The father and stepmother insisted that the proposed change in living arrangements would be too disruptive for little Karl and that any judge or social worker or psychologist would see it their way."

"Did they actually state that or is the birth mother making that up?"

"I've look at e-mails and they actually did say that."

"How convenient for the father. He has no more child support to pay now that the boy lives with him . . . *and* his live-in sex partner serves as a free nanny for the boy. How very convenient eh?"

"Without a doubt."

"Constable Wangelin . . . we need to look more closely at the father . . . he's a piece of work. Interesting how he arranges people like pieces on a chessboard . . . to be moved around for his pleasure and convenience."

"He's big into '*people management*' as he calls it . . . he gave me a long boring lecture on that topic when I asked him what he does at work. Nokia is apparently thinking of sending him to finish his business school education at Harvard or Yale in America. His library is filled with tons of books on that topic."

"How can Gunnar Haugen work as a people manager at a big corporation when he can't even manage the location or safety of his own son?"

"I guess . . . Chief Inspector . . . that big corporations have their own version of reality that is the opposite of reality."

"Absolutely. That's why absolute idiots thrive in big corporations. Anything else on the biological mother?"

"She eventually gave up on getting custody of Karl. She worked for a time as a secretary here in Oslo . . . then two years after she returned from Sweden she went to Trondheim to visit relatives. That's where she met Police Inspector Arvid Engen of the Sør-Trøndelag district. They married and live in Namsos. Karl visited them every two weeks for the weekend during the school year . . . and he spent most of his summer vacations with them."

"Do the birth mother and her husband Arvid Engen have alibis for June fourth?"

"Airtight. She was at work at the courthouse in Trondheim. Arvid was also at work . . . chasing down and arresting a gang of burglars all during that Friday with four other officers."

"Has the Engen house been checked and searched in Namsos?"

"Nothing turned up."

"Could Karl have been taken by a friend or relative of Maya or Arvid?"

"I doubt it . . . not after the commotion in the media over the boy. Anyone would have to be pretty stupid to keep little Karl Haugen after all that publicity . . . and the massive five-hundred-thousand kroner reward that Karl's father posted for Karl's return or clues leading to his whereabouts."

"Constable Wangelin . . . another thing I've been thinking about . . . was Karl supposed to be seeing his mother Maya Engen on the weekend after the Friday when he disappeared?"

"No . . . the next weekend. . . . Now that I think of it . . . the Engens and Haugens had some rather strange arrangements for those weekend visits."

"Strange how?"

"Every other weekend Inspector Arvid Engen or Maya Engen drove down from Trondheim on the E-Six and they picked Karl up at a gas station in the small town of Otta . . . which is about the halfway point between Oslo and Trondheim and Volda."

"Why Volda? . . . Isn't Volda a little town on the coast . . . about two hundred miles south of Trondheim?"

"Yes. Volda is where Maya Engen's first husband lives with her first son. The man owns a goat farm that sells goat milk for a cheese factory. So . . . every two weeks . . . on the same day that Maya and Inspector Arvid Engen drove south to Otta . . . the goat farmer drove east from Volda with his son on Highway Fifteen to Otta. . . . They all met at the same gas station . . . at the same time . . . with Karl and his father Gunnar Haugen and his stepmother Agnes."

"So every two weeks this woman . . . Maya Engen . . . reunites for the weekend with the two sons that she abandoned to their fathers? How cozy."

"It gets better. Karl doesn't come alone on the hand-off trips with his father and stepmother Agnes. Oh no. He comes along with Thor Jenssen . . . who is the first son of Agnes from her third marriage . . . actually her second marriage . . . but she got the dumb and wealthier third husband to adopt Thor as his own child."

"Agnes Haugen . . . has been married four times before she's forty? . . ."

"Indeed. We found out quite a lot about her from her ex-husbands. Her first husband she married right after graduating from high school . . . she married him so she could get out of her parents' house and away from their control. Her own friends and family agree that she pursued him hard in high school and did her best to bed him down."

"I know the type," said Sohlberg as he thought of Margerete Frederisksen his old high school vixen on Ulvøya Island.

"You do?"

"Constable Wangelin . . . believe it or not I was young once upon a time."

"Well . . . anyway . . . Agnes Haugen's friends and family all agree that the young man wouldn't spend much time with her because his parents were wealthy real estate developers who were adamant about Agnes not hanging around their son or their house. They hated her . . . still do with a passion."

"So how did she get around the young man's parents?"

"Agnes's own friends told us that she lied to him about being pregnant . . . and how she might even press rape charges against him. So he was forced to marry her. Then . . . when no baby bump showed up on her belly she claimed that she had a miscarriage. That's when his parents swooped in and paid her off handsomely to get a divorce."

"This belongs in some Hollywood tabloid."

"Happens all the time Chief Inspector."

"Not when I was growing up. That would've been extremely unusual. A young woman sleeping around like that to get a monied husband. Huh!" Sohlberg immediately noticed that Wangelin gave him a pity look as if saying, "*Boy did you lead a sheltered life. You need to get on with modern times and not be an old-fashioned prude.*"

"Now Chief we have Agnes's husband Number Two . . . a good-looking hunk but not too smart. She used the divorce pay-off and her parents' money to try to get him set up in several businesses . . . but they all failed. He's broke . . . a ne'er-do-well who's failed in too many business ventures . . . but he does succeed in impregnating her."

"Don't they always."

"They have a son Thor . . . but by then the marriage is an unhappy disaster . . . each spouse accusing the other of infidelity . . . seems they each had lots of casual sexual liaisons. Then she marries husband Number Three. He seems to know the most about her . . . he has quite a lot of dirt on her . . . on account of him being in contact with all of the husbands . . . including the current Number Four . . . who is of course . . . Karl's father."

Sohlberg nodded in glum silence as Constable Wangelin proceeded to tell him about the many lies that Agnes had used to ensnare Gunnar Haugen into an unhappy marriage. Sohlberg wondered if someone—a former husband or her current husband—was trying to frame Agnes Haugen. After all the stepmother had a salacious if not controversial past. Solhlberg sighed and said:

"I'm not surprised about her lies to get this man Gunnar Haugen since . . . as you can imagine . . . I've come across far worse marriages in my more than twenty years of investigations . . . but my head is still spinning from all these crazy family relationships."

"They are complicated."

"What bothers me the most Constable Wangelin . . . is that these adults meet twice a month to trade kids as if they were collectors who meet to trade Pokémon or baseball cards or some other collectible. So . . . who picks up Agnes Haugen's son Thor?"

"Her third husband's parents . . . the paternal grandfather is retired Navy . . . they live near Trondheim."

"Alright. Do this today . . . since I doubt Nilsen ordered this. I want to find out what happened at the gas station where the parents met to trade the children. Call whoever's in charge of policing Otta . . . get whatever constables are necessary out there today or tomorrow at the latest . . . have them find any witness who may've come into contact with this sad bunch of *parents*. Also . . . have them check out all of the closed circuit cameras at or near the gasoline station . . . maybe a camera filmed something interesting on the Friday of Karl Haugen's disappearance . . . or the Saturday after."

"But it's more than a year later."

"I know . . . I doubt if they'll find anything . . . but it's worth the long shot that someone saw something suspicious . . . or that some camera captured a picture of someone else with Karl Haugen. At least see if they can get any video. Look for bank ATMs nearby. They usually keep their video much longer. We need to focus on the parents before we look at anyone else."

"I agree. Chief Inspector . . . it's not good that we turned a blind eye on these parents . . . and grandparents. But that was Nilsen's decision. The team had to go along. Look . . . I'm relatively new in the force . . . a newbie with little experience and yet I knew that Nilsen was not doing a good job. You should have heard Nilsen praising Maya and Arvid Engen as solid members of the courts and the police. He heaped even more praise on Maya's first husband the goat farmer for raising their son alone while making great cheese.

"I almost puked when Nilsen about got on his knees to worship the two retired university professors in Stavanger who are the parents of Agnes Haugen. As you can imagine . . . Nilsen couldn't say enough nice things about Thor's paternal grandparents as *honorable citizens and a Navy captain*."

"We'll see how honorable all these citizens are in reality. Also . . . did the team bother checking out the activities and whereabouts of Maya Engen's first husband the goat farmer on June four?"

"No."

"What about the paternal grandparents of the stepmother's first son Thor . . . who live up in Trondheim?"

"No."

"What about the stepmother's parents . . . the retired university professors in Stavanger?"

"No."

"I want their homes searched top to bottom and their whereabouts for Friday June fourth and Saturday June fifth thoroughly examined. Call headquarters right now and let them know that we need this done immediately."

"Yes. Chief Inspector."

While Constable Wangelin placed the call to Oslo on her cell phone Sohlberg thought about the infinite possibilities that existed for mischief—and murder—as a result of the messy relationships of the adults around little Karl Haugen.

The minutes passed by slowly as Wangelin made several more phone calls to launch the re-invigorated investigation. When the calls finally ended Sohlberg let out another exasperated sigh. He shook his head and said:

"Did the team check the phone and computer records of Maya and Inspector Arvid Engen?"

"I don't think so . . . let me think. . . . Actually no."

"What? That's outrageous."

"Nilsen said it was ridiculous to even think that a police officer or a goat farmer or a retired Navy captain or retired university professors would kidnap Karl or help someone do that."

"Get the records for all of them . . . six months before June fourth and six months after."

"Anything else?"

"Did Nilsen get the phone and computer records for Karl's father and the stepmother?"

"No. Again Nilsen said it was a waste of time to think that the mother or father or stepmother would take or harm the child. According to Nilsen, '*These are good people. Not the criminal element.*'"

"Get me the phone and computer records for the father and the stepmother . . . six months before and after June fourth."

"Not that I mind Chief Inspector but . . . that's a lot of stuff for me to look into. . . ."

"Just look for frequently called phone numbers . . . or e-mail addresses that show up a lot. I'm sure that KRIPOS has some software to do that in minutes. If they don't then just go on the Internet. I'm sure you'll find some company somewhere selling that software."

"Of course. I'll call or go to a company called Alta Soft . . . I think they're still up on Adolph Tidemandsgt in Lillestrøm . . . about twenty minutes northeast of downtown Oslo. They have very good stuff."

"I wouldn't be surprised if Steen and Strøm sells

software next to linens and housewares. Everything is available nowadays on the Internet . . . especially software."

"I'll look at altasoft's website and see what they carry. Then I'll call them to find out if their software can help us."

"Good," said Sohlberg. He started to frown. "There's something else."

"What?"

"I'm really bothered by Karl's mother . . . so this Maya Engen woman gave birth to two sons and then she abandons the two boys to her two husbands? . . . Maybe she wanted back what she had so carelessly given away."

"Nilsen never considered that angle Chief Inspector. Everyone saw her more as a pitiful victim."

"Could be she's a pitiful victim . . . as you call her. It could also be that she arranged for Karl's kidnaping."

"Yes . . . could be."

"Alright then . . . after you get the phone and computer records I want you to give me a list of every single one of the friends *and* family of Karl's mother . . . of Karl's father . . . and of Karl's stepmother . . . who had frequent phone or computer contact with these three people."

"The three people closest to Karl Haugen . . . I always thought they were our best suspects."

"Exactly Constable Wangelin."

"I think we're finally getting closer to solving this."

"Actually we'll be much closer after the Smiley Face Killer tells us *who* is his Number One suspect."

~ ~ ~

"Why did they take me? . . . Where's my Daddy?"

No answer. He looked but could not see his father at all.

"Mom!"

He was hurt and bewildered beyond measure as to why his mother and father had not come for him. Maybe just maybe he was going to have to live without his parents. He remembered the woman who had recently come to visit him. She said:

"Sometimes we have to do things on our own. Like when we go to school alone without Mommy and Daddy. That's kind of what you're doing here right now. . . ."

No. He would keep waiting for his mother and father. Surely they would come for him.

Chapter 9/Ni

HALDEN PRISON,
AFTERNOON OF 1 YEAR AND
24 DAYS AFTER THE DAY,
FRIDAY, JUNE 4

"I think we're almost at the exit," said Constable Wangelin excitedly. "Is that it?"

"Yes."

"I can't believe we're about to visit the Smiley Face Killer . . . Norway's forgotten serial killer."

Sohlberg checked his map one more time and read aloud the instructions on how to get to the maximum security prison. A few minutes later they got off the E-6 at the exit for Highway 21 east to Halden. Less than a mile later they turned left and went north until they reached Road 104 and headed east on Torpumveienen.

"Are we on the right road?"

"This is it," said Sohlberg who felt a stressful tension he had not felt in a long time.

They turned left to the ironically named Justice Road.

Despite his growing tension Sohlberg looked forward to visiting Halden Fengsel. He wanted confirmation that his investigation was on the right track.

Who better than a serial killer and a child predator to let Sohlberg know if he had narrowed down the list of suspects to the most likely culprit?

Sohlberg desperately wanted to solve the Karl Haugen case and not make any mistakes. His investigation had to be flawless or close to flawless or he would probably never be able to leave Norway and get back to Interpol. But the main motivation in solving the Karl Haugen case was the little boy himself. Innocent. Defenseless. Taken and gone. Whoever took Karl Haugen had so far made no mistakes or at least no discernable mistakes. That meant that Sohlberg could make no mistakes.

He thought aloud and almost started shouting as a result of his excitement over the true nature of the case:

"You know Constable Wangelin . . . everything . . . and I mean *everything* . . . that took place on that Friday was essential . . . critical . . . to the kidnaping of Karl Haugen. It was all so *intricate* . . . like a Swiss watch filled with dozens of tiny springs and screws and sprockets that all have to work together in perfect harmony and timing.

"Karl Haugen would *never* have vanished so easily if any one single event had gone wrong. It's hard to believe . . . but we're dealing with a master criminal in a boring suburb of Oslo . . . a criminal genius who put as much work and thought into the kidnaping of Karl Haugen as a Swiss watchmaker does into the best time mechanism."

"Yes . . . that's the word for the abduction . . . intricate."

"Now think about this . . . a Swiss watch is intricate . . . but it's intricate for only *one* single solitary purpose . . . to accurately tell time . . . the same goes for this kidnaping . . . it was . . . it *is* so intricate . . . executed with the greatest care and precision . . . and planned months or maybe even years in advance . . . and yet despite its intricacy the entire kidnaping was only for one purpose. . . ."

"To take Karl Haugen."

Sohlberg paused for a long time before he spoke. "That's the obvious purpose . . . but could the kidnaping be for some other hidden purpose that we can't see or fathom or understand?"

"Oh . . . I see what you mean."

"If we find out what is the *sole* purpose of all of the events on that June fourth then we will find out who is the kidnaper and what was the kidnaper's motivation."

"I agree . . . *that* is the key to solving the case Chief Inspector."

"The purpose of the abduction . . . the goal of the kidnaping . . . reveals the who and the why since we already know the how."

Four miles northeast of the town of Halden a clearing in the forest revealed the prison. It left Sohlberg speechless.

The taupe-colored prison walls rose out of the forest. A psychologist had picked the calming and warm gray-brown tint of the concrete walls. Interior decorators had picked elegant modern art to fill all of the walls and all of hallways of the prison. The outer prison walls were covered with large murals of inmates wearing prison stripes in humorous situations such as playing volleyball. Ten years and $ 260 million had gone into building Norway's super-modern and second largest prison. In Sohlberg's eyes the maximum security facility for 252 inmates looked more like a modern spa in Los Angeles or Palm Springs.

"I'm sorry Constable Wangelin . . . but this is rather luxurious for people who don't deserve luxury accommodations as punishment for rape or murder. I can't believe the government spent ten million dollars per prisoner to build this luxury retreat."

"Well . . . you know the Norwegian way," she said alluding to the low 20% re-offending rate of Norwegian prisoners in comparison to the 50% to 60% rate in Britain and the USA. "Don't forget Chief Inspector . . . we have less than five thousand men and women in Norway's prisons . . . that's less than seventy convicts per one hundred thousand people versus the American rate that's one thousand percent greater."

"True . . . and yet. . . . You can murder or rape in Norway as many times as you want and you nevertheless get a maximum sentence of twenty-one years. Think about it . . . you can kill fifty or sixty or more people and yet you only get twenty-one years in Norway."

"Well that's changed Chief Inspector . . . since a few years ago . . . when was it? Two thousand eight? . . . Since then criminals can get charged with the new law of crimes against humanity."

"What's the penalty?"

"A maximum penalty of thirty years. And there's an anti-terrorism law that allows for the indefinite prolongation of sentences . . . in blocks of five years at a time . . . each renewed by a judge if the convict is deemed dangerous to public security."

"How many times has that law been applied? . . . How about zero times? How about never?"

Wangelin nodded slowly in reluctant agreement.

Sohlberg waved at the 75-acre facility where inmates enjoy a music studio and a rock climbing wall and hobby rooms and recreational areas and jogging trails and a superb library and two-bedroom cabins where inmate families can stay during overnight visits. "I wish you could see some of those miserable French or Russian prisons . . . or the truly horrible ones in Peru or Brazil."

Constable Wangelin nodded. "I know about those hellholes . . . but we have a low enough crime rate and more than enough oil money to pay for this."

"I . . . I don't know . . . is this fair? Is this justice? . . . I mean this prison here is a country club for millionaires compared to San Quentin in California or other American horrors like SuperMax in Colorado."

"I've heard they're absolutely awful."

"Of course they're all topped off by the ultimate nightmare of Louisiana's Angola State Penitentiary."

"Bad?"

"I went to pick up a prisoner for extradition . . . hope to never be back there again . . . ever."

"But don't you think Chief Inspector that we are a little more civilized than the Americans?"

Sohlberg said nothing. But his hand gesture left no doubt as to his contempt for any prison that provided a soft life for a felony convict.

The inspector and constable checked in and wended their way through security checkpoints. A deputy warden joined them as an escort. He showed them how the prisoners' cells were arranged in units of 10 to 12 rooms "just like college dorms".

"I don't think so," said Sohlberg. "The cells in this prison are far better than most college dorms."

"Why do you say that?" said the clueless deputy warden.

"Because each cell has a private bathroom and a flat-screen TV and a mini-fridge and lovely views of the forest. The windows don't even have bars on them . . . and each group of cells shares a living room and kitchen. That's far better than any college dorm."

"That is true Chief Inspector," said the deputy

warden with pride.

Sohlberg shrugged. Over and over he kept repeating: "What the heck is this place . . . a luxury hotel?" Sohlberg pointed to the stainless-steel counter-tops and wraparound sofas and birch-colored coffee tables that seemed straight out of an Ikea catalogue. "What the heck is this place . . . a luxury hotel for felons?"

The oblivious deputy warden continued his lecture about the *strong and positive* relationship between the prison staff and the inmates and how the guards do not carry weapons. The man pointed out how the prison was not depressing to the inmates thanks to more than $ 1,000,000 worth of original artwork that graced every location that inmate eyes might happen to fall upon.

Sohlberg was about to make a rude comment when they were ushered into the elegant office of the Prison Warden Henrik Birkeland.

"Harald Sohlberg! . . . I'm glad you're in this part of the world. How long has it been since we last met? . . . I think you had just been promoted to Inspector when I last saw you."

"I don't remember . . . but I'd say it's been at least fifteen years since we've seen each other no?"

The two men briefly spoke of a few cases that they had worked on when they had started out in the police force as rookie constables in Oslo.

"Why Henrik did you ever join the kriminalomsorgens correctional services?"

"Rehabilitating criminals is much less stressful than catching them. The K.S.F. lets me spend lots of time with my wife and kids. I'm a grandfather now! . . . What about you . . . are you—"

Sohlberg evaded the personal question especially with Wangelin at his side. "I'm here just for a short visit.

This is a temporary assignment. I'll be back to Interpol soon."

"I see," said Warden Birkeland. "Is that why you're visiting the Smiley Face Killer? . . . Your temporary assignment? The one that's so hush-hush? . . . When they told me you were coming out here I asked and no one in Oslo wanted to tell me exactly what your visit is all about."

"I'm sorry . . . but we have to keep the investigation under wraps."

"Alright. So be it. Are you ready to see him?"

"Yes."

"With those boxes?" said Warden Birkeland. He pointed at two boxes that Constable Wangelin cradled in her arms.

Sohlberg nodded and said, "Those boxes are for Rønning."

"You know the guards will have to see what's inside them."

"Of course," said Sohlberg. "As you know Anton Rønning has helped me before in other cases . . . in exchange for big and small perks."

"It's always been a mystery to me *how* and *why* you got him out of prison in Spain where he was . . . correct me if I'm wrong . . . serving the equivalent of a life sentence—"

"For raping and murdering three boys in Mallorca."

"So tell me Sohlberg . . . how did you and your friends at Interpol manage to convince the Spaniards to let Rønning out of that very well-deserved hellish pit of a prison he was in? Why did you coddle that sick pervert?"

Sohlberg's face and neck darkened. "What? What did you say?"

"I'm sorry . . . I shouldn't have said it that way . . .

but why did you bring Rønning up here to this country club when he was living in hell in that Spanish prison and getting daily beatings and worse. I understand he stopped taking showers after he was gang-raped.

"Now he's here in Norway enjoying our prison's nature trails and pottery classes. Sooner or later he will get his twenty-one year sentence cut down by at least a third . . . like everyone else.

"Everyone says you got him a sweet deal . . . a pretty good life up here . . . quite cozy."

"Don't ever accuse me of that! I'm no friend of perverts . . . and that's not why I arranged for his transfer up here."

"Really Sohlberg?"

"Matter of fact . . . after Rønning ran away to Spain the Spaniards caught him . . . they gladly traded Rønning for Mohammed Kumar . . . one of our lovely Norwegian Muslim immigrants from Pakistan."

"Oh yes," said the warden. "I remember him . . . an extremist Islamic terrorist we were holding up here in our prison system after we caught him funding and planning the murders of two hundred killed in the Madrid bombings."

"Well then . . . I hope you see the insanity of accusing me of coddling criminals."

"Please Harald . . . I didn't mean it that way."

A minute passed while the men gathered their composure. Sohlberg's volcanic anger almost got the better of him because he had to keep an ugly secret. No one could ever find out that his mentor Lars Eliassen had called him out of the blue and asked him:

"What do you think of a man who rapes and kills dozens and dozens of children?"

Sohlberg's memories transported him to the distant

past which felt as real as if it was taking place in the present.

~ ~ ~

"What do you think of a man who rapes and kills dozens and dozens of children?"

"He's a monster," said Sohlberg who was surprised that Inspector Lars Eliassen had called him out of the blue with such a question.

Eliassen paused. "In the old Viking days he'd be cut to pieces."

"Naturally."

"What do you think of such a man when he's . . . released on bail and runs away to another country?"

"A coward."

"I need a favor then . . . I remember that you know how to speak Spanish."

"Yes. I do."

"Listen . . . I have a hunch," said Eliassen, "that Anton Rønning is hiding down in Spain after jumping bail."

"Why?"

"Because a long time ago . . . at the start of the investigation . . . I interviewed a distant Rønning relative . . . who mentioned that she sometimes lent Rønning her condominium in Mallorca and that he even had a key to the place."

Sohlberg could hardly talk with excitement and let alone cooly say, "So what is the favor?"

"The favor is you driving down to Stockholm Sweden . . . buy a calling card . . . then use the card on an anonymous public pay phone to call the Spanish *guardia civil* ."

"I see. What do I tell them?"

"That you have an anonymous tip."

"What tip?"

"That *El Maton Loco* . . . The Crazy Killer of children in Madrid and Mallorca is a Norwegian citizen . . . Anton Rønning . . . he's staying at a certain posh condo unit in Los Caballos . . . a gated community in Mallorca . . . and that they might want to catch him before he decides to take a flight to Oslo Norway were he would . . . at most . . . serve a light prison sentence in a comfortable if not luxurious Nordic prison."

"I understand."

"Sohlberg . . . I hope you do. Spain doesn't have life sentences or the death penalty. But it has a couple of horrific prisons more in tune with the Turkish model than the Norwegian model. In other words . . . Anton Rønning will rot in a Spanish prison straight out of the medieval Inquisition or Dante's *Inferno*."

~ ~ ~

The overwhelming reality of Halden Fengsel pulled Sohlberg out of his reverie. He walked to a credenza and served himself a glass of water from an elegant decanter made by the Swedish glassmaker Kosta Boda. He drank most of the glass and then said:

"Henrik . . . you need to consider the *facts* before you ever again accuse me of coddling criminals like Anton Rønning."

"Such as? . . . "

"We had a five-year investigation at Interpol that was going nowhere fast into an international pedophile ring . . . members of the ring bought and sold and traded children including infants all over the world . . . and they of course bought and sold and traded videos and pictures of their criminal acts with children.

"Many of the victims were their own biological or adopted children. We couldn't solve the case . . . then I remembered a comment that Rønning once made to me . . . I visited him in Spain and he gave me a tip that eventually lead to a webmaster in Amsterdam who secretly posted and hid the videos inside legitimate websites."

"I didn't know that. I doubt if anyone knows . . . right?"

"That's right . . . thanks to Anton Rønning we exposed dozens of businessmen and women . . . accountants . . . bankers . . . lawyers . . . judges . . . senior police officers . . . NATO generals . . . you name it. . . . A Norwegian Supreme Court justice who likes to watch the raping of young girls . . . a top Chinese diplomat at the United Nations . . . a deputy director at the F.B.I. and at the B.A.T.F. in the United States."

"I'm not surprised."

"We even caught a former Deputy Assistant Secretary of the United States Navy who was good friends of Senator Kerry the presidential candidate. . . . And of course we had plenty of top level people at UNICEF and the World Bank and the International Monetary Fund. The cream of society . . . caught red-handed in the sewer. We saved sixty-three children . . . took them into protective custody."

"I don't remember any arrests of the perverts."

"Of course not. Only two got arrested. None got convicted."

"Why?"

"The ususal . . . the perverts got their friends in government to drop any charges. Only one got charged .

. . that former U.S. Navy official. The rest? . . . They resigned or retired. You know the usual phony corporate doubletalk . . . they left to pursue other interests . . . *to spend time with family*."

"But the perverts—"

"The perverts got off because they knew too much about the people in power . . . the affairs . . . the financial frauds . . . the perversions . . . you name it."

"I know whose club you're talking about . . . the lifestyles of the rich and powerful club. These high-placed perverts have their protectors and friends who gladly turn a blind eye as long as these perverts are of use to them."

"Yes," said Sohlberg. "You know . . . the *Too Big To Fail* crowd. . . ."

"That's the reality," said Warden Birkeland sadly. "I know very well how that works. Remember the case of the mayor and his teenage boyfriend?"

"Exactly. See what I mean?"

"All too well. Anyway . . . I hope you didn't put dynamite in the boxes for Rønning to blast a hole in the wall and escape."

"No. They're Freia chocolates. Our Smiley Face Killer is crazy for any Freia chocolate confection. The melkesjokolade milk chocolate bars are his favorite . . . as are the Kvikk Lunsj Quick Lunch chocolate wafers."

"How charming . . . chocolates for a killer . . . like visiting a relative . . . like me visiting Grandpa Birkeland this weekend."

"Rønning is now what . . . seventy-eight?"

"Eighty. This visit should be interesting. . . . Just don't get too near him. He attacked a guard two months ago and broke her wrist."

~ ~ ~

Anton Rønning had a good tan. The portly 80-year-old seemed rather hale and quite serene on the patio where he was taking the sun on a lounge chair. The monster listened to music piped into his earphones by an MP3 player. He smiled and looked the epitome of an old retiree enjoying a comfortable government pension. The serial killer reminded Sohlberg more of a retired accountant or a genial grandfather.

"Hello Sohlberg. I'd get up but I hurt my back two months ago . . . I had to show this disrespectful guard how to respect me . . . so I gave her the proverbial slap on the wrist. . . . I'm sure some tattle-tale already told you the gossip about the guard's broken wrist."

"Yes."

"What have you there?" said Rønning. He pointed and cast a leering glance at Constable Wangelin and the boxes in her arms

"Your favorite."

"Ha! That's not exactly what I meant . . . who's the pretty lady . . . your daughter?"

"No."

"My my my . . . well she's not your wife . . . you're not the kind of man to dump an old wife to marry a newer gal half your age. A mistress? You have a mistress? . . . No. That's certainly not your style . . . my straight straight arrow. Don't tell me . . . she's just a co-worker?"

Sohlberg nodded.

"Interpol? . . . No. She looks like one of ours. Home-grown I'd say. Quite lovely."

"She's Norwegian . . . from the Olso district . . . if that's what you mean."

"That so? . . . Are the Police and the Ministry of Justice finally figuring out that it's best to catch criminals with honey and not with vinegar?"

"I wanted to ask you—"

Anton Rønning raised his hand. "One minute please . . . let me hear the end . . . oh . . . oh . . . this is so good . . . Vivaldi . . . The Four Seasons . . . played by Fabio Biondi and Europa Galante. Oh my! How they play . . . so much energy . . . how exciting.

"I can almost see that redheaded priest Vivaldi playing the violin in Venice like the devil himself! I'm surprised the church didn't burn him at the stake for such outrageous music . . . it just *burns* with passion . . . and lust for life. Just like me . . . don't you think?"

Sohlberg shrugged and said, "I wonder what the world would be like if we brought back burning at the stake for society's heretics."

"Hot my boy. The world would be hot for devils like me." The old murderer laughed lustily at his own joke. "Anyway . . . what goodies have you brought me in those boxes?"

"Your favorite chocolates."

"How kind. How lovely. You know . . . I have always depended on the kindness of strangers . . . just like Blanche Dubois in A Streetcar Named Desire."

"I need your help."

"Again . . . so soon?"

"Yes."

Anton Rønning laughed and took one of the milk chocolate bars and it disappeared into his cavernous mouth in one stealthy move. "Sohlberg I'd like to get transferred out of here. Don't get me wrong. I'm grateful very grateful to be here. After my last beating I probably had days to live in Spain before you got me out.

"But I'm getting old Sohlberg. I've spent what? . . . The last thirty years in prison? More than fifteen years in

Spain and more than ten here."

Sohlberg removed his glasses and carefully cleaned them with a small soft blue cloth that he used only for that purpose. "Crime and punishment. Acts and consequences. One follows the other . . . no? As night follows day."

"But another day follows the night. Doesn't it? . . . Sohlberg I'd like to spend my last days without looking at any walls. I want to move to Bastøy Prison."

Sohlberg was not surprised. The minimum security prison on Bastøy Island was an idyllic resort-like facility less than 50 miles south of Oslo. Inmates could easily swim to the mainland but did not for fear they'd be sent to less hospitable lodgings. Bastøy Island held 115 inmates who lived in cozy wood cottages when they were not working in the organic farm or horseback riding or fishing or swimming or playing tennis.

"I'll be honest with you," said Sohlberg. "Halden is as good as it gets. I will not be personally recommending that you get transferred to Bastøy."

"Fair enough. Will you at least let them know that's *my* request if I help you?"

"I'll let them know about your request. Now . . . will you help me?"

"Of course. You got me out of that nightmare down in Spain. We have a good working relationship."

"I and the constable here are going to tell you everything about a case we're working on."

"The Karl Haugen case?"

"Oh?" Sohlberg raised his eyebrows. "You heard anything about the case here in prison?"

"Yes but not what you think. Most of the inmates are outraged that someone would take or harm the boy. We were even more outraged at the incompetent police investigation."

"We're going to lay out some basic facts for you to consider about the case."

"Alright."

"You can ask me all the questions you want. Constable here will answer what I can't."

"What do you want to know?"

"Who is the person most likely to have taken the boy."

"What's the other thing you want to know?"

"I'll tell you after you hear us," replied Sohlberg who was thrown off balance by the question and by the killer's lifeless flat eyes which stared out at odd angles like one of those horrid Picasso portraits.

How did Anton Rønning know that he wanted another piece of information from him?

The killer had a knack for always being one step ahead of everyone around him especially law enforcement. Rønning had only been caught because of one little slip-up—a parking ticket that linked Rønning's car to the scene of another molestation. Sohlberg's mentor Lars Eliassen had noticed and persistently investigated the parking ticket and Rønning himself long before Inspector Eliassen got to arrest Rønning for crashing a getaway car while fleeing from one of his victims. Like an obsessed bloodhound Eliassen had single-mindedly followed the trail of clues that ultimately unmasked Anton Rønning as the Smiley Face Killer.

An hour went by. Then another. Rønning listened intently to Sohlberg and Wangelin. At the start of the third hour the killer said:

"Enough."

Constable Wangelin started to speak but Sohlberg held up his hand.

Rønning lapsed into silence. Fifteen minutes passed.

Sohlberg and Wangelin waited in the growing shadows thrown by the forest around them. The lonely sun moved to the far west. Finally the killer spoke from the darkening shade:

"I seriously doubt if the boy was taken by a stranger . . . least of all for deviant entertainment purposes like mine. . . . No. . . . Everything you've told me tells me one thing . . . that one of the parents took the boy. The father or the stepmother. But you I think already suspected that."

"Yes," said Sohlberg. "But *why* . . . *why* do this?"

"The third oldest motive in the world after lust and greed. . . . Revenge."

"I see."

"Do you?" said Anton Rønning while another chocolate bar disappeared into his mouth like so many of the hapless victims who fell into his voracious pit of depravity. "Sohlberg . . . these chocolates remind me of my sweet grandmother . . . when she wasn't beating the life out of me she always quoted me an old saying. . . . *Revenge converts a little right into a great wrong.*"

PART THREE: DOORS OF PERCEPTION

To get a confession the police detective must offer the suspect a series of doors that must be attractive enough for the suspect to open and step through. Each door should open the path to a damaging admission or a provable lie.

— Lars Eliassen, Police Inspector

Ask me no questions, and I'll tell you no fibs.
— Oliver Goldsmith (1730–1774)

If the doors of perception were cleansed everything would appear to man as it is, infinite.

— William Blake,
The Marriage of Heaven and Hell

Chapter 10/Ti

MORNING OF 1 YEAR AND 25 DAYS
AFTER THE DAY, FRIDAY, JUNE 4

The evidence room in the basement smelled as all
evidence rooms smell: moldy. The clerk handed Sohlberg
a numbered box with Karl Haugen's backpack which the
police had picked up at the school at 11:02 PM on the
Friday that he disappeared. The red backpack held the
usual collection of a child's school supplies and life: pens
and pencils and notebooks and books and rocks and
Pokémon trading cards and chewing gum and a blue
plastic grasshopper.

Sohlberg looked around the bag and noted that Karl
Haugen's lunch box or pail was not in the backpack. He
checked the list of evidence and it did not mention any
school lunch.

In the elevator that took him back up to his office
Sohlberg wondered why Karl Haugen did not have his
lunch with him that day if the parents were correct in
telling the investigators that Karl was supposed to be at
the school all day long and that they always prepared a
lunch for Karl to eat at school.

Why send a boy off all day to school without his
lunch?

Was it because one parent or both parents never
expected Karl to eat his lunch or come back home?

The question had intensely bothered Sohlberg ever

since he had formed a mental outline of other troubling questions that he needed to ask the parents.

"Hei," said Constable Wangelin cheerfully as she walked into Sohlberg's cubicle at 9 AM. He had given her permission to come in one hour late because they had returned exhausted to Oslo after midnight from their excursion to Halden Prison. "Chief Inspector . . . I just got a return call from one of the constables who worked on the early stages of the investigation. He says that we must talk to Karl Haugen's teacher . . . Lisbeth Bøe."

"Why?"

"According to him she's always been very angry about being made a scapegoat and blamed by everyone for not alerting the school administrators early enough about Karl Haugen's disappearance."

"Why was she blamed?"

"Because she saw Karl Haugen early that day at the science fair . . . and yet she did not raise the alarm when Karl was absent from her class at nine o'clock when she took roll."

"But you previously told me that she marked him absent. Obviously she did not find his absence that strange."

"That's correct Chief Inspector . . . and that's the key . . . why didn't she find it unusual that Karl Haugen was there earlier for the science fair and then gone from the class?"

Sohlberg rubbed his eyes. "My suspicions are coming true . . . we are dealing with a brilliant devious mind. . . . Do you now see Constable what I meant when I said that this case is *intricate* . . . brilliantly designed with a purpose that we still cannot even come close to understanding?"

"True . . . but we have an inkling . . . do we not . . .

that the taking of Karl Haugen was probably for purposes of revenge?"

"Yes. But by who . . . why . . . over what minor slight or great injury or wrong?"

"Chief Inspector . . . you agreed with Anton Rønning that it was most likely one of the parents."

"I did agree it was one of the parents . . . but in this family just who is the *parent*? . . . We have the birth mother *and* all of these messy entangled relationships . . . such as the ex-husbands of Agnes Haugen who'd love to get even with her from what you've told me. The stepmother has left behind a small army of angry ex-husbands."

"That's true . . . shall we leave now and go interview this school teacher who's being blamed for Karl's disappearance?"

"By all means. I've always found that scapegoats offer unique truths from their down-and-out point of view."

~ ~ ~

"I want to see my Dad and Mom. Please . . . I have to see them."

The man said and did nothing but the woman smiled.

"I wanna go back home!"

The woman shook her head.

Karl refused to believe that he could not go back home to his father or mother. He no longer got angry about not seeing his father or mother. But he got ever so sad whenever the woman hugged him and told him:

"It's going to be alright."

~ ~ ~

By the time they drove into Holmenkollen the entire Oslofjord had clouded up. A cold front moved in from the North Sea and furiously dropped an inch of chilled rain.

"This almost feels like autumn," said Sohlberg. "I wish I'd brought my parka."

"We'll have more sunny warm days."

Sohlberg nodded but he wondered if his fellow countrymen felt as surprised as he was at how quickly the promise of summer had disappeared. Nature seemed intent on reminding him that the long grim dark days of winter would be back soon.

Hairpin switchbacks led all the way to the top of Pilot Hill. The school's one-floor red building seemed cheerful enough as did the surrounding playground ringed by grass and then forest.

"Very nice school up here," commented Sohlberg. "But I expected more rural surroundings. I remember this was all farms and ski slopes back when I was a kid."

"You had no idea the area was so built up?"

"No. I can't believe all these buildings have been put up here on top of the high hills of Holmenkollen."

"Well Chief Inspector . . . the Holmenkollen ski festival is still up here."

"But this urban sprawl is hideous." Sohlberg looked sadly at another piece of Norway's rural splendor chewed up by long rows of two- and three-floor luxury condominiums and apartments.

"You can't blame people for wanting to live up here . . . this suburb is very nice. I could never afford to live here."

"Let's take a walk," said Sohlberg. "I need to get a feel for the crime scene."

The school offered spectacular views of Oslo and Oslofjord. Sohlberg noted that the school sat between two dead end streets: Grindbakken and Måltrostveien.

"What's the street that passes below the school grounds? . . . I hear traffic on it."

"Oh that? . . . It's Olaf Bulls vei."

"Could someone have parked down there and come up here to take Karl Haugen?"

"Highly unlikely. They'd be blocking traffic even if they parked on the shoulder."

"I can also see why a stranger is unlikely to have walked or driven to the school to take the boy in broad daylight. Look at all these condos and apartments around us . . . anyone on a terrace or window on the second or third floor would've seen something suspicious."

"Chief Inspector . . . that's why we interviewed every single person living within a half mile of here. And . . . nothing. Absolutely nothing. No one inside or outside the school that day saw anyone who did not belong here."

"What about Bogstad Lake . . . it can't be more than a half-mile from here. I imagine Nilsen had the lakeshore searched?"

"Yes."

"Was the lake dragged for a body?"

"Of course . . . we sent in boats with sonar and scuba divers. Nothing. Not a shred of evidence by the lake or anywhere else."

"Interesting . . . if this abduction was for revenge then why not plant a false clue out there . . . place one of Karl's belongings out by the lakeshore . . . a shirt or a toy . . . that would have thrown the investigation into confusing turmoil . . . and led us down a wild goose chase. Wouldn't it?"

"Yes . . . you'd think so," said Constable Wangelin

hesitantly.

"And yet the criminal did *not* plant red herrings to shift the investigation in any particular direction. How brilliant . . . and how cruel since those who love Karl are left permanently in a *daily* agonizing state of suspense as to whether he's dead or alive . . . tortured or hurt."

"Diabolical."

"And . . . at the same time our criminal has been arrogantly confident that he or she will *never* get caught. . . . That's the genius of this criminal. He or she tortures the family *and* stumps the investigators."

"What a monster."

A chill crept into Sohlberg. He had half-expected to find something unusual about the school's location or something else that would explain how a child could vanish in the middle of a school that was filled with more than 200 adults and children that fateful Friday. But Grindbakken skole at 106 Måltrostveien seemed no different than any of the other well-kept elementary schools in Oslo's suburbs.

They met Karl's teacher at a conference room near the principal's office. Karl Haugen's 26-year-old teacher Lisbeth Bøe was no different than any of the other young elementary school teachers. She was caring and competent and supremely confident about her skills. The cares and disappointments of life had not yet aged her.

Constable Wangelin made the introductions.

"I hope this won't take too long," said the doe-eyed teacher. "School's almost over and I have a lot to do to. I wish your people had paid more attention to what I told them. Your Inspector Nilsen brushed off what I said as if I was nuts or lying. You could tell a mile away that the man was stupidly infatuated with Agnes and Gunnar Haugen."

Sohlberg raised his hand and said, "How so?"

"Your Inspector Nilsen believed everything that the Haugens said and he discounted everything I said. He and the parents made it look like I was careless about Karl . . . that is not true. And I resent how I was forced to waste a lot of time getting interviewed by that idiot Nilsen."

"Frøken Bøe," said Sohlberg sternly, "I don't waste *my* time and I promise you that I won't waste yours. Alright?"

"Alright."

"Now . . . what's this business about the parents making it look as if you were careless about Karl."

"If the parents had not tricked me then I would have reacted differently at roll call when I saw that Karl was not in class and marked him absent. You see . . . I would have immediately called the administration and told them to look for Karl or call Karl's home because I had indeed seen him earlier at school during the parent and family portion of the science fair."

"Okay . . . so what was the parents' *trick* to not arouse your concern or alarm?"

"Simple. Both parents told me several times . . . in the two to three weeks before the science fair . . . that Karl had a doctor's appointment on the Friday morning right after the science fair. They said that he would only come in early to school to drop off his exhibit . . . and then leave at nine to go visit the doctor . . . who needed to run several tests on him."

"Isn't it normal for the school to require written notice from the parents if a child is absent?"

"Oh yes we do. But here's the cute and sick part of their trick. They turned in a written notice to the administration on Tuesday . . . and that signed piece of paper only said '*Karl will be out on a doctor's visit on*

Friday.' At no time did they specify which Friday. The Haugens later claimed that they clearly told me many times that the excused absence for the doctor's visit was for the following Friday. They told everyone that I had obviously gotten *confused*."

"Who signed the note?"

"The father."

"Do we have a copy of the note Constable Wangelin? . . . I'd like to get the original if possible."

"I think we have the original back at headquarters. If not then I'll get the original from the school later today."

"Frøken Bøe," said Sohlberg. He almost always used the formal address that most Norwegians dislike and rarely use because almost everyone in Norway likes being on a first name basis to show off Norway's so-called social equality. "Can anyone testify that *before* Karl disappeared you actually mentioned or told them about Karl Haugen being pulled out of class by his parents on Friday June fourth because of a doctor's visit."

"Oh yes. I told eight . . . maybe nine colleagues here at the school . . . all of them will testify that I complained *before* Karl disappeared about his parents wanting him excused from school on June fourth . . . and not on Friday June eleven as the parents later claimed."

"What was your complaint to your colleagues?"

"I told several teachers earlier that week that it was unfair for the Haugens to take Karl out of school on the day of the science fair when he was probably going to win a special award for his excellent project on red-eye tree frogs. . . . I can give you a list of five teachers and three administrators that I complained to after Karl put so much work into a project that his parents shoved on him."

"What do you mean by *shoved on him*?"

"Karl wanted to do a project on icebergs. That's all he talked about that year. He loved how icebergs float around before melting. He was fascinated by the fact that icebergs are mostly hidden under the surface . . . and how an iceberg sank the Titanic. But his parents forced him to change his project to frogs."

"In a nutshell . . . are you telling us that *both* parents misled you into believing that Karl would only attend the science fair from eight to nine in the morning?"

"Yes."

"And . . . you're telling us that both parents misled you into believing that Karl would take an excused absence and leave school at or a little before nine in the morning to be at a doctor's appointment that Friday June fourth?"

"Exactly."

Sohlberg smiled and said, "Please write your witness list now."

Frøken Bøe wrote furiously on a notepad while she frowned and said:

"Also . . . I didn't like them pulling Karl out of school because I don't think Karl really had anything wrong with him that needed a doctor visit."

"Why do you say that?"

"They made up his symptoms. They kept saying he had seizures during those two to three weeks before June fourth. That's a lie. I never once saw him have seizures. At most he was a little space-y the two weeks before he disappeared. He looked sleep deprived . . . if not stressed. I asked him what was wrong and he just shrugged.

"I then asked the parents why Karl looked so stressed. That's when they told me they had called a doctor . . . and that she had told them that he was having seizures and needed to come in for an examination.

"But then I thought . . . what doctor would diagnose seizures over the phone? And since when can you talk to a doctor over the phone just like that? . . . You're lucky if you get to talk to a nurse on the phone."

"Do you know the name of the doctor?"

"Julie Heldaas. She's a pediatrician. A lot of children in the school go to her."

Sohlberg nodded and rubbed his cold hands. He knew that he would solve the case quickly if he could find out whether the father or the stepmother was the source of the clever trick to mislead the administrators and teachers into believing that Karl was leaving school to visit a doctor that fateful Friday June fourth.

"Frøken Bøe . . . would you say that Karl was a happy boy?"

"Over all yes . . . but you know . . . children from divorced homes have a lot of stress . . . I noticed he got very sad whenever he came back from visiting his mother up in Namsos . . . I figured he wanted to stay up there and not come back to his father and stepmother."

"Did he say anything in particular about wanting to live with his mother?"

"No . . . he wouldn't talk a lot about his home situation . . . I always felt that someone at home had told him not to talk with me or other teachers . . . I did notice that he seemed distressed during the two or three weeks before he went missing . . . he could not focus on class assignments . . . he forgot everything he had to do . . . he would stare out into space. . . .

"Karl even got into a fight with another boy . . . that was a first for Karl since he was a very sweet and good natured boy. The even more weird thing about the fight was that he kept screaming at the other boy, '*I hate you. I hate you.*' Now that was very very unusual for Karl . . .

it was almost as if he was a little tape recording that just kept repeating something he heard at home . . . I've seen that before with my children. They repeat what they hear at home from the adults."

"Any signs of physical abuse?"

"No. Had there been I would've immediately called the police . . . especially with his stepmother pestering me every single day to let her know *exactly* how Karl was doing at school as far as his academics and behavior. It's no secret . . . Chief Inspector . . . that I found Agnes Haugen a little too much to handle. But . . . I must admit that I have two other former elementary school teachers who also go nuts in micromanaging their children and their education."

"One last thing Frøken Bøe."

"Yes?"

"Did Karl Haugen usually bring his lunch from home?"

"Agnes always packed his lunch."

"Did he have a separate lunch box or did he carry his lunch in his backpack?"

"Let me think . . . Karl . . . in his backpack. He had small plastic tubs . . . like tupperware . . . that held his food. So the answer is no . . . he did not have a separate lunch box or pail . . . he took his lunch straight out of his backpack."

"Thank you Frøken Bøe. We'll be in touch."

"Oh . . . I almost forgot."

"Yes?"

"During the first few weeks after Karl disappeared we found out that Karl's parents . . . especially the stepmother Agnes . . . had made an outrageous statement to the newspaper and televison reporters."

"What statement?"

"Agnes Haugen insisted that she saw Karl talking to a science fair volunteer who was monitoring the children when she left the school that morning after the fair ended."

Sohlberg nodded. "I read somewhere in the files . . . that the school had several parents who volunteered to watch over the children in the hallways and the auditorium."

"That part's true. The lie is that Agnes Haugen insists that the volunteer was a man wearing a volunteer badge. That's simply not true . . . there were *no* male volunteers at the science fair that day."

"Are you sure?"

"Of course. It was the first time that had happened in several years . . . we've always had male volunteers at the science fair . . . but not last year when Karl disappeared . . . all the teachers and administrators made comments about that."

"Could anyone sneak in wearing a badge?"

"Not really. Inspector . . . don't forget . . . I was there. I never saw a man posing as a volunteer . . . or wearing a volunteer badge. Trust me . . . all of us teachers would've noticed that immediately."

~ ~ ~

Karl didn't know how much longer he could hold out. He desperately wanted to see his father and mother. A few days ago he had fallen asleep and suddenly he had woken up and heard his mother's voice calling him with wild despair:

"Karl! . . . Karl! . . . My son!"

She was after all still looking for him!

But she could not see him. Eventually her voice and

her presence faded away and so did his hopes of ever seeing his beloved mother. His father had stopped looking for him. That made him even sadder. How could his father have given up so easily!

"Dad! . . . Mom!"

~ ~ ~

Wangelin drove four miles southeast to the giant Rikshospitalet National Hospital campus of Oslo Universitessykehus University Hospital. Dr. Julie Heldaas was on the last of her late morning rounds. She had agreed to meet them as soon as she was finished.

Sohlberg and Wangelin waited for the doctor at her small office. Sunlight poured in through the window now that the rainstorm had passed.

"This is quite a view," said Sohlberg. He was surprised that although the hospital was at a much lower altitude than Holmenkollen the hospital still had lovely views of the broad Oslofjord which looked more like a vast lake surrounded by low mountains.

"It's nice isn't it?" said Constable Wangelin. "What with all the sunshine and the water sparkling like that. I wish I could be out there today."

"Do you—" Sohlberg interrupted himself. He was about to ask her if she liked water sports but that would have breached Norwegian office etiquette which meant avoiding friendships at work and not sharing any confidences or personal information. He missed people's overall friendliness in Canada and the USA as well as the meaningful work friendships that he had made in those countries. Prosecutors and law enforcement officials in Mexico and Latin America had also befriended him to a degree unheard of in Norway.

"Do I what . . . Chief Inspector?"

"Do you think the doctor will be here soon?"

"She told me to be here at five minutes past noon."

A minute later at exactly 12:05 PM the doctor walked in and shook hands while Constable Wangelin made the introductions. The petite 60-year-old doctor invited them to sit down.

Sohlberg started off with:

"Thank you for meeting us Dr. Heldaas. We have a few questions about your patient . . . the minor Karl Haugen."

"Has he been found?"

"No. By the way . . . I'd appreciate you not informing anyone of this visit or this conversation."

"Inspector . . . that's unusual . . . you do understand don't you?"

"Understand what?"

"That I won't lie if the parents ask me about this visit. You need to understand that I also can't reveal any confidential medical information about the boy unless I have a release from the parents."

Dr. Heldaas was not subtle about her dislike for the police. She looked down on Sohlberg from the tip of her long pointy nose as if he was some contagious infection to be avoided. Over the years Sohlberg had met too many highly-educated professionals who looked down on the police. She struck him as the kind who hated the police but would not hesitate on calling the police if anyone as much as scratched her brand-new CL 600 Mercedes coupe.

"Doctor Heldaas . . . I'm not asking you to lie to anyone . . . or for anyone. What I want . . . and expect from you . . . is for you *not* to interfere with a police investigation. I don't think you want to ruin your reputation or drag the university hospital into a major headache on charges that you obstructed an official government investigation."

"I'm cooperating am I not?"

"Yes you are . . . and I thank you for that. Now . . . this little boy . . . Karl Haugen . . . has been missing for more than a year. Would you agree it's important to find him?"

"Undoubtedly."

"So we are on the same page."

"Yes we are."

"Alright," said Sohlberg in a friendlier manner. "First . . . I need to know if you had an appointment to see Karl Haugen on June four of last year."

"No. It was for June eleven."

"Are you sure? . . . Do you want to check your calendar?"

"No need. I've gone over that matter with Gunnar and Agnes Haugen several times."

"Please explain that."

"Explain what? . . . I don't understand you."

"Explain when and how you went *over that matter with Gunnar and Agnes Haugen several times*."

"I don't remember setting up the initial appointment . . . you'd have to talk with my appointment secretary . . . or the call nurse. But after Karl went missing the mother and the father called me several times to make sure that we had the appointment written down for June eleven."

"Didn't you find that odd . . . them asking for confirmation of Karl's appointment when Karl was already missing?"

"I did find it odd . . . until they explained that Karl's teacher was trying to evade responsibility for not informing the administration that Karl was missing at roll call on the morning of June fourth. . . . Apparently the teacher is telling people that she was misled by the parents into thinking that Karl had an excused medical absence that Friday June four."

"Did you have a conversation with Karl's parents about him having seizures?"

"Seizures? No. Never. He was perfectly normal from a medical perspective."

"Did anyone at the hospital or your practice . . . perhaps a call nurse on the telephone . . . speak to the parents about him having seizures?"

"No. Absolutely not."

"You're that sure?"

"Yes. Right after your constable called me I checked the charts to refresh my memory about Karl . . . there's nothing in his charts about seizures . . . no one ever mentioned anything about seizures to any of his healthcare providers."

"Could someone have lost the note or not even written a note about him having seizures?"

"No. We're totally paperless . . . we enter every medical note or observation into his computerized chart . . . including telephone calls from the parents."

"Would you put your professional reputation on the line and declare under oath that without a doubt Karl Haugen did *not* suffer from seizures?"

"Yes. Again . . . he was perfectly normal from a medical and physical point of view."

Sohlberg thanked the doctor and left the room with Constable Wangelin. They stood in the hallway. Sohlberg put his ear to the doctor's door and heard nothing. He wondered if the door might be too thick for eavesdropping or padded for soundproofing.

"Please run down to the corner of the building . . . and find any room with a window that's opposite hers and see if she's making a call."

Wangelin sprinted down the hallway. A few minutes later Wangelin met him by the elevators.

"She was on the phone."

"Of course she might've been calling someone else on an unrelated matter . . . but I doubt it."

"Do you think Chief Inspector that she called one or both of the Haugens . . . even after you warned her?"

"Yes. I think she called one of them at the very least if not both. Never trust doctors or lawyers. They think they're gods . . . far above the laws and morality of mere mortals."

"You shouldn't get so angry . . . you look like you could explode."

"I'm not angry over Dr. Heldaas!"

"Then what are you angry about?"

"The parents planted the topic of Karl having seizures into the investigation. . . . Don't you see? . . . They manufactured an issue that was bound to confuse us . . . *and* they set up very fertile grounds for a criminal defense down the road that lets one or both of them claim that Karl fell . . . or got lost . . . or had amnesia . . . or drowned because of his so-called *seizure*."

"These parents are unbelievable . . . Chief Inspector . . . as you said before . . . the abduction was brilliantly planned from the get go."

"We're being outsmarted even now . . . a year later. We're being played for idiots . . . morons. That's why I'm about to explode."

Sohlberg noticed that Wangelin almost smiled when he punched and broke the elevator button. He was sure that Wangelin must have heard plenty of rumors about him and now he had proven one of the rumors to be true—he had a volcanic temper barely kept under control.

Chapter 11/Elleve

AFTERNOON OF 1 YEAR AND 25 DAYS
AFTER THE DAY, FRIDAY, JUNE 4

Police officers and staff hurried up and down the
hallways of the seventh floor at 12 Hammersborggata.
Hushed but rushed voices could be heard everywhere.
Sohlberg and Wangelin could not but help notice that the
atmosphere had radically changed at headquarters since
they had left earlier that morning.

"The unmistakable air of a breaking development in
a major case," said Sohlberg. "Wonder what's going on?"

Thorsen's secretary waved at them to come into the
commissioner's office.

"Sohlberg!" shouted Ivar Thorsen. "There you are.
Well . . . well . . . well. While you've been off gallivanting
who knows where today I am proud to report that the Karl
Haugen case is almost solved."

"Ahh . . . you don't say so? How wonderful," said
Sohlberg with unconcealed sarcasm that went over
Thorsen's head.

"Isn't it great?"

"You found the boy?"

"No."

"Someone saw the boy or heard from him?"

"No. But—"

"Someone confessed. Right?"

"No! Stop interrupting me Sohlberg. We arrested Jo

Haugen . . . the thirty-year-old biological brother of Gunnar Haugen . . . Jo Haugen is the uncle of the missing boy . . . we arrested him for child molestation."

"Molesting what child . . . Karl Haugen?"

"No. The uncle's girlfriend left town because her elderly grandmother is close to dying . . . the girlfriend left her fifteen-year-old daughter alone with Karl's uncle. The girl woke up to find him fondling and kissing her while trying to undress her. She screamed . . . hit him with a lamp and ran out of the house to a neighbor."

"What does he say?"

"Nothing. Said he was too drunk to remember. But he said he probably did it because his own grandfather raped and molested him and his brother . . . Gunnar Haugen . . . when they were boys."

Sohlberg nodded and merely said, "I need to think about this. Let's go Constable Wangelin . . . we have work to do."

Commissioner Thorsen abruptly shouted:

"Wait . . . where are you two going? Don't you want to interrogate the uncle?"

"Is the grandfather still living?"

"No."

"Then I don't want to see the uncle for now. Just make sure that the uncle is not allowed to talk to or meet with Karl's father or stepmother. If you let that happen then we could lose the case and never solve it."

"Alright but do you mind telling me. . . ."

"No. Not yet," said Sohlberg. He strolled nonchalantly out of Thorsen's office.

Once they got to Sohlberg's office Constable Wangelin made sure that no one was around to hear her while she whispered:

"What was that all about? . . . Isn't this a major

break in the case? Shouldn't we be meeting with the uncle? . . . I thought it'd mean a lot to you."

"It does . . . but not in the way that you expect."

"But Chief Inspector . . . there's no denying it . . . the case dynamic has radically changed with the uncle's arrest and . . . the allegation that the Haugen grandfather sexually imposed himself on Karl's uncle and father."

"But at this point in our investigation Karl's uncle is a distraction. You're forgetting a basic principle of investigating a cold case . . . which is to focus focus focus. You see . . . to bring a cold case to full boil you need to apply the heat of investigation to one spot for as long as it takes. In other words we can't afford to run around like headless chickens."

"Well . . . you know best."

"Thank you. You see Constable Wangelin . . . experience does have its rewards."

Sohlberg grabbed his suit jacket from the coat stand.

"What's next?" said Constable Wangelin.

"We're off to Nokia . . . their research lab."

"To interview the father?"

"Yes . . . they returned our call . . . we first have a meeting with their I.T. department . . . which has some information for us on the father's computer use. Then we'll interrogate him . . . catch him by surprise . . . and hopefully throw him off his guard."

"Chief this is going to be interesting . . . and a long day."

"Did you get the information on the most frequent phone numbers that the father has made calls to or received calls from during the past two years?"

"I did. It turns out that he only uses a company phone . . . from Nokia of course . . . they have a record of all of his incoming and outgoing calls and text messages."

"Does anything stand out?"

"No. Nothing unusual except for the past two weeks . . . he called his parents a lot."

"We'll pay them a visit. What about the most frequent e-mail addresses he's written to or been written from?"

"We also have those from Nokia since Nokia owns the only computer that Gunnar Haugen uses."

"Even his personal e-mail address?"

"Yes. Employers like Nokia can see and copy whatever is on a company computer . . . even if it's a laptop that the employee has at home. . . . The only unusual activity is a recent spike in e-mails to his parents . . . something about using his grandfather's old barn for a painting project."

"Really? . . . Call headquarters and have them find the barn's location . . . have several officers check it out *today* . . . it's urgent that this be done now . . . as soon as possible. Also have someone go out and interview his parents. Make sure that Gunnar Haugen's father and mother are interviewed separately about the barn . . . and the grandfather's molestation of their sons."

"Chief . . . could Karl be at the barn?"

"Maybe."

"This might be our lucky break!"

"I don't know," said Sohlberg in a glum tone while he thought about the most recent developments in the case. "If Gunnar Haugen is involved in his son's kidnaping then he's gotten rather careless by using a company phone and a company computer as his only means of communications."

"But Chief Inspector don't you think the barn is important?"

"Definitely. That's why our men have to be there

today. Have the officer-in-charge contact us immediately with whatever they find. Go ahead . . . call them now and have them be out looking in the barn while we're at Nokia with Gunnar Haugen."

"Chief Inspector . . . could Karl Haugen be alive somewhere in the farm? . . . Or is he buried under the barn?"

"We'll find out soon . . . won't we?"

"What makes you so sure Chief Inspector?"

"We're about to let the father and the stepmother clear or incriminate themselves."

"How?"

"Watch and learn Constable Wangelin. I'll lead them to several doors that point to guilt or innocence . . . of course they won't know whether guilt or innocence is behind each door."

"What if they refuse to answer?"

"Silence itself is always an answer to a question."

~ ~ ~

Constable Wangelin took the eastbound lanes of Ring 3 or Highway 150 that circles Oslo. Heavy traffic slowed down their trip to Nokia's headquarters at the suburban Nydalen office park in the Nordre Aker borough of northern Oslo. They got off the freeway on the exit for southbound Maridalsveien. While maneuvering through a maze of narrow streets Wangelin got lost looking for Nokia's building on the east bank of the Akerselva River.

"These streets are so confusing," she said hoping that Sohlberg would not get angry or question her competence.

"They always have been in this neighborhood. I just can't believe how this area has changed . . . it used to be an ugly run-down industrial site . . . along with a few modest homes . . . now it's all modern condos and office buildings . . . it looks just like some rich suburb in the U.S.A."

After several wrong turns Wangelin finally found Sandakerveien which she took northbound. They spotted Nokia's building just before reaching Ring 3 or Highway 150. Nokia's offices reminded Sohlberg of all the corporate campuses and corporate headquarters that he had visited throughout the world—bland and impersonal. Just like the top executives of major corporations.

The head of Nokia's Human Resources department in Oslo greeted them at the lobby. She escorted them to a conference room where a nervous young man sat in front of a large laptop computer and an even larger white binder filled with about eight inches of paper.

"Please show the police what you found on Gunnar Haugen's computers."

"We have remote access to all computers that Nokia owns. We monitor all computers that we own to prevent industrial espionage and other unauthorized uses . . . which includes pornography . . . computer games . . . and other recreational uses."

Sohlberg—impatient as ever—said:

"We get it. What did you find?"

The computer technician worked the keyboard and got into screens that meant nothing to Sohlberg.

"We found that Gunnar Haugen installed a key logging software on his computer . . . it lets him spy on other computers into which he has secretly loaded the key logging software . . . the software lets him see everything a person is typing on that computer."

"Is this software a Nokia product . . . does it belong to Nokia?"

"No. Anyone can buy this type of software at a store or on the Internet."

"Who was he spying on?"

"His wife. Agnes Haugen. Actually her laptop computer. You can see her using it right now."

"Was he spying on anyone else?"

"No. But I also found that he installed in her cell phone a similar but much more advanced software that lets him spy on cell phones including all Nokia models."

"How?"

"He secretly loads a special software into the phone's SIM card . . . it's a tiny piece of hardware . . . the subscriber identification module . . that's inside every cell phone. The software lets him hear every call and see every text message and image sent or received on the phone."

"Is this software a Nokia product . . . does it belong to Nokia?"

"No. This is really advanced. He must've designed it himself or gotten it from one of his friends or contacts in the industry."

"Whose phone did he spy on?"

"His wife's phone. He was snooping on her calls earlier today."

"Agnes Haugen's phone?"

"Yes . . . she's always had our top-of-the-line phones."

"Why?"

"Because Nokia gives the newest models to senior technology managers like Gunnar Haugen . . . the idea is to get managers and their families to use them a lot . . . and test them for free so that we can find out if the phones have any software bugs or hardware defects."

Sohlberg's mind raced as he tried to figure out the twisted relationship between Gunnar and Agnes Haugen.

"So . . . Herr Haugen knows who contacts his wife . . . and whom she calls or texts or sends images to?"

"Yes. The software lets him read every phone number that calls in and that she dials out . . . and he can see all of the text messages and images sent and received on the phone."

"What kind of information did he find on his wife's computer and cell phone use?"

"Well. . . ."

"Go ahead . . . tell the officer," said the HR apparatchik.

"Apart from the normal use that one would expect of her contacts with friends and family and various businesses from time to time . . . his wife . . . his wife . . . well . . . she uses her computer and cell phone to communicate with a lot of men in a . . . a sexual or erotic context . . . she arranges meetings with them at their homes or at hotels and other locations. She also sends a lot of nude pictures of herself to men . . . a few of the men also sent her nude pictures of themselves."

"Can we see whom she wrote to and when?"

"Yes. He stored everything that he's spied on her for the past two years in his hard drive. We copied his entire hard drive last night as you requested since we own the computer and all content on the computer. This binder has a plastic pouch with a portable hard drive that contains everything in his computer's hard drive and . . . as requested . . . we've included a flash drive that stored everything she's ever done on every Nokia cell phone she's used for the past two years."

"Excellent. Thank you. What are all those pages in the binder?"

"A sample print-out on everything that he's seen on *her* computer and *her* cell phone during the past four weeks."

"Let me go over one point . . . you copied everything on his computer . . . including everything that he's gathered from spying on her in his company computer?"

"Yes."

Sohlberg mused over the explosive and intrusive nature of the material that Gunnar Haugen had collected on his wife. The chess player and lawyer in Sohlberg needed to make sure that a criminal prosecution or conviction would not be set aside by a court because he had illegally obtained the computer and cell phone information. He said almost casually:

"And . . . technically and legally . . . all that information belongs to Nokia . . . right?"

The techie said nothing. Instead he turned and looked at the Nokia Human Resources manager. The self-important but utterly forgettable manager cleared her throat and said:

"Technically and legally all that information belongs to Nokia. . . . Every Nokia employee signs an agreement that specifies that *everything* on any company computer or phone or digital equipment belongs to Nokia . . . and that includes any and all personal non-company information that the employee may have knowingly and unknowingly placed in the company's computers or phones . . . whether intentionally or accidentally."

"Very good." said Sohlberg. He pointed at the Nokia techie. "Constable Wangelin will you please give him your business card with your e-mail and phone."

"I will . . . as long as he's not able to spy on me or the force."

Sohlberg wasn't sure if Constable Wangelin was joking or serious. Either way Wangelin made her point because the HR person immediately interjected with:

"Oh . . . of course not . . . we'd never snoop on the police."

Sohlberg wasn't so sure. But he had an investigation to complete and an arrest to make. "Ah . . . before I forget . . . what can you tell me about Gunnar Haugen's computer activity on June fourth of last year? . . . The day his son disappeared."

"He was logged into one of our servers from eight in the morning to three in the afternoon. But the activity was not continuous . . . only sporadic . . . sometimes as much as half an hour would go by before he was active typing on the keyboard . . . designing and testing software. You will find in the binder a minute-by-minute timeline of his computer activity for that day."

"Thank you. Now . . . please take us to Gunnar Haugen's office."

Constable Wangelin's phone buzzed while they rode the elevator up to Gunnar Haugen's offices on the top floor. When they got out on the lobby Wangelin pulled Sohlberg aside and said:

"Chief Inspector . . . they're on the way to the grandfather's farm . . . it's near Hov . . . on the shores of the Randsfjorden."

"Is the grandfather still alive . . . does he live at the farm?"

"No . . . he died two years ago," said Wangelin. "But let me pull up a map on my phone and have you take a look at this coincidence."

"Come now Constable Wangelin . . . there's no such thing as a coincidence in a major crime case."

"I know."

The map on her cell phone screen showed Hov to be a small town located about 80 miles north of Oslo. Like Wangelin he noticed that Hov—a small cluster of homes and businesses next to the E-16 Highway to Bergen—was also about 20 miles southeast of the E-6 Highway to Trondheim.

"Well now," said Sohlberg. "The grandfather's farm and barn are near the E-Six Highway that Gunnar Haugen takes to drop off Karl Haugen with his mother."

Wangelin nodded and smiled.

"Excuse me," said Sohlberg to the Nokia HR manager. "We need to go back and ask a few more questions of your technical person."

Twenty minutes later the techie confirmed that during the last three months Gunnar Haugen's cell phone had received and transmitted several calls from a cell tower near the grandfather's farm at Hov. Before that 3 month period Gunnar Haugen's cell phone records showed no activity near the grandfather's farm.

"Do you want me to check out the wife's cell phone to see if she's used her phone in that location?"

"That was my next question. Yes. Please."

The techie said, "No. I don't see anything the past three months in that area with her phone."

Sohlberg frowned. "What about further back in time?"

After tapping at the keyboard a few times the techie said:

"Wait. There's one hit on that tower thirteen months ago."

"When exactly?"

"Noon on Saturday . . . May the eighth."

Sohlberg wondered why Agnes Haugen had been at the farm one month before the boy's disappearance. Of course her husband or anyone else for that matter could have taken her cell phone out there.

But other than her husband who would've done that?

He needed to find out from Gunnar or Agnes Haugen or someone else if one or both of them had been at the grandfather's farm shortly before the fateful day of Karl's disappearance.

"One last thing," said Sohlberg urgently. "I noticed you said Gunnar's phone showed that several calls were recently made and received in the area around Hov . . . and yet for Agnes Haugen's phone you said a *hit*. What's the difference?"

"A hit is when the person has the cell phone turned on but does not answer it."

Chapter 12/Tolv

INTERROGATION OF GUNNAR HAUGEN, AFTERNOON OF 1 YEAR AND 25 DAYS AFTER THE DAY, FRIDAY, JUNE 4

"Gunnar Haugen . . . I'm Constable Wangelin and this is Chief Inspector Sohlberg. We have some questions for you. Can you come to the conference room with us?"

"Am I under arrest?"

Sohlberg found the father's question astonishing if not incriminating. Sohlberg looked him in the eye and said:

"Should you be?"

A clearly shocked Gunnar Haugen instantly looked away. He paled and stared at the floor and said nothing more.

"Come this way Herr Haugen," said Sohlberg grimly.

Gunnar Haugen hesitated.

Sohlberg then did what he rarely did. He only used this tactic to impress upon people the seriousness of his investigation and the possibility if not probability of an arrest. Even long-time criminals did not like what Sohlberg was about to do in such a personal and invasive manner. Sohlberg put a forceful grip on Gunnar Haugen's forearm. The father's arm jerked involuntarily.

"Let's go Herr Haugen. Now."

"Yes," replied the engineer meekly as his co-workers

stared.

Sohlberg was pleased. Everything was going according to plan. It was time to move from keeping the investigation quiet to putting pressure on a group of suspects. He could have questioned Gunnar Haugen quietly and in private after work or had him called down to the Human Resources department. Instead the public scene of Gunnar Haugen being questioned at work by the police guaranteed that the father's co-workers would immediately call family and friends and that within an hour the media would issue reports about 'breaking developments' in the Karl Haugen case. The media frenzy would put intense pressure on Sohlberg's next best suspects—the mother and the stepmother.

Sohlberg's newest goal was to force the suspects to point the finger at each other. This tactic never failed with criminals and their accomplices. Of course the exception to the rule was the rare case of family members—or lovers—who had very tight bonds of love and trust.

"This way," said Constable Wangelin. She pointed to a hallway where the HR manager waited for them.

The HR manager escorted them to a windowless conference room and left. Wangelin took out a tape recorder and dictated the date and time and the identity of the persons in the room.

"Are we going to be here long?"

Sohlberg glared. "Do you have something more important Herr Haugen than answering questions about your missing son?"

"No . . . I was just wondering how long this will take. I have classes after work . . . down the street . . . on Nydalsveien."

"What classes?"

"I'm enrolled in the executive M.B.A. program of

the B.I. Norwegian School of Management."

"Oh really?" said Sohlberg as he took off his coat and sat down. "Well . . . to answer your question . . . I have no idea how long we're going to be here. I guess a lot depends on your cooperation and answers. Yes?"

"I . . . I don't know what you want from me. I've cooperated with everything that the police have asked of me."

Gunnar Haugen appeared to be worried. Sohlberg's initial strategy of surprise was working despite the likelihood that Karl's doctor had already called one or both of the parents.

A thought struck Sohlberg: if the doctor had indeed telephoned a warning then had the warning only gone to the stepmother and not to the father? After all the man's bewilderment had been obvious since first approached in his office by the inspector and constable.

Had the stepmother kept the warning to herself?

If that was the case then why did she not pass the warning on to her husband?.

"Herr Haugen . . . before we discuss whether you have actually cooperated with us let me first explain why I'm here since I noticed you did not bother asking me why we're here."

Gunnar Haugen said nothing. Instead he assumed the stoic look that everyone in Norway knew from watching Gunnar Haugen's image on television and newspapers and magazines.

"I have two assignments Herr Haugen. First . . . I'm here to make an arrest."

Haugen blinked nervously.

"Second . . . I'm here to make sure that we have more than enough evidence to convict."

"Wait," said Gunnar Haugen as if waking up from

an afternoon nap. "Where's Nilsen? I thought he was in charge of the case. He knows I cooperated."

"Nilsen is out. I'm in charge now. All I can tell you is that after carefully reviewing all of the case files . . . I don't see how you can claim that you've cooperated. Quite the opposite."

"Nilsen knows that we helped as much as we could."

"You helped yourselves . . . not your son. Anyway . . . as I was saying . . . I reviewed the case files and all of the interviews with you and your wife and I could only come to one conclusion. You and your wife bamboozled Nilsen with lies and half-truths."

Haugen stared at the table.

"Unfortunately for your son Chief Inspector Nilsen took everything you and your wife said at face value. He questioned nothing. Anyone who hears the interviews or reads the transcripts immediately realizes that you live in a fantasy world or are a lousy liar . . . or both. *Nothing* that you and your wife have ever said to the police makes any sense."

Sohlberg expected an indignant outburst or at the very least a protestation of innocence. He got neither from Haugen who remained wrapped in his silent stoic mantle.

"Why didn't you go into work on the Friday that your son disappeared?"

"Our daughter had been up all night crying. I felt too tired to put in an honest day's work."

"And yet you supposedly worked all day on your computer at home from eight in the morning until three in the afternoon."

Haugen said nothing.

"Whose idea was it for you to stay home that day?"

"I . . . I don't know. I guess both of us. My wife

needed me to stay with the baby while she took Karl to the science fair."

"Who packed Karl's lunch for that Friday?"

"I . . . I don't know."

"Who usually packed his lunch?"

"Well . . . it depends . . . some days I did . . . others day my wife."

"So you're a top up-and-coming manager at Nokia . . . and you're also going to Business School and yet you have the time to prepare his lunch?"

"I . . . well . . . yes. I have time to pack his lunch."

"Why doesn't your wife prepare his lunch all the time?"

Silence.

"Herr Haugen . . . your wife's unemployed. She has all the time in the world to pack his lunch. She seems to be in very good health. So . . . tell me . . . why doesn't your wife prepare Karl's lunch *all* the time."

"That's just the way it is."

"I see. We just have to take your word for it. Right?"

Silence.

"Can anyone corroborate your claim that you sometimes packed his lunch?"

"I. . . ."

Sohlberg took out a Polaroid picture of Karl's backpack. The picture was taken by the police at Frøken Bøe's room on the day of the disappearance. Sohlberg pointed at the picture and said, "Is this your son's backpack?"

"I think it is. Yes. . . . Maybe."

"I've looked inside that backpack . . . and guess what? There was no lunch in the backpack."

Silence.

"No lunch . . . that means only one thing Herr

Haugen. You or your wife or both of you never expected Karl to be around to eat his lunch at school. That's why one of you didn't pack his lunch. That was a major slip-up. Do you care to explain it?"

Silence.

Sohlberg noticed that Gunnar Haugen's right eye flickered wildly.

Was Gunnar Haugen trying to figure out what lie to tell about the missing lunch?

"There's another very odd thing that I found," said Sohlberg who switched topics to keep Gunnar Haugen off balance. "I read the transcript of your third interview and found something rather unusual."

Silence.

"You stated that your wife Agnes Haugen is a very good mother. Is that true?"

He nodded.

"Please answer me with words Herr Haugen. The tape recorder can't pick up your head nodding . . . so I guess for the record that means yes. Anyway . . . you told us that your wife taught Karl sign language at age six. Yes?"

"Yes."

"And yet Karl is not deaf . . . his doctor told us that he is a perfectly normal child from a medical and physical point of view."

"He is."

"So he's not deaf?'

"No."

"Then why would your wife teach him sign language?"

"I . . . well . . . you know . . . she's a teacher . . . she has a master's degree in education and a license to teach elementary school."

"But she's not licensed to teach deaf children . . . is she?"

"I . . . I don't know."

"She never taught sign language to Thor . . . her first son . . . did she?"

"I . . . I don't know."

"One last time Herr Haugen . . . why would your wife teach your son sign language when he's not deaf?"

Silence.

"Herr Haugen . . . did your wife teach sign language to Karl so that they could communicate in secret?"

Gunnar Haugen's eyes dimmed.

Sohlberg's throat tightened as he realized how out of touch this man was to the reality of his home life where his wife led a separate parallel existence.

"Herr Haugen! Look at me. Did your wife secretly and silently send your son instructions in sign language for him to leave the school that Friday June fourth?"

Sohlberg looked straight into Gunnar Haugen's eyes. But the engineer had shut down. His tightly closed eyes told Sohlberg and the world one message:

"Leave me alone!"

Wangelin and Sohlberg could literally see that the man was withdrawing to some distant place where no one could intrude.

"Herr Haugen," said Sohlberg. "You and your wife both told investigators that your son suffered from seizures and yet his doctor says that is not true and has never been true. So tell me . . . whose idea was it to create the fake illness about seizures?"

Silence.

"Whose idea was it to use a non-existent illness to confuse the teacher and the school about which Friday Karl would not be at school but on a doctor's visit?"

Silence.

"Constable Wangelin . . . please arrest Herr Haugen if he does not answer my questions."

The tinkling sound of Wangelin's handcuffs brought Gunnar Haugen back into the room.

"What? . . . What do you want to know?"

"Why did you sign that vague letter to the school telling them that your son would miss school on Friday because of a doctor's appointment and yet you did not date the letter . . . nor did you specify exactly which Friday he would be gone from school."

"Well . . . that's just the way it was written. I can't change the past."

"But you Herr Haugen are a senior high-level manager at a huge multinational corporation . . . *and* you are going to a major business school . . . surely a sharp up-and-coming executive like you doesn't write such vague communications . . . or is this what you do at Nokia . . . or learn at business school?"

"My wife typed the letter. I just signed it."

Sohlberg wanted to smile. The father had finally opened the door that offered him a way to implicate or blame Agnes Haugen in the disappearance of his son.

"Herr Haugen . . . it's incredible that you of all people signed such a vague note . . . a piece of nonsensical verbiage that resulted in so much confusion . . . thanks to that misleading note of yours the school was not able to react fast enough to your son's disappearance. Thanks to your note the search for *your* son was delayed by more than six hours. How do you think *that* will look before a court considering your conviction and sentence?"

Silence.

"You also made verbal statements to the teacher that made her think that your son Karl was visiting the doctor on Friday June four instead of Friday June eleven. Then you switched your dates and statements and told the school and our investigators that you had always told the teacher that Karl would be at the doctor on the *next* Friday . . . June eleven."

"I never spoke to the teacher before Friday June four. My wife handled all school matters for Karl."

Sohlberg stared at Gunnar Haugen. Sohlberg was elated that the father had taken another step to implicate or blame Agnes Haugen in a felony crime. But now the time had arrived to change topics before Haugen could carefully think about Sohlberg's questions and even more important Haugen's own answers.

"Herr Haugen . . . children repeat whatever they hear their parents say at home. They are little tape recordings. Wouldn't you agree Herr Haugen?"

"I don't know."

"You son repeated many interesting things at school about you and your wife. Did you know that?"

"He could've been repeating things he heard at his mother's home up in Namsos."

"So you do admit that children repeat what they hear at home."

"You're talking about a hypothetical . . . that Karl supposedly repeated what he might have heard at my house. So I offered you an alternative that's reasonable. Anyway . . . this is all theory."

"Actually it's not Herr Haugen. Your son yelled '*I hate you. I hate you.*' Now. . . where would he have heard that?"

"I . . . I don't know."

"But you do know Herr Haugen . . . you know but you just won't tell me the truth . . . that's part of your family's many secrets . . . right? . . . Never tell . . . just keep quiet and pretend to be happy . . . right?"

Silence. Sohlberg worried because he could again see Gunnar Haugen literally withdrawing from the room in mind and soul if not body. Sohlberg moved quickly to offer another door to Gunnar Haugen. This door offered Gunnar Haugen an excuse for kidnaping or harming his son. Sohlberg shrugged and said:

"Herr Haugen . . . I know how people live with deep horrible secrets . . . then one day they just can't go on and they go crazy and explode. You see . . . I know one of your secrets. . . ."

Silence.

"Your wife. I know all about her."

Haugen's eyes narrowed and then closed shut.

"I know all about her many many lies to trap you in a loveless marriage."

Silence.

"I know about her lying to you about being born to a wealthy family."

Silence.

"I know about her playing on your sympathy for those who are adopted like you."

Silence.

"I know about her playing on your feelings about being a single father who needed a care-giver for his son . . . and who better than an elementary school teacher?"

Silence.

"I know about her pretending to want a career in education only to turn down a good job offer teaching at a school because she instead preferred your offer of marriage . . . which meant she no longer had to work for a living. I also know that she lied to you about not being materialistic when she has a long track record of using men to get material possessions."

"I love my wife and she loves me."

Sohlberg wondered if the statement was part of Gunnar Haugen's natural instinct to deny the reality of his loveless marriage.

Was Gunnar Haugen's profession of love meant to protect Agnes Haugen? Or was it maybe meant to protect Gunnar Haugen by making his marriage appear to be that of a loving couple?

"Herr Haugen . . . what kind of woman tells lies about not being able to have children and then magically cranks out a baby that will keep you paying child support for a long long time if you get a divorce."

Silence.

"I know about your wife pretending that she wanted to be a stay-at-home wife when . . . in fact . . . she likes to party around with other men."

Silence.

"I know about the many men she has had sex with while you were here at Nokia working hard."

"I . . . I love my wife and she loves me," said a robot-like Gunnar Haugen.

"I know for a fact that your wife sent x-rated e-mails and nude pictures to one of your best high school friends who showed up to help search for your son."

Silence.

"I also know that she sent text messages to one of her men friends and offered to pay him half of your life insurance proceeds if he'd *erase* you out of the picture."

"She jokes around a lot."

"Why are you protecting this woman?" shouted Sohlberg who grew increasingly furious at Gunnar Haugen's refusal to cast suspicion on his wife. "Is she blackmailing you?"

"She loves me."

"She can't blackmail you any more because we just arrested your brother for molesting a teenage girl . . . he told us about your grandfather molesting him and you at the barn in his farm near Hov."

Sohlberg expected more silence and withdrawal. Instead he got an angry reaction from Gunnar Haugen who yelled:

"That never . . . never happened to me!"

"Why would your brother lie?" said Sohlberg who was amazed at how this man could live with so many painful secrets. "Why would a pedophile like your grandfather only molest your younger brother and leave you alone?"

Silence.

"Has your wife ever threatened to tell the police that you molested your son because your grandfather molested you and your brother?"

Silence.

"Is that your non-answer? . . . I've read one of her e-mails to one of her men friends . . . she wrote him that she was worried that you may've harmed Karl or kidnaped him because you probably molested Karl . . . she wrote that molestation victims tend to be molesters themselves."

Silence and a blank stare.

"What would you say was Karl's demeanor and behavior during the four weeks before he was kidnaped?"

"Normal."

"Really? . . . Normal? . . . That directly contradicts what you and your wife told the school and the teacher . . . you told them that Karl was acting strangely . . . staring into space . . . distracted . . . and even angry."

"I only repeated what my wife observed . . . she spent much more time with my son than I did. She was . . . *is* a professional . . . a school teacher trained to observe these problems."

Sohlberg looked as if he had just swallowed a spoonful of lutefisk. Just the thought of the traditional Norwegian dish made Sohlberg feel like retching. He hated the gelatinous cod fish cooked with caustic lye and lots of boiling.

"Herr Haugen . . . you're feeding me a lot of lies." Sohlberg studied Gunnar Haugen's stoic stone-face which meant that the engineer was either gullible in the extreme or a brilliant manipulator.

"I'm not lying to you. My wife carefully observed Karl. She knew what she was talking about when she said he was acting strange . . . having seizures."

Sohlberg shouted:

"Is she a doctor? How would she know if he was suffering from seizures? . . . Don't you know Herr Haugen . . . what your wife was doing behind your back when she went around telling people that Karl was acting strange?"

"No. What? You tell me!"

"She told everyone at the school and your gym club and all of her friends . . . and Karl's mother . . . that Karl had begun behaving oddly . . . . *weird* when he started the second grade . . . that he was distracted . . . that Karl was *staring off into space* . . . that was her favorite quote . . . that he seemed irritated or upset . . . she said all those were the typical symptoms of molestation."

"I. . . ."

"Don't you want to contradict the misleading lies and misinformation she's planting about you?"

"I love my wife and she loves me."

Sohlberg felt horrible about the amount of punishment he had dealt to Gunnar Haugen in the interview process. But Sohlberg had to get critical information out of the father. This was after all a cold case about a missing boy.

"Herr Haugen . . . we interviewed several people at the gym and they all told us that your wife complained about your coldness and lack of attention and the ugly ways that you criticized her weight gain after having your baby daughter."

"Not true. I never said a word about her weight. She's the one obsessed with her body and looks. She's the one who made me pay for her implants. She's the one who went overboard in training to become a champion bodybuilder."

"She says these were all your ideas."

Silence.

Haugen's silence puzzled Sohlberg. Usually by this point any other man would have begun spilling a flood of negative information about his wife and her involvement in a little boy's disappearance. But not Gunnar Haugen.

Sohlberg tried again. "She's told friends that you're a very controlling person . . . that you controlled her spending."

"Her spending? Whose money is she spending? Mine. She was out of control spending *all* of my money. Yes. . . I controlled her spending all of *my* money. I plead guilty to that charge. Does that finally make you happy Chief Inspector? Do you think that you're going to solve this case by dragging me through mud? All of this is nothing more than vile and idle gossip about some minor marital discord that we've had . . . *all* marriages have their ups and downs. But I was . . . I *am* happy in our marriage"

"Perhaps. But not all up-and-down marriages have missing children. Do they?"

Silence.

"You and Agnes always painted a pretty picture of

your happy marriage and home life to your friends and family . . . and later to us. This is the first I've heard of your marriage with ups and downs. All of your social media postings on Facebook and Biip and elsewhere paint the picture of your family being a perfectly happy *blended* family."

Gunnar Haugen coughed and was about to say something but he stopped himself.

"Herr Haugen! You claim you have a happy and stable marriage. But Agnes Haugen has sent dozens and dozens of e-mails and text messages to her family and friends about how she was fed up of taking care of Karl and that you refused to discipline him."

"Maybe she did go overboard with controlling Karl . . . but she does that with everyone else . . . if Karl did not bring a green slip or note from school *every* day then she wanted me to punish him by locking him up in his room for the evening without any play time. She often refused to let him watch television or any movies even after I said he could. There was no room for error."

Sohlberg felt sorry for Gunnar and Karl Haugen and anyone else who lived in a family with *no room for error*. A chill crept into Sohlberg's hands which no amount of rubbing could warm up.

"After the birth of our daughter eighteen months ago my wife grew even more impatient with everyone and everything . . . even with the baby."

"What about the baby?"

"She would get angry that our baby would wake up at all hours and not stop crying."

"What else?"

"My wife started bombarding Karl's mother and stepfather up in Namsos with several e-mails a day complaining about Karl and how difficult life was at our home with the baby . . . of course she did the same with Karl's teacher . . . sending her e-mails complaining almost every day about Karl and me and the baby . . . and even her first son Thor who never gave us any problems when he lived with us."

"Whose idea was it to kick Thor out of your house?"

"Not mine. I came back from a business trip to Helsinki and . . . boom! . . . I find out she sent Thor to live with her parents even though Thor and I were getting along very well."

"Would Thor agree with that statement?"

"Yes. Call him up right now. Anyway . . . I complained to her about her sudden and disruptive action but what can I do? . . . He's not my son. It was her idea to kick him out and send him to live with her parents . . . she was fed up with him not obeying her and talking back at her all the time. She and Thor . . . who's now fourteen . . . they got into awful fights . . . her postpartum depression led to her into big fights with Thor all the time . . . as all parents do with teenagers."

"Your son Karl went missing less than two weeks after Thor left your home."

"So? . . . That's just a coincidence."

"Really Herr Haugen . . . don't you tie the two events together? You don't think your wife did something to your son Karl in retaliation for you kicking her son Thor out of your home?"

"No."

Sohlberg glanced at Gunnar Haugen as if saying "Are you that naive or stupid?"

"Look Inspector . . . my wife has postpartum depression. That's the reality we've had to live with."

"What doctor diagnosed her with postpartum depression?"

"I . . . I don't think she mentioned . . . but it's common knowledge that many women get severely depressed after delivering their baby. She told me she has postpartum depression. Wouldn't she know best what she has?"

"She's not a doctor . . . is she?"

"No."

"On the other hand maybe she does know what's best if she's setting up an insanity defense."

"What? . . . Why would she want an insanity defense?"

"So she can walk away scot-free from whatever crimes she committed against your son."

"No!" said Gunnar Haugen who slumped into his seat.

"Herr Haugen . . . I need you to help us . . . the investigation uncovered irrefutable facts that point to you or your wife or both of you taking Karl that Friday."

"You have no grounds to say that."

"Oh . . . but I do . . . you have an unhappy marriage filled with resentments and betrayals."

Sohlberg was not surprised that Gunnar Haugen refused to admit that he had been spying on his wife's electronic communications. What surprised him profoundly was Gunnar Haugen's next statement.

"Inspector . . . you're making my marriage appear to be what it's not. We were managing our relationship and working through all our issues in a positive manner."

"Herr Haugen . . . you're just giving me a lot of phony corporate doubletalk . . . *managing the relationship . . . working through issues in a positive manner. . .* you do realize . . . I hope . . . that we're on the same planet . . . planet Earth. . . . We're talking about a deeply troubled marriage with infidelity and resentments and lies. We're not talking about some employee's performance review for the year."

"Sir! Everything was fine in our marriage until some sick perverted stranger took our little boy. Why aren't you out looking for that criminal?"

Sohlberg almost sneered when he noticed that Gunnar Haugen was returning to his stoic martyr look and possibly withdrawing or shutting down for good.

"Chief Inspector . . . why are you harassing me . . . saying all these ugly things about our good marriage?"

Sohlberg felt like jumping across the table and slapping Gunnar Haugen. But Sohlberg then realized with immense sadness that at some level Gunnar Haugen actually believed that he had a good marriage to Agnes Haugen and that his wife loved his son and that somehow everything would be alright if he repeated often enough the Big Business and Big Government mantra of *working through issues in a positive manner.*

"Herr Haugen . . . I'm saying all these ugly things about your so-called good marriage because I know that you've been spying on your wife . . . I know that *you* are very well aware of her many betrayals and deceptions. I . . . like you . . . know everything that she's been doing behind your back."

Sohlberg's phone buzzed. Before leaving the room he said, "Constable here will look after you and make sure you don't escape or injure yourself or try to call anyone."

The call from headquarters stunned Sohlberg. The police had found—at the remote farm of Gunnar Haugen's grandfather—a large barrel for the disposal of acid waste. Even more stunning was the discovery that Karl Haugen's lunch box had been buried under the barn. Fifteen minutes later Sohlberg walked into the conference room and said:

"Herr Haugen . . . stand up please so that we can handcuff you."

"Why?"

"You're under arrest for the kidnaping and murder of your son."

Chapter 13/Tretten

INVESTIGATION FOLLOW-UP,
EVENING OF 1 YEAR AND 25 DAYS
AFTER THE DAY, FRIDAY, JUNE 4

Two hours after delivering Gunnar Haugen into booking Constable Wangelin placed five hurried phone calls to verify her information before she walked into Sohlberg's office and announced:

"I confirmed from the lab that Agnes Haugen made several interesting phone calls. We need to discuss the calls. Also . . . Constable Rhode just called me. . . ."

"What about this Constable Rhode?"

"He was one of the first investigators at the scene of the crime on the day of Karl's disappearance. He's been on vacation . . . just got my message about whether he remembered anything unusual in the case . . . and did he ever."

"Great . . . give it to me."

"First he interviewed this cranky old coot who lives near the school."

"Where does he live?"

"At a dead end . . . where Orreveien ends in a circle. That location is less than a half mile from Karl's school. The old man hates people who come down his street to drink and party. So he writes down the day and time of the event and the make and color of the vehicle whenever he sees anyone parked on the dead end . . . and if he's able to he uses his binoculars . . . he looks through them and writes down as much of the license plates as he can see from his home."

"Very good . . . sounds promising."

"Sometimes he can see all the letters and numbers on the license plates or a little or nothing . . . based on how and where the cars are parked and the position of the sun and the shadows from the nearby trees."

"Very good. This is what we've needed to help solve this case."

"Listen to this . . . during the two week period before Karl disappeared . . . the old man twice saw a green Volvo SUV . . . the XC90 model . . . park at the dead end on Orreveien. The driver . . . a short pudgy woman with short curly light brown hair in her early forties got out of the car and went into the forest all alone for about twenty-five minutes. The old man was able to read the first two letters and numbers of the license plate . . . and. . . ."

"And?"

"And those partial plates match an Oslo vehicle that matches his description of the car. I looked up the owner's name and . . . lo and behold . . . Danica Knutsen turns out to be a bodybuilding friend of Agnes Haugen."

"So. . . ."

"It turns out that this Danica Knutsen has no reason for being on that dead end . . . she lives in Togrenda . . . a suburb off the E-Six Highway."

"Where about . . . more or less?"

"Fifteen miles south of where you live."

"So she does *not* even live close to Holmenkollen."

"That's right Chief Inspector . . . and she does *not* have any children at Karl's school."

"None?"

"None. She has no priors. Never married. But I did

find a newspaper article on her. . . . She sued a drug company a few years ago and won a substantial judgment in the United States against a California drug company because she can't have children . . . seems she fried both of her ovaries with all of the steroids that she took beginning in high school and kept taking until she turned forty.

"I did more research and found out that within a year of getting her lawsuit award she had spent all of it and fallen into debt . . . she then got a job as a secretary at a law firm but was fired a year later . . . also she's known for promoting organic farming."

"Anything else on her?"

"No. That's it for now."

"Find out more about her . . . find out exactly what she did the month before and the month after Karl Haugen disappeared. Find out . . . hour by hour . . . what she did and where she went on the day that Karl vanished."

"There's more I need to tell you about the old man."

"Go ahead."

"On the day that Karl disappeared he saw . . . from nine in the morning to nine-thirty . . . and from three-fifteen to three-thirty . . . a woman drive a large white vehicle into the dead end . . . his description of the vehicle matches the description of the Toyota pickup truck owned by Karl's father."

"Did he get the license plates?"

"No . . . the car was parked in such a way as to make it impossible for him to see the plates with his binoculars. He said it was almost as if the driver knew the old man was watching from his vantage point."

"Who did he see in the car . . . a man and a woman . . . was there a passenger . . . maybe a little boy?"

"He didn't see a child that afternoon but then again the child may've been too low inside the truck to be seen and the child could've come out the passenger side door which the old man could not see from his vantage point . . . the woman had long hair in a ponytail and she wore a cap and sunglasses . . . he again said it was almost as if the driver was doing everything possible to avoid being identified."

"You said he didn't see a child that afternoon . . . when did he next see the vehicle?"

"Are you ready for this Chief? . . . He saw the white pickup at two in the morning of the following day."

"What?"

"Yes. The same pickup parked at the dead end . . . the driver again left the engine running for almost half an hour . . . from two to about two-thirty that morning. Now . . . the interesting thing is that one of his neighbors . . . a young mother with a baby saw the same white pickup in the afternoon and again at two in the morning. That night she got a creepy feeling with the pickup truck being there again at two in the morning so she let her dogs loose . . . they went barking down the street . . . a few minutes later the pickup left in a hurry . . . speeding at over fifty miles-per-hour up the street."

"So the old man's not inventing this. Did the old man or young mother see the driver or any passengers the second time at two in the morning?"

"No Chief . . . the tree shadows fell right over that spot."

"Too bad. These two incidents at the dead end on Orreveien confirm our theory that the entire kidnaping was carefully planned down to the last detail."

"Did you notice something interesting Chief? . . . It's Agnes Haugen who drives her husband's pickup on the day Karl vanishes."

"I want this Danica Knutsen put under round-the-clock surveillance. The same goes for the stepmother Agnes Haugen. I want to know *exactly* what these two women are up to because they'll soon find out that Gunnar Haugen has been arrested in the kidnaping of his son. So please focus on putting together a minute-by-minute timeline showing the whereabouts of both women that day."

"I'll go and look at the binders. I think someone in the force interviewed Danica Knutsen because she repeatedly kept showing up at the Haugen home during the days after the kidnaping. Anything else?"

"No . . . but the timeline is urgent. Haugen will be out of jail in two days or less. We have forty-eight hours or less to prepare for our interrogation of Agnes Haugen and her friend Danica Knutsen. Get as many people as you need to help you. If you have to— "

"I know Chief . . . if I have to I'll work on it all night long."

"Thank you. Please call me anytime as soon as you finish. . . . even if that's at four in the morning."

"Are you sure?"

"Yes. I doubt if I'll be getting much sleep anyway . . . the case is always on mind."

Sohlberg spent the next two days at home. Fru Sohlberg knew better than to engage in any conversation with her husband. He spent most of his time reading binders on the case down at the guest cottage by the beach. Their conversations consisted mostly of him saying "Of course dear. . . ." and "Oh?"

A few months later Sohlberg found out that Fru Sohlberg had wisely cancelled her parents' visit because she knew that they'd probably feel ignored if not slightly insulted by her husband's mental and physical absence during the investigation.

Chapter 14/Fjorten

INTERROGATION OF AGNES HAUGEN,
MORNING OF 1 YEAR AND 28 DAYS
AFTER THE DAY, FRIDAY, JUNE 4

A media firestorm broke out during the two days
after the arrest of Gunnar Haugen. The headlines said it
all: IS IT MURDER? ARRESTED FATHER WILL NOT
SPEAK ON KARL HAUGEN CASE SAYS DEFENSE
LAWYER.

Most of the tram's passengers in the 7:15 AM
commute on Line 18 into downtown Oslo were reading
newspapers with the latest about the Karl Haugen case.
Those who were not reading about the arrest managed to
steal a glance at the man who got on the tram and walked
straight into a pole near the compartment's middle doors.
He bounced off the pole and kept on walking as if in a
trance.

"Drunk at this hour in the morning," said an elderly
woman loudly. "Imagine that at his age."

But the man was not drunk. It was Sohlberg lost in
thought and oblivious to his surroundings. He always got
that way at the end of every investigation when all the
loose ends had to be tied down and fully explained.
Sohlberg was legendary for his absent-mindedness when
thinking about how to wrap up an investigation.

One question after the other swirled in Sohlberg's
mind.

How much did Gunnar Haugen know about the facts leading to his son's kidnaping?

How much did the man know about the kidnaping itself?

Why did Karl's father refuse to make any statements against his wife Agnes Haugen with respect to the disappearance of his son?

Most other parents would have cooperated with the police when confronted with evidence that their spouse was likely to be involved in a crime against a stepchild. But not Gunnar Haugen.

Why didn't Gunnar Haugen implicate Agnes Haugen *after* he was arrested and given plenty of chances to finger her as the main suspect in his son's disappearance?

Did the father and stepmother act together in the boy's disappearance?

Was one of them perhaps an after-the-fact accessory?

Why did Gunnar Haugen have an acid disposal barrel that was more the right size for a large adult body than for a small child's body?

Sohlberg was jolted back into reality when the tram braked to a complete stop at the Jernbanetorget station near the Oslo Central Station. He meandered over to downtown Oslo's loveliest boulevard—the Karl Johans gate—and he sauntered over to its northern point. Tree leaves shimmered in the gentle end-of-summer sunlight. Strollers cast wary looks at the man with a pinched face and narrow eyes and an enormous flopping raincoat. His mind churned over the case facts. He tried to connect all the facts together to make sense of the kidnaping of Karl Haugen.

How could someone as smart and educated as Gunnar Haugen have made so many obvious and dumb mistakes in marrying and staying married to Agnes Haugen?

Sohlberg was surprised at the immense pity he felt for Gunnar Haugen. The man reminded him of so many others who mistakenly think that their education and their income and their titles and their success outside the home would render them immune to failure inside the home.

What wise man had once said, *No success outside the home can compensate for failure in the home*?

Sohlberg wondered if the man had instead perhaps said, *No other success can compensate for failure in the home*.

Regardless of the exact words the underlying thought bothered Sohlberg.

Had he been too quick to seek success at the expense of his first wife Karoline?

Sohlberg remembered the many evenings and nights and weekends and holidays that he had abandoned Karoline to stay working at the law firm. He also remembered how often he had also abandoned Emma and their now-dead son when he investigated crimes.

After bumping into a group of tourists Sohlberg looked up and was shocked to see the Royal Palace up on the hill. Sohlberg muttered a curse when he realized that he had missed his turn and was now far off course. Even more embarrassing he got lost in thought again and took several wrong turns as he tried to find his way back to the police offices at 12 Hammersborggata.

The increasingly agitated Sohlberg walked up and down the narrow and odd-angled and confusing streets for almost 30 minutes before someone kindly pointed him to the corner of Hammersborggata and Torggata.

As soon as he got out of the elevator the receptionist sent Sohlberg to Ivar Thorsen's office.

Commissioner Thorsen sat behind his desk smug and preening. He said in the most patronizing way possible:

"Sohlberg you've done good. An arrest so soon! Excellent. Excellent. I knew you'd pull the proverbial rabbit out of the old hat. Good job. Good job."

"Not so fast."

"What? . . . Oh you're always so . . . so . . . how shall I say it? . . . Nitpicky? . . . Crossing your t's and dotting your i's. Alright. Go ahead. You deserve it in this case. Besides . . . we'd like to get a rock solid conviction on the father."

"Look Thorsen . . . we may have found bottles of acid . . . and a large barrel to store acid waste at the barn . . . all plastered with Gunnar Haugen's fingerprints. But that doesn't prove by a long shot that Gunnar Haugen kidnaped or killed his own son. Why would he need such a large barrel for such a little boy?"

"Well. . . ."

"We also found from Nokia's records that several mysterious telephone calls were placed to and from Agnes Haugen's cell phone on the day of the boy's disappearance. The calls to and from her phone started at around twelve-thirty and ended at about one-thirty in the afternoon.

"Nokia traced the calls from pings on cell phone towers and their records show that all of the calls took place along Sørkedalsveien near Ring 3 . . . there's a bunch of stores and businesses down there in the Smestad neighborhood.

"Several calls were placed in or near a furniture store . . . Hus and Hage . . . where Gunnar and Agnes Haugen did a lot of shopping."

Thorsen scratched his head and then his groin and

said, "Aha . . . these calls would support the stepmother's afternoon alibi . . . that she was driving around in the afternoon trying to calm her baby down after she went to the gym."

"Maybe. Seems that way."

"Alright then. It's obvious that the father did it."

"I don't know that for sure. Look Thorsen . . . you need to let me *finish* the investigation . . . let me nitpick. Seems to me that the father only needed a barrel that was a quarter as large to dispose of Karl Haugen's little body.

"It looks more to me like he had plans to dispose of an *adult* body . . . but even if that's what he planned on doing you have to ask yourself . . . where's the body he wanted to put in the large barrel? . . . And even more important . . . where's Karl's body?"

"It's there Sohlberg. It's there. Sooner or later we'll find the boy's body. I have no doubts he's somewhere in that farm. Right now we've got forty-two police officers and crime scene investigators out there at the grandfather's farm. We've dug up the barn. We already found the boy's lunch pack . . . a key item that you noticed was missing from the boy's backpack. Really . . . what more do we need?"

"Anyone could have put the boy's lunch box out there . . . matter of fact we have cell phone records showing that the stepmother Agnes Haugen was there at the barn one month before the boy's disappearance. Seems she forgot to turn off her cell phone . . . it rang and sent a ping off a cell tower near the barn."

"Her husband could've gotten the call at the farm with her phone."

"Nope. At the time he was traveling on a long business trip with another Nokia manager."

Thorsen frowned. "Well then why in the world did

you arrest the father if you haven't finished the investigation?"

"Because the arrest is part of the investigation . . . the father's arrest will set off a chain reaction on the part of the other suspects . . . especially the stepmother . . . as I told Constable Wangelin . . . to get a cold case to full boil you need to turn up the heat and concentrate it where it'll get results."

"The arrest of the father is more like a blowtorch."

"You said I could use any means . . . do whatever it took to solve this case . . . right?"

"Yes. But be careful Sohlberg . . . because if you fail . . . you're on your own."

"I see that nothing has changed."

"Obviously not when I see that you're playing with fire *again* Sohlberg."

~ ~ ~

Constable Wangelin drove Sohlberg straight to the residence of Agnes and Gunnar Haugen on Ryghs vei. A short distance from the Haugen house Constable Wangelin stopped the car at the corner of Ankerveien and Ryghs vei to review one more time with Sohlberg the phone records of Agnes Haugen and the timeline for Agnes Haugen and Danica Knutsen on that fateful June fourth. They also went over reams of other information that Wangelin had mined from the massive amounts of material in the binders at the Karl Haugen room back at headquarters.

"One more thing Chief Inspector."

"What?"

"You asked me to look into Agnes Haugen's statement that she used her husband's pickup on June fourth because Karl's science project would not fit in her Audi sports car. I measured the car . . . and it turns out that his exhibit could have fit in the back with room to spare."

"How interesting," said Sohlberg slowly as his eyes got that misty far-away look that he was famous for when he was about to tackle and try to solve the most complicated aspects of a crime. "I think we're ready to pay Agnes Haugen a visit."

Secluded and surrounded by trees and pasture at the end of a long private driveway the massive Haugen home could just as easily have been in the middle of a remote rural area. Sohlberg noted that Karl's school was less that 2,500 feet northwest of the Haugen household.

Constable Wangelin pointed and said, "Ah look there she is. . . ."

Agnes Haugen sat on the grass in her bikini bottom and she read a celebrity magazine while sunbathing topless by the side of her enormous two-story home. Wangelin was sure that Sohlberg had not noticed the woman's exposed breasts so Wangelin scooted ahead of him and warned Agnes Haugen to put on her bikini top which came on the implanted Vesuviuses one second before Sohlberg came upon them.

Frowning Sohlberg said rather sternly:

"Fru Haugen . . . since we're not here for a picnic shall we move inside your house where we can all sit down in more formal surroundings?"

"Why of course. Whatever you say."

Sohlberg was not surprised that the expensive home was decorated with gaudy furniture and tasteless accessories which all shouted one thing: "Look at how rich we the Haugens are and you're not."

They sat on an oversize sofa covered with a faux

tiger-stripe fabric that was monumental in proportion and tackiness.

"I'm glad I'm meeting you at last Fru Haugen. I'm Chief Inspector Sohlberg and this is Constable Wangelin whom you've met before."

"Where's Nilsen? Isn't he in charge of the case anymore?"

"No. He's been permanently removed." Sohlberg was disappointed that her face showed no expression at that bit of news. "I'm in charge now and I've been assigned to bring this case to a close . . . to a final resolution. In other words to an arrest and a conviction . . . ending in a prison cell for the monster who took Karl Kaugen."

"Is that so?"

Sohlberg studied her demeanor and saw nothing but the fading looks of an unhappy 40-year old suburban housewife whose stone-cold poker face betrayed absolutely no worry or fear.

"Yes . . . I will arrest the shameless monster who killed Karl Haugen . . . that innocent little boy."

Sohlberg's last sentence sent a shadow of worry across her face.

Or was it anger?

Or sorrow?

If she had sorrow then for whom?

Sohlberg waited for the next move from Agnes Haugen. He desperately wanted to see if she would open the door he had just presented to her. If she went along with him and did not object to his stating that Karl Haugen had been killed then she was the culprit or she knew who had killed the boy.

"Did you say killed? . . . Is he dead?" Agnes Haugen spoke barely above a whisper. Then she got louder as she firmly rejected the trap offered by Sohlberg. "Did you find a body? . . . I can't believe he's dead. No. It can't be."

"Karl is dead."

"How . . . when?" Her stupendous blue eyes glistened with appropriate tears.

"We'll get to that later," said Sohlberg who was fuming and at the same time admiring the brilliant ease with which Agnes Haugen had cleverly evaded his first trap.

"How can this be?" said Agnes Haugen. "How can Karl be dead?"

Sohlberg offered Agnes Haugen his second trap. He invited her to open the door that would lead to her husband's conviction. He said:

"Fru Haugen . . . I'm here to gather evidence to convict your husband in the kidnaping and murder of his son . . . the minor Karl Haugen."

"You've already decided it's Gunnar?"

Agnes Haugen reminded him of a mouse sniffing the bait on the trap. Sniffing but not nibbling. "I don't decide anything Fru Haugen . . . the evidence decides for me."

"What's the evidence?"

Sohlberg almost smiled. He was surprised at her cleverness and boldness. Parry and thrust.

"That's not a matter for your consideration Fru Haugen . . . is it? . . . Unless of course you yourself have. . . ."

Sohlberg said nothing more. He threw a blank look at Agnes Haugen and then he set up his third trap—the silent treatment.

Seventeen very uncomfortable minutes passed by in complete silence. Sohlberg had used this silent treatment quite effectively over the years. More than 2/3rds of all homicide suspects had started talking to Sohlberg out of nervousness and guilt when he gave them the silent treatment. Talkative suspects soon progressed from small talk to asking questions or making comments and their questions or comments always led to damaging admissions or confessions of the full or partial variety.

Agnes Haugen fidgeted when minutes 18 and then 19 and 20 came and went by. She could stand it no longer and suddenly blurted out:

"Well . . . what's this all about? . . . What do you want?"

"Fru Haugen . . . don't you know what this is all about? . . . This is all about a little boy . . . your stepson. Remember him?"

"Of course."

"Then why ask me what this is all about? . . . Don't you know Fru Haugen that it's all about Karl Haugen and not about you? . . . Can you . . . for a minute . . . stop thinking about yourself? . . . Don't you see? . . .

"It's all about an innocent and defenseless boy who did not deserve to have his life cut so short. It's all about a little seven-year-old boy who became an inconvenience to his father and his mother and then to you the stepmother."

Agnes Haugen looked away but only to stare impassively out the window—as impassively as if Sohlberg had been boring her with a dull sales pitch for a new Electrolux vacuum cleaner.

Sohlberg's anger exploded. He even surprised himself when he yelled:

"Fru Haugen! . . . This case is all about a shy little boy who changed his science fair project to the red-eye tree frog just to please you."

"Wait just a minute . . . *both* my husband and I made that decision. It was not just to please me."

"That's not what your husband says." Sohlberg studied her reaction to his fourth trap—creating conflict between the spouses. "He says that you forced Karl to abandon his project on icebergs. The little boy loved icebergs and he wanted to report on them at the science fair. But you did not let him. Why would you do that Fru Haugen?"

Agnes Haugen sat poker-faced and said nothing to the seemingly trivial question that had been increasingly bothering Sohlberg for reasons that he could not describe.

"So Fru Haugen . . . please tell me . . . why did Karl switch his science exhibit from icebergs to red-eye tree frogs?"

Silence. He was impressed by her cunning intelligence. She had walked away from the fourth trap as quickly and cleverly as she had walked away from all his other traps. Sohlberg felt embarrassed at how easily she was defeating him. He decided to confront her with the evidence.

"Fru Haugen . . . please read the timeline that Constable Wangelin is handing you. It details on a minute-by-minute basis your whereabouts that Friday June fourth. Take your time reading it. Let me know if anything is wrong with the information. If you don't point out any errors then we will assume it's correct."

After ten minutes Agnes Haugen said, "It seems to be right."

"Good. Now if you will please look at the time when you say you left Karl at the school. You say you left him and the school at about nine in the morning . . . right?"

"Right."

"Then you drove around looking to buy medicines for your sick baby."

"Yes."

"After driving around and stopping at two stores you then drove back home."

"Yes."

"That's when you posted Karl's science fair pictures on Facebook."

"Yes."

"Then you picked up your sick baby and went with the sick baby to the gym from eleven-twenty to twelve-twenty."

"Yes."

"All this in your husband's white pickup truck?"

"Yes."

"Why?"

"Why what?"

Sohlberg again found himself almost smiling at the stepmother's crafty evasions. "Fru Haugen . . . why did you drive your husband's pickup when you have your own car . . . the red Audi sports car?"

"I don't know . . . I guess I like the pickup more for driving the baby around town."

"Even though the baby was sick?"

"I wanted to give my husband a break . . . he needed some time to do work from home on the computer. So I took the baby with me to the gym."

"Was that his idea?" said Sohlberg who again offered her the door to start incriminating her husband.

"I . . . I guess so."

She had opened the door. He wondered if she'd step in all the way through the proffered door. Sohlberg said almost casually:

"Was it his idea to *not* go into work that day . . . and stay at home?"

"I'm not his boss. He does whatever he wants when it comes to his work at Nokia."

"Speaking of his work at Nokia . . . I noticed that he travels quite a bit for them all over Europe and the United States."

"That's right."

"On one of those trips . . . a month before Karl disappeared . . . you took a call on your cell phone at a farm that belonged to your husband's grandfather."

Her eyes glazed over. He had finally caught her off balance. He could see her thinking and trying to stay one step ahead of him. She lapsed into silence.

"Fru Haugen. We know all about that call . . . a call that you did not answer but that your cell phone picked up when you were at the farm."

"I lend my phone out quite a lot."

"Oh really? . . . Who got your loaner cell phone on May third of last year?"

"I don't remember. . . I might have lent the phone to my husband's brother."

Sohlberg almost nodded but not in agreement but rather in amazement at how subtle she was in now trying to drag in her husband's brother into the short list of suspects.

"Your husband's brother?"

"Yes."

"The one who got arrested for molesting a teenage girl?"

"That one."

"The one who said his grandfather raped him and your husband in the barn?"

"Yes."

"But why would you lend him your phone when he has no real relationship with you . . . I understand he's only met you once or twice during the past five years."

"Gunnar's family are leeches . . . they want our

money . . . they smooch off of us all the time."

"You mean his family wants *his* money . . . don't you?"

"Well yes. I'm on unemployment."

"Let's see if I got this right . . . are you telling me that you lent your cell phone to your husband's brother?"

"Yes. I must have."

"And you're telling me that your brother-in-law was at his grandfather's farm when he got a call from one of your friends?"

"Yes. He must have."

"That's going to be rather difficult because your husband's brother was down in Copenhagen that week with his girlfriend and her family."

"He could've lent my phone to someone else."

"Like who?"

"I don't know. Ask my brother-in-law. Who knows what shady characters he lent my phone to. . . ."

"We have. He's never borrowed or used your phone or your husband's."

"Then I don't know what to tell you."

"How about the truth?"

"I've told you the truth."

"So you say. Tell me Fru Haugen . . . how is it that the neighbors happened to have seen your car in the farm on the day that your cell phone received that call?"

"My car?"

Agnes Haugen looked slightly confused.

Had she forgotten whose car she had driven up to the Haugen farm to plant the lunch box in the barn? Or was she merely pretending to be confused so as to force Sohlberg into revealing exactly which car the neighbors had seen at the Haugen farm?

"Yes," said Sohlberg. "Your car."

"I don't think so Detective. Not my car."

"Oh . . . did you think Fru Haugen that I was referring to your red Audi sports car? . . . No. I was referring to your husband's white pickup . . . which you drove to Grindbakken Skole . . . with Karl the day that he disappeared."

"I rarely drive that car."

"The neighbors at the farm saw you . . . a redhead with long hair . . . driving your husband's white pickup truck."

"My husband must have taken another woman up there with him."

"I doubt it."

"He's no saint."

"Are you Fru Haugen?"

"What are you implying?"

"I'm not implying anything. I'm letting you know the facts . . . the evidence . . . you drove the white pickup truck to the farm."

"Have you considered my husband?"

"Don't you worry if we're considering your husband. . . . Besides . . . we know that at the time he was traveling with another Nokia executive in rather distant locations. Now I'd like you to tell me why someone other than *you* would take *your* cell phone up to a farm owned by your husband's grandfather?"

"I don't know. . . ."

"Did you know Fru Haugen that several neighbors also remember seeing your red Audi sports car up there several times in the months of April and May of last year?"

"I lend my car out quite a lot."

"Who got your loaner car on May third of last year?"

"I don't remember. . . like I said . . . I lend my car

a lot."

Constable Wangelin threw Sohlberg a look that said, "You see! I told you that the Haugens make the unnatural seem normal."

"Fru Haugen . . . why would someone take your car up to a farm owned by your husband's grandfather?"

"I don't know. . . ."

Sohlberg leaned forward as if he was actually throwing her such a difficult curve ball that she would not be able to return his volley. He said:

"How did your stepson's lunch box wind up buried in the farm that once belonged to your husband's grandfather?"

Sohlberg would later write down in his final report to the prosecutor that a smile briefly crossed Agnes Haugen's face when he told her about the lunch box. During the interview however Sohlberg was not sure if she had indeed smiled.

After a long pause Agnes Haugen said:

"That's a good question."

Agnes Haugen's brilliant response left Sohlberg dumbfounded. He had rarely met a suspect who could make such unresponsive *and* evasive answers to his questions while at the same time leading him on to other suspects. Sohlberg fell back on his time-tested question of 'Why?'

"Fru Haugen . . . why is it a good question?"

Another long pause. "Because the farm is where my husband and his brother were raped by their grandfather."

Sohlberg let out a short and silent sigh. Agnes Haugen had finally opened the door to incriminating her husband. He asked as informally as he could:

"So . . . you think that the rapes are linked to your stepson's disappearance?"

"*You* could say so."

He admired her sly response. He offered her another door to further implicate her husband. "Actually . . . Fru Haugen . . . he was not their real grandfather . . . right?"

"Yes."

"Your husband and his brother were adopted . . . were they not . . . after being abandoned by their birth parents?"

"Yes."

"Abandoned . . . thrown away like garbage by the birth parents . . . and then abandoned a second time by their adoptive parents . . . who left them in the hands of the predator grandfather. Abandonment . . . that's life for the adopted."

"Yes . . . I know it first-hand because I too was adopted."

"So . . . Fru Haugen . . . do you think that your husband or his brother or both of them took and killed your stepson Karl because your husband and his brother were abandoned and molested?"

"*You* could say that. I couldn't."

"Why not?"

"I . . . I'm not qualified . . . am I? . . . I'm not a detective. I'm not a shrink. I studied to be a teacher . . . not a psychologist or a psychiatrist . . . or a detective like you."

Sohlberg's had never felt as frustrated by a suspect's answers. It was time to throw her another curve ball to keep her off balance. He shrugged and said:

"Fru Haugen . . . you are not trained as a psychologist . . . psychiatrist . . . or detective. But you are trained as a teacher. Is that why you taught Karl Haugen sign language?"

For the second time Sohlberg saw a dark and sharp

look of worry or anger cross the soft almost chubby peaches-and-cream complected face of Agnes Haugen.

Her silence triggered another Sohlberg inquiry. "Fru Haugen . . . why did you teach sign language to a boy who was not deaf or hearing impaired?"

"My husband and I thought it would be a good learning experience that would prepare Karl for school . . . and increase his learning capacity. Some parents have their children learn music at an early age for the same reasons. We just happened to pick sign language."

Sohlberg had finally caught her in a lie. Gunnar Haugen and everyone else had e-mails and other documents showing that Agnes Haugen was the only person who had decided to teach sign language to Karl. The lie would be useful in a prosecution. Therefore Sohlberg did not ask the follow-up question that he desperately wanted to ask Agnes Haugen as to whether she had in fact taught sign language to her stepson so that they could communicate in secret without anyone else knowing what she was telling the boy.

Sohlberg stared at Agnes Haugen. He switched his line of questioning back to the timeline to keep her off balance. "Fru Haugen . . . let's go back to the timeline for your whereabouts on June fourth. . . . Exactly where did you go from twelve-twenty when you left the gym to two o'clock when your husband saw you in the house after he came back from buying his lunch?"

"From twelve-twenty to two o'clock? . . . I'm sure that I was driving around . . . trying to get my baby to sleep."

The clever evasion irked Sohlberg. "You're *sure* you were driving around? . . . I need you to be more than sure."

"That's the best I can do."

Sohlberg wondered if she meant that was the best she could do as far as lying and misleading. The double meaning of her response was not lost on Sohlberg. He frowned and said:

"Fru Haugen . . . *where* did you drive around?"

"I don't remember. It was all a blur that day. I just drove around to calm down my baby daughter."

"Your husband says that he's never *ever* seen you driving around to calm the baby or get the baby to sleep."

"He doesn't know much . . . he's too busy . . . too wrapped up in his work to notice these things at home. He manages a large department at Nokia. . . . By the way . . . have you asked my husband where *he* was at that time?"

"We have . . . it turns out that *several* closed circuit cameras caught him not just buying his lunch that day but also driving to and from the store."

"I'm sure Detective that you will find plenty of video evidence that will show exactly where I was during those one-and-a-half hours if you work hard at it . . . and treat me just like my husband."

"Rest assured I will . . . but first you must tell me *where* you went around driving . . . did you go to downtown Oslo? . . . Or downtown Lillehammer? . . . Did you drive in the city or a small town . . . or into a rural area . . . maybe Lake Bogstad?"

"I don't remember."

"Maybe you drove north a couple of hundred miles to Trondheim?"

"I don't know."

"Or maybe you drove down south a couple of hundred miles towards Copenhagen?"

"I don't know."

"Or did you drive a couple of hundred miles out to Stockholm?"

"I don't know."

"Alright. But don't say that I didn't try to help you Fru Haugen."

"How? . . . How would you help me?"

"I gave you a chance . . . to give me the information that would send your husband to prison. But you decided to play coy with me. You thought I'd come running after your lies and half-truths if you dangled some small piece of information in front of me. Big mistake."

"Big nothing. . . . I saw that you Mister Big Detective had already made up your mind. There was nothing I could say. I know your type. You're the kind of man that makes people lie . . . you ask questions that you know will get lies for answers."

"You should've tried telling the truth for once Fru Haugen."

"I know men like you . . . you manipulate women with your questions . . . your innuendos."

"You have anything else to say?"

"No. Not to you. Ever."

"Fine. Stand up Fru Haugen. You are under arrest. Constable Wangelin . . . please handcuff her."

Three hours later at 12 Hammersborggata Chief Inspector Sohlberg and Constable Wangelin sat down in an interview room with a much more subdued Agnes Haugen.

Like most middle class suspects Agnes Haugen had been humbled if not humiliated by the fingerprinting and the mug shots and the obligatory strip search and the regulation jumpsuit. At Sohlberg's instructions the guards kept him informed of all of the abuse and insults and taunts and threats of hardened ex-con female prisoners who wanted a piece of the woman arrested for kidnaping the little boy Karl Haugen.

Sohlberg studied Agnes Haugen as gently and carefully as a man inspects a rattlesnake at close range.

"What do you want?" said Agnes Haugen with contempt. "I told you Mister Detective that I would never tell you anything about the case. Never. I want my lawyer."

"Fru Haugen . . . I'm not here to ask you questions or listen to you. You are here to listen and listen good to what I'm going to say."

"I want my lawyer."

"He's on his way. But first you will hear me out."

Agnes Haugen crossed her arms and hummed a ditty.

"Fru Haugen . . . you made several mistakes . . . mistakes that will defeat your ultimate plan of framing your husband for *your* criminal acts . . . which include the kidnaping and murder of Karl Haugen."

"You're a disgusting imbecile . . . a moron with a badge."

"Maybe. But *you* brilliantly planned the kidnaping and murder of that innocent little boy months if not years in advance. Your problem was choosing the wrong accomplice."

Chapter 15/Femten

INTERROGATION OF OLAV TVIET AND INTERROGATION OF DANICA KNUTSEN, AFTERNOON OF 1 YEAR AND 28 DAYS AFTER THE DAY, FRIDAY, JUNE 4

Everyone on the top floor of 12 Hammersborggata felt the frenzied activity that was typical of a major case drawing to a close. Sohlberg sent out five teams of two detectives each to gather evidence at the Haugen residence and at the school and at the condominium of Danica Knutsen. A harried and exhausted Wangelin coordinated the incoming and outgoing telephone calls and text messages. A secretary ordered sandwiches and beer.

"Ah . . . perfect," said Sohlberg as he picked up four egg salad sandwiches from a tray of gargantuan open-faced sandwiches that older Norwegians favor. "I miss these sandwiches. I can't think of many other countries where they make open-faced sandwiches. Aren't you having any?"

Wangelin smiled and shook her head. "I'm having a salad."

Sohlberg felt old and old-fashioned upon realizing that Wangelin and the younger detectives had ordered salad bowls from a nearby health food store. "I should've had a salad like you."

Sohlberg and Wangelin ate silently together in his cubicle office. He devoured his four sandwiches in less than 10 minutes but he did not touch the beer.

Wangelin twice started to say something but she immediately stopped herself. Sohlberg felt that she wanted to ask him why he never drank any alcohol—an oddity for a senior detective. Or perhaps she wanted to warn him of the increased risk of heart attack from his four egg salad sandwiches. Either way Sohlberg felt more than ever like the proverbial odd fish out of water in his own country. He looked forward to returning to America with Fru Sohlberg.

A few minutes after two o'clock Sohlberg and Wangelin took the elevator down to the third floor to interview 43-year-old Olav Tveit. The man had called headquarters the day before and insisted on speaking with the detective in charge of the Karl Haugen case.

Unlike other detectives who ignored or turned away potential witnesses Sohlberg was always accessible to talk with anyone who wanted to discuss a case with him. Of course this led to many bizarre interviews with unhinged citizens who claimed to be psychics or that aliens from outer space had committed certain crimes. Sohlberg had nevertheless gleaned many valuable tips and evidence from walk-in interviews.

The modestly dressed man shambled into the room with a defeated and sad air. He reminded Sohlberg of drastically diminished men who retain the smidgen of dignity that is just enough to avoid suicide or a murderous rampage. Wangelin made the obligatory introductions and legal statements after turning on the video and microphones.

"I'm here," said Olav Tveit, "because I should have told you . . . about some information . . . I had it a year ago when you people were investigating the Karl Haugen case. I don't know why I withheld it . . . I was unemployed . . . depressed . . . I wasn't thinking straight . . . I needed time to think about everything that had happened."

"What information?" said Sohlberg. He tried not to sound too excited about the proffered information.

"I dated Danica Knutsen for three years . . . we met at the gym . . . she used to be full of energy . . . she was mostly vegetarian and ran marathons and used to compete in iron-man contests with fifty miles of swimming and running and bicycling.

"She was smart . . . full of curiosity about the world . . . and very very honest. But about eighteen or maybe nineteen months ago . . . her personality completely changed after she lost her job as a receptionist at a downtown law firm.

"She bragged that she'd get a job in two weeks . . . of course that never happened. I mean . . . who over age forty finds a good job in today's economy? . . . After three weeks she went on unemployment . . . she grew obsessed over finding ways to get the most welfare benefits . . . she soon refused to leave her apartment . . . or look for a job . . . or keep her diet . . . or do any exercise."

Although Wangelin appeared bored Sohlberg certainly was not. The information fit perfectly with the background check on Danica Knutsen and the resulting psychological profile that Sohlberg had drawn up for the woman that he felt was the key to solving the case. Sohlberg nodded and said:

"Would it be fair to say that she was depressed?"

"Yes! . . . By all means. She started making poor decisions."

"Like what?" said Sohlberg who moved closer to the edge of his seat.

"She quit taking classes at a cooking school . . . she

was preparing for a new career. I joined the same school after I lost my reporter job in a round of layoffs at *Aftenposten* about the same time that she lost her job.

"We needed to get new careers that would pay decent salaries. I was stunned when she quit. I reminded her that the school guaranteed placement at a good job . . . I begged her to come back to school but she would not."

Sohlberg felt sympathy for the man before him. He wondered what he would do if he was unemployed and struggling to find a new career. A chill went down Sohlberg's spine—he realized that he could never work at anything other than as a police detective.

"Thank you Herr Tveit," said Sohlberg with genuine gratitude, "for sharing this information. . . . Every detail no matter how seemingly trivial is important. Anything else?"

"Danica seemed obsessed with living in extremes . . . she went from a strict vegetarian to round-the-clock overeating on ice cream and cakes. . . . She used to exercise all day long and spend a lot of time running marathons and then suddenly she does nothing all day long except sit in front of the television for weeks and weeks. . . . Or she'd get involved in projects that only wasted her time and energy . . . projects that would never help her find a new job or get a new career started.

"I lent her a lot of money that I badly needed myself . . . I asked her not to but she went ahead and she ran and got elected to the unpaid position of president at her condominium association where she wasted forty or more hours each week on stupid squabbles and trivial decisions. . . .

"She then decided she'd become an organic gardener even though she doesn't own any land and has no funds to rent or buy any land on which to grow organic produce.

. . . She refused to get any old job to pay me back my loans . . . instead she took this unpaid internship . . . it required her to work more than forty hours a week at an organic farm . . . the internship was basically unpaid slave labor at the organic farm."

"What organic farm?"

"Anabel's Organic Farm . . . owned by that restaurant chef who's on television . . . she writes all those organic food cookbooks . . . the farm's out near Lake Bogstad . . . just west of Holmenkollen."

Sohlberg nodded. The farm was less than two miles from Karl's school and it had come up in the background investigation that Sohlberg had ordered of Danica Knutsen. Earlier that day at five in the morning Sohlberg had dispatched a team of detectives and crime scene investigators and a canine unit to the organic farm to gather evidence and search for Karl's body.

"Did she mention anything else about the organic farm Herr Tveit?"

"Not really."

"What did she tell you about Agnes Haugen?"

"Well that's the strange thing. She never mentioned Agnes while we were together those three years . . . even though it now seems that those two are very very good friends according to what I've read in the newspapers . . . I was stunned when I read that Danica had literally moved in to live full-time at the Haugen residence for fifty-two days after Karl Haugen's disappearance."

"She never mentioned Agnes Haugen?. . . Think carefully before you answer."

Olav Tveit frowned and then said:

"Maybe once or twice after she first met Agnes Haugen at the gym . . . that was a month or so after Danica and I started dating."

"What did Frøken Knutsen say?"

"Just that she had met this redhead at the gym who worked out a lot and wanted to be a world champion bodybuilder. She also mentioned that Agnes Haugen had ridiculously large breast implants. We laughed about that quite a bit since a lot of the men at the gym used to ogle at Agnes working out in very tight t-shirts."

"Did they see each other socially outside of the gym?"

"No. At least not the first couple of years after they met. But they got much closer when Danica lost her job . . . that's when I noticed changes to Danica's personality and outlook . . . all of the sudden she hated men . . . men were controlling good-for-nothing abusers of women.

"Danica went around repeating whatever Agnes spouted . . . like saying that women should stick it to men and make sure men suffer for dominating women. I'm pretty sure that Agnes tried getting Danica to think she was a lesbian or bi-sexual or at the very least that she has lesbian tendencies that she needs to explore."

"Do you think that Agnes and Danica had an affair or physical relationship?"

"I . . . I . . . I'm not sure. I don't think so.

"I saw right through Agnes's brainwashing campaign. I warned Danica when I found out that Agnes had taken Danica to lesbian bars and left her with lesbian magazines and feminist books.

"I was amazed at how quickly Danica started repeating and believing a lot of poisonous garbage that Agnes planted inside her head. I think that Agnes Haugen played on Danica's insecurities and Danica's need to be loved unconditionally now that she started losing her athletic looks."

Sohlberg nodded and wondered when was the last

time that he had come across someone as manipulative and cunning as Agnes Haugen.

Olav Tveit shook his head and moaned. "Agnes Haugen destroyed my relationship with Danica."

"Why do you say that?"

"Because I was forced out of a very good relationship with Danica soon after Agnes got close to Danica. You see . . . we had even spoken of marriage. That became impossible when Danica told me she was not going to pay back my loan."

"Why not?"

"Because Agnes told her that I should've gotten the loan down in writing . . . and that since I did not do that then it meant that I intended to give her the money as a gift. In other words . . . I tricked Danica into believing it was a gift and that now I'd be able to force her to do whatever I wanted by claiming the gift was a loan."

"How much was it?"

"Six months of my old salary . . . I had saved so much over the years."

"I'm sorry to hear that. Do you want to file a criminal complaint against Frøken Knutsen for taking your money under false pretenses?"

"No. No. I still love her. I'd never do that."

"Then why did you come here?"

"To let you know that Danica would never ever harm a little boy like Karl Haugen . . . no matter what you think Danica did or might have done in the disappearance of Karl Haugen.

"You see . . . Danica Knutsen is smart but very gullible when it comes to other people manipulating her. She once had a boyfriend who made her buy him a motorcycle and tons of other things a few days before he left her for another woman.

"I just cannot emphasis strongly enough that Danica would never harm Karl Haugen."

"I appreciate you coming here to put in a good word for Frøken Knutsen."

"Are you going to charge her in the kidnaping of Karl Haugen?"

"It's too early to tell . . . but you helped put a lot into context."

A call came through to Wangelin's cell phone. She turned to Sohlberg and whispered in his ear:

"They just drove in . . . Danica Knutsen is down in the basement. They want to know if you want her brought up to interrogation room number one."

"Yes . . . put her in there." Sohlberg turned to Olav Tveit and made a short bow that showed the policeman's respect and appreciation for the informant. "Thank you so much for coming in Herr Tveit. We have to go now. I will see how I can help Danica Knutsen."

"I knew you would . . . I just knew it the minute I walked in and saw you . . . you're a good man."

~ ~ ~

Sohlberg and Wangelin turned down the hallway just as Danica Knutsen was ushered into a special interview room that Sohlberg had requested. The room had a one-way mirror that looked out into the hallway so that the police in the room could observe the reaction of witnesses and suspects inside the room to those witnesses or suspects who were made to walk past the room's window without the walking witness or suspect knowing that they were being seen from inside the interview room.

Constable Wangelin turned on the video and microphone and made the obligatory statements.

Frumpy and arrogant Danica Knutsen did not present a pleasant picture. She did not acknowledge Sohlberg when he walked into the claustrophobic room. He noticed that Danica Knutsen cast a lustful if not lewd look at Wangelin.

Sohlberg sat down and looked straight into Danica Knutsen's eyes and said:

"Frøken Knutsen . . . the game is over. We know what you did."

"What?"

"We know what you did. Let's start off with what you did three days ago when Gunnar Haugen got arrested."

"It was high time you arrested him. He's responsible you know."

Sohlberg kept a bored look that said, "I know everything there's to know about this case but I have to go through the motions and tell you this stuff because of police bureaucracy."

Danica Knutsen shook her head in disgust. "That monster Gunnar Haugen. He's done so many horrible things. . . . I'm glad you brought me here . . . I want to help as much as I can to put him in prison."

The interrogation was progressing far better than Sohlberg had hoped for in his wildest dreams. Danica Knutsen was opening doors as soon as he offered them. She was the opposite of the recalcitrant father and stepmother of Karl Haugen.

"What has Karl's father done that's so monstrous?" said Sohlberg. "What horrible things has he done?"

"Uhhh! . . . You name it," yelled Danica Knutsen. "He's verbally and physically abusive to Agnes. He ignored her and treated Karl as if he didn't exist. He's a controlling manipulative man."

Sohlberg noticed that even while Danica Knutsen cast aspersions on Karl's father she was sneaking appreciative glances at Constable Wangelin. He wondered how badly Agnes Haugen had lied to Danica Knutsen about the so-called *monstrous* behavior of Gunnar Haugen. He also wondered how Agnes Haugen had taken advantage of Danica Knutsen's obvious preference for women.

"Frøken Knutsen . . . please be more specific about the horrible things Gunnar Haugen has done . . . especially as to Karl's disappearance."

"For starters he's the one who made Karl switch his science fair project from icebergs to red-eye tree frogs . . . that's the kind of insensitive beast that he is."

"What else?"

"He's the one who suggested that Agnes drive his pickup truck that day . . . he's the one who insisted on staying home from work that day . . . he's the one who wanted Agnes to take Karl to the doctor on a Friday . . . he's the one who told Agnes not to pack Karl's lunch for that Friday . . . he's the one who asked Agnes to drive around town for the baby's medicines . . . he's the one who suggested she take the baby on a long drive to calm the baby down. . . . He planned everything that happened that Friday . . . don't you see?"

"No. Please explain."

"He did all of that just so he could stay home and spy on Agnes. He wanted to find out if men would come to the house if they saw that his pickup truck was gone and her red car was in the driveway."

"That's very clever of him," said Sohlberg who knew that the opposite had to be true because Danica Knutsen was merely repeating what Agnes Haugen wanted the world to believe about her husband. He admired the

intricate and cunning plan of Agnes Haugen to frame
Gunnar Haugen for his son's disappearance. "But . . .
Frøken Knutsen . . . I need you to explain one small
matter."

"What matter?"

"You say that Gunnar Haugen planned and carried
out a very complicated plan that would allow him to stay
at home and spy on his wife . . . yes?"

"Yes."

"Then when did Gunnar Haugen have time to
kidnap his son and make him disappear?"

"That was the diabolical brilliance of the plan . . .
Gunnar Haugen had his brother the pervert pick Karl up
at school so that he and the brother could molest Karl . .
. just the same way that their grandfather had molested
them as kids."

"But," said Sohlberg patiently, "Gunnar Haugen's
brother was not even near Oslo or Holmenkollen that
Friday."

"Oh he was . . . you just haven't looked into it."

"We have. That's why we know for a fact that
Gunnar's brother was working down south in
Kristiansand . . . that's over two hundred forty miles
away. We have several credible witnesses who saw him or
met with him that day between seven in the morning and
four in the afternoon."

"Hah! . . . Mister Detective you are so gullible.
These people are lying for him. These so-called *credible*
witnesses are friends of Gunnar and his brother. They're
all in cahoots. They're lying!"

"What about a bank's ATM camera . . . do they lie?
An ATM took a picture of Gunnar's brother getting cash
at seven-fifteen in the morning in downtown
Kristiansand."

"Bah. You are so gullible. But then again . . . you're a man . . . always controlling women."

Sohlberg pounded the desk and yelled:

"Frøken Knutsen . . . are you a parrot? . . . Why do you have to repeat everything Agnes Haugen tells you or puts inside your head? . . . Don't you understand that you're going to go to prison for a long long time?"

"Why?"

"Because you did her bidding . . . you obeyed her orders . . . you believed her lies. Don't you understand that Agnes Haugen used you to help kidnap and murder the boy *and* frame her husband? . . . Are you really that gullible?"

Sohlberg noticed that for the first time in her interactions with the police Danica Knutsen grew somber. He was glad that the seriousness of her situation was starting to dawn on her. He felt sorry for the naive woman. But he still had to deliver the first of two punches designed to knock down Danica Knutsen's relationship with Agnes Haugen.

"Frøken Knutsen. How many cell phones do you have?"

"One. Why do you want to know?"

"Because I just caught you in a lie. Three days ago we followed you after you received a telephone call from Agnes Haugen. We know where you went. We know what you did."

"What?"

Sohlberg moved closer to observe her ever-widening eyes. "Our detectives saw you throw away a disposable prepaid cell phone at a garbage can next to a restaurant near your home. We of course retrieved the phone and downloaded all of the incoming and outgoing telephone numbers and text messages. And guess what?"

"What?" said Danica Knutsen as she visibly shrank away from Sohlberg.

"All your calls and text messages in and out of that phone went to another prepaid disposable cell phone owned by . . . Agnes Haugen."

Danica Knutsen moaned.

"Our detectives," said Sohlberg loudly as he got closer to her, "followed Agnes Haugen after she called you three days ago . . . and just like in your case they saw her throw away her cell phone . . . in a dumpster by a bus stop . . . and just like in your case they also retrieved the phone."

A pale green color shaded Danica Knutsen's face.

"Now Frøken Knutsen . . . why would two women . . . in the middle of an investigation into the kidnaping of a child . . . happen to buy and use two cell phones in addition to their own cell phones?"

"We needed our privacy . . . Agnes told me the police were listening in on her phone after Karl disappeared."

"Really?"

"Agnes also told me her husband was spying on her . . . and trying to frame her for Karl's disappearance."

"That's rather interesting since you and Agnes Haugen bought and used the prepaid cell phones more than ten months *before* Karl disappeared. The police were not involved back then."

"You're right. But that evil controlling twerp of her husband kept tabs on her all the time. . . . Agnes told me that he was listening in on all of her calls because he ordered her to only use the cell phone that Nokia had given him to test."

"Actually Frøken Knutsen no judge is going to buy that pathetic lie as an excuse for your secret telephone relationship with Agnes Haugen. The court will see that your secret telephone calls months *before* Karl Haugen disappeared are part and parcel of your conspiracy with Agnes Haugen to kidnap and murder the little boy."

"No!" shouted Danica Knutsen. She squirmed in her seat and pulled her short wavy brown hair with both hands.

"We know what you did that fateful June fourth."

"No," she said with a whimper.

"You went to do your internship work at Anabel's Organic Farm . . . but you conveniently vanished in the afternoon from twelve-twenty to one forty-five and then you—"

"No! . . . No. No. No. I never left."

"Oh yes Frøken Knutsen. Your boss and her assistant have submitted sworn statements declaring that you got a phone call at fifteen minutes past twelve and that you then took off with no explanation and that they looked for you all over the farm but never found you."

"I was there."

"That's another lie Frøken Knutsen. Your boss and her assistant walked all over the grounds looking for you . . . they went to the main house and saw that your car was gone from the parking lot and driveway."

"I . . . I . . . had to get lunch. I was feeling faint."

"Where did you *get* lunch?"

"There's a little vegetarian restaurant . . . I don't remember the name right now. I paid cash."

"Vegetarian? How can that be? . . . You quit eating healthy foods after you lost your job. Your friends and your ex-boyfriend and your boss and her assistant have all declared that they only saw you eating junk food since last year."

"They're mistaken."

"No Frøken Knutsen. They're not mistaken."

"Then I don't know what more I can tell you. I have nothing more to say."

"Actually . . . Frøken Knutsen . . . I don't need you to tell me anything more since *you* obviously want to take the blame for the kidnaping and murder of Karl Haugen."

"What are you talking about?"

Sohlberg took a calculated risk. He wanted to get an immediate reaction from her. So he presented his theory of her conduct that day as a set of proven and known facts. "Don't you understand Frøken Knutsen? You set up the perfect alibi for Agnes Haugen when you took her call at twelve-fifteen . . . you then abandoned your internship job the organic farm so that you could meet Agnes Haugen nearby . . . you took her cell phone and drove down to Smestad . . . you drove up and down Sørkedalsveien near Ring 3 so you could take and place calls on *her* cell phone from twelve-twenty to one forty-five in the afternoon."

"How ridiculous."

Sohlberg nodded at Wangelin who sent a text message from her cell phone. A minute later Agnes Haugen walked down the hallway past the one-way mirror.

"Do you see her?" said Sohlberg laying down the trap with a bait of truth. "Agnes Haugen will testify that *you* kidnaped and killed Karl Haugen because *you* have a lesbian obsession with her."

A deep moan rumbled from the horror-stricken Danica Knutsen. She shrieked and cried and shook uncontrollably.

Sohlberg knew the symptoms of suspects electrocuted by the truth. He shrugged and said:

"Constable Wangelin will you please take Frøken

Knutsen downstairs for booking . . . give her a moment to compose herself so she can be fingerprinted and photographed and then taken to be charged before a judge—"

"No! I would never harm little Karl. Never! Never! Never! Agnes told me to drive up and down Sørkedalsveien and use her cell phone so she could go spy on her husband and see what he was doing to Karl."

"It'll be your word against hers."

"You may think I'm really stupid . . . but you see . . . I decided to prove where I was at the time because Agnes acted really weird that day . . . Agnes looked so freaking happy . . . something just wasn't right about what she was asking me to do. So I bought a snack on the way down to Smestad and I bought gasoline on the way back to the organic farm."

"Where?"

"At the Shell Seven-Eleven store . . . at the corner of Stasjonveien and Hollmenkollveien. I have the receipts. I had no cash so I paid for both with my father's debit card."

"Frøken Knutsen . . . are you willing to testify against Agnes Haugen?"

"Yes! . . . I won't let Agnes get away with it. She won't make a fool out of me. I can't believe how easily she tricked me."

"You're not the only one Frøken Knutsen."

~ ~ ~

Sohlberg met with Thorsen and Gunnar Haugen and Haugen's lawyer upstairs at Thorsen's office. Sohlberg stood by the doorway and he waited for Thorsen to take full credit for solving the case and he did not have to wait long.

"Thank you for coming," said Commissioner Thorsen. "This case has been one of the most difficult ones in my career but I decided to throw everything at it . . . to fully dedicate myself completely to finding the criminal who took your son. . . ."

Sohlberg was not surprised when Thorsen went on to summarize the case by reading straight out of the executive summary that Sohlberg had written in his final report to Thorsen.

"Agnes Haugen meticulously planned and rehearsed and executed the kidnaping and murder of Karl Haugen for the sole purpose of tormenting her husband and then framing him for her own criminal conduct.

"We know from eyewitnesses and phone and text and e-mail records that she rehearsed every phase of the kidnaping and the murder. For example we have three credible eyewitnesses who saw Agnes Haugen park her husband's white pickup truck several times at the dead end of Orreveien in the days leading up to the kidnaping on June fourth.

"We know from circumstantial evidence . . . and from credible eyewitnesses or from forensic evidence the following facts and circumstances . . . that she used sign language to order the little boy to meet her in the school's parking lot right after the science fair ended at 9 A.M.

"We also know that she drove Karl to the dead end at Orreveien and then strangled or smothered him in the forest where she had lured him with the promise of studying more frogs before going to the doctor's appointment. . . . And we know that she hid Karl's body near the pond in a temporary grave.

"We know from eyewitnesses and circumstantial evidence that Agnes Haugen returned that same day in the afternoon to the dead end at Orreveien where she was seen parking her husband's white pickup truck . . . she walked into the forest that afternoon from about twelve thirty to one thirty. We also know that at the same time Danica Knutsen . . . having been duped by Agnes Haugen . . . used Agnes Haugen's cell phone so as to create an electronic alibi for Agnes Haugen.

"Agnes Haugen claimed that she spent most of the morning and early afternoon driving around town to pick up medicines and to calm down her sick baby daughter. Her claim was a half-truth that she used to cause confusion around the fact that she brazenly returned to the pond that afternoon so she could move Karl Haugen's body to his permanent grave.

"Using previously gathered bark and twigs and leaves Agnes Haugen did a superb job in expertly hiding the boy's body in the cracked trunk of a fir tree. The crack begins almost three feet above the ground and it measures four feet in length . . . and one foot across . . . with a depth of almost two feet. No one could see the crack.

"Cadaver dogs and canine tracking units were not brought out to sniff the area around the pond because huge areas were already being searched at the time . . . areas where Agnes Haugen sent investigators and search-and-rescue teams on wild goosechases as a result of her false and misleading statements to investigators that her stepson might have gone exploring in those areas when in fact the boy was afraid of being alone or in the woods. She also claimed that the boy may have left school thinking that he'd perhaps meet with his father and explore the woods but the factual record conclusively shows that Gunnar Haugen never had time to go on excursions with his son."

Gunnar Haugen cast his eyes down in shame and

regret.

Thorsen cleared his throat and continued reading out of Sohlberg's report. "Insects and wild animals and the elements destroyed any evidence that may have been on or in or near Karl Haugen's body. The exact cause of death will probably never be determined because of the extreme decomposition of the boy's small body after more than one year in the forest. The forensic team will probably find more bones. The forensic team has already collected one of Karl's front teeth and a small bone chip probably from his shoulder bone from inside the tree trunk."

Gunnar Haugen raised his hand and said, "How did you know that my son was in that tree?"

Commissioner Thorsen blushed. "I . . . I . . . I'll let *my* assistant Chief Inspector Sohlberg answer. . . ."

"Well," said Sohlbergh, "from the very beginning I was bothered by the fact that Agnes Haugen forced Karl to study the red-eye tree frog for his science fair project. Why should she care so much about his science fair exhibition?

"I was always curious as to why she forced him to study frogs when he only liked to study icebergs. I was even more curious about the frogs when I observed that *everything* that Agnes Haugen ever said or did was for one purpose only . . . to benefit her . . . and usually at someone else's expense."

"That's the truth," said Gunnar Haugen barely above a whisper.

"I also got interested in the area around the pond after I discovered that we had already interviewed a witness . . . an old man . . . who had seen some strange comings and goings by a white pickup truck that matched the one owned by you Herr Haugen. That's when I decided to focus on that area . . . especially after a Google satellite map search by Constable Wangelin revealed that there was a small pond on Dag Svendsen's property."

"Dag? . . . Who?" said a devastated Gunnar Haugen.

"He's a lonely old man who lives where Orreveien becomes a dead end . . . he saw your wife park your pickup truck there for half an hour at nine in the morning right after the science fair and later that afternoon . . . from about twelve thirty to one forty-five.

"I went to visit Herr Svendsen the day after we arrested you Herr Haugen. I spent two hours with the old man. We spoke about everything under the sun and that long talk turned out to be critical. He informed me that the pond is surrounded by a lot of trees that have split or cracked trunks. Herr Svendsen made the off-hand comment that children like to hide in the '*kid caves*' . . . as he calls the hollow trunks. That's when I got the idea that your son's body was probably hidden in one of those trees near the dead end."

"Isn't the dead end at Orreveien near the school?" asked Gunnar Haugen's lawyer.

"Yes," said Sohlberg. "That's where Agnes murdered and hid Karl . . . less than a quarter mile from the school."

"She's a sneaky one," observed Thorsen. "She hid everything so well."

"Yes," said Sohlberg. "That's typical of the most brilliant criminals . . . they operate right under our noses. That's what makes them so hard to identify and catch."

"That woman," said Gunnar Haugen in a weak pitiful voice. "She destroyed me!"

"That might be Herr Haugen," said Sohlberg with his eyes solemn and mournful. "Just don't forget . . . a man can be destroyed but not defeated."

Gunnar Haugen nodded. But he didn't seem to really

understand what Sohlberg was telling him. Haugen was a broken man. The lawyer asked more questions.

Sohlberg took a few steps back and left the room. He looked forward to spending the evening with Fru Sohlberg. He was grateful that he had a loving home to go to that evening because Sohlberg knew that no amount of money or success could buy a happy marriage or a loyal spouse.

"I'm done . . . finished," said Sohlberg to his wife on the cell phone as soon as he left the ground floor lobby of 12 Hammersborggata.

He walked out into the street with a spring to his step. The burden of the little boy's sad life and death lifted temporarily off his shoulders. Of course the burden would return from time to time and weigh Sohlberg down. The dead always came back to him. He remembered all of the homicide victims whose cases he had worked on. Even if strangers to Sohlberg the dead and gone visited him in the labyrinths of his mind.

"Solve the case?"

"Yes. It's time to go home and leave Norway."

EPILOGUE: HOMEWARD BOUND

Karl Haugen heard barking. A puppy ran up to him. He played and kissed the dog which licked his cheeks. Karl felt much more happy than he had in a long long time. He suddenly realized that his father and mother wanted him to stay where he was playing with the dog.

A man and a woman who seemed kind and familiar came up to him and said:

"Karl . . . are you ready to go back home?"

He looked at the endless beautiful fields of incredible sun-drenched flowers and he laughed when his puppy ran off to play in the distance. He finally had the puppy that he had wanted for so long.

Karl ran after the puppy and finally entered the Eternal Sunshine of the Spotless Mind of God.

THE AUTHOR

Jens Amundsen is the pen name of an attorney whose literary anonymity protects him and his clients from the powers that be.

THE PUBLISHER

Nynorsk Forlag stays true to its roots as an independent publisher bringing the best of Nordic crime novels to the public. From its humble beginnings as an underground press, the company intentionally remains small so as to stay focused on its authors and readers.

[*sample chapter*]

WHITE DEATH IN TROMSØ: AN INSPECTOR
HAROLD SOHLBERG MYSTERY
by
JENS AMUNDSEN

Published simultaneously in the USA and Norway.

ABOUT THE BOOK

Chief Inspector Sohlberg investigates a mass grave near Tromsø, the most northern city of Norway, just 1,242 miles from the North Pole. He uncovers more than nine murdered victims in a suspenseful investigation that involves the ultimate threat to Western civilization.

Ch. 1/Én

MORNING OF THE DAY,
TUESDAY, JULY 6

Only 1242 miles separate Tromsø from the North Pole. The same amount of miles separate Alaska's Prudhoe Bay from the North Pole. Tromsø however is much warmer and more hospitable to human life than Prudhoe Bay thanks to the Gulf Current which brings warm waters to Norway all the way from the sunny hot climes of Florida and the Caribbean. But geography like the stars is not at fault for human events.

"I've never seen so many bodies," said Constable Lars Rasch of the Troms politidistrikt. He did not exaggerate. Rasch had never even seen one single homicide victim during his five years as a policeman in the northernmost city of Norway. He stared at the row of frozen bodies buried in the permafrost.

"Look like sardines in a can . . . don't they Rasch?"

The constable said nothing. Instead he looked in disgust at Per Moen the owner of the fish shack that had become the tomb for nine corpses. Rasch turned his gaze upon the sea. The morning's storm had washed the sky and the ocean and the islands in depressing shades of gray that seemed to merge into one mournful salute to the dead.

"Hey Rasch . . . how soon can you move the stiffs out? . . . I need to have a place to store my stock out here.

It'll cost me a fortune if I have to move my inventory elsewhere. . . . I imagine I'll be compensated for my building getting torn apart to get these popsicles out of here . . . no?"

Rasch grunted. He had always heard and now knew for a fact that Moen was a man obsessed by one thing only—the bottom line.

"Look . . . we'll discuss this later."

"No. Now. Let's talk now. I don't want your people ripping up my land digging up stiffs. I swear I'll sue the police if you don't put everything back to the way it used to be. This might just ruin my fishing operations if you keep blocking me from access to my land and fish shack and dock.

"Rasch . . . don't you understand?

"I need this shack to keep my fish cold in the permafrost below . . . I can't afford refrigeration. My great-grandfather found this spot . . . and now you're going to ruin me! . . . I swear I'll sue for millions and get you fired if I'm not allowed back in tomorrow."

"Do whatever you need to do. But right now you need to leave this crime scene."

"Hey Rasch you little jerk . . . ever since you joined the police you've been acting like you're a real big man in town. I remember when you went to school with my little brother and he used to beat the daylights out of you."

"Are you leaving or not?"

"Alright . . . alright. Save the tough guy looks for someone else."

Rasch sighed as soon as he was alone. He knew that he too would soon have to leave the area that he had cordoned off in police tape. Forensics promised him they'd be over to start processing the shack within the hour. He wanted to but decided against ripping up the rest of the wood floor planks that he and Moen had pulled up.

One of the corpses caught Rasch's attention. A large white towel covered a barefoot man. The blood-soaked frozen-stiff towel read:

WELCOME TO TROMSØ!

Constable Rasch could not help thinking that Tromsø had turned out not to have been all that hospitable or welcoming to the nine bodies that he had found shot point-blank in the back of the head and buried quite unceremoniously under Moen's fish shack in a remote location on the island of Reinøya.

"Let's see," said Rasch to himself, "if I can get the old city slicker out here."

The constable took out his cell phone and dialed his boss who was at headquarters just 30 miles south of him. While Rasch dialed he noticed what appeared to be a square booklet next to one of the bodies.

~ ~ ~

"What . . . nine bodies?" said Chief Inspector Fredrik Waldemar Hvoslef of the Troms politidistrikt. "Shot in the head? . . . Are you sure?"

"Yes," said Constable Rasch while he stared at the nine corpses. "All of the bodies have one hole in the back of the head . . . and big exit wounds in the front or the top of their heads."

"Arrange for the autopsies . . . call in forensic services to help you."

"I already did. Aren't you coming?"

"I . . . I can't," said Chief Inspector Hvoslef. He did not like leaving his comfortable and warm offices at 122 Grønnegata in downtown Tromsø. Nor did he want to travel on a small boat to the crime scene because he easily got seasick. In fact Hvoslef a transplant from Oslo rarely left the small island of Tromsøya where most of the city was located.

"You can't?"

Hvoslef could almost hear the contempt on the other side of the telephone call. The constable seemed to ignore the fact that Tromsø sits 186 miles *north* of the Arctic Circle. In Hvoslef's mind this cruel geographical fact meant that he faced imminent death year-round if he left the city limits to venture into the Arctic wastelands. Even during the summer months Chief Inspector Hvoself felt threatened by the vast empty wilderness that surrounded him.

"Sir . . . I think you need to come out here. I found a passport and an Interpol badge next to one of the bodies."

"What?"

"The pictures on the badge and passport match the dead man's face perfectly."

"Where's the passport from?"

"Russia."

Chief Inspector Hvoslef realized that he'd have to venture out of his warm safety zone. He absolutely hated the outdoors with a passion especially in the Arctic police district that he had been assigned to three years ago. He was obsessed with the idea of his freezing to death in the Land of White Death. But he had no choice.

"Sir? . . . Can you hear me?"

"Yes! . . . I'll be over there."

~ ~ ~

"I told you not to get involved."

"It's done. Besides . . . I had to. What do you think?

. . . That I could just walk away?"

"Yes."

"That's not me."

"Since when are you . . . a poaching thief . . . such a moral and upstanding citizen?"

"Enough."

"You steal cod and halibut and salmon . . . other men's catch for a living. I told you to stay away from Moen's place. He's always suspected you."

"Stop."

"This will bring us trouble. Big trouble."

"Enough."

"They will find out it was you."

He looked out to the sea and scanned the horizon. His blue eyes burned with Viking vigor. "No one will find us."

"They will find us."

"Enough."

"You'll see . . . you can't stop this. I can't believe you got us into such a mess. This is not good. We're in big big trouble."

He shook his head and started planning how to ambush and kill anyone who landed on his island.

~ ~ ~

Seasickness tormented Chief Inspector Hvoslef. Nausea continued to plague him even two hours after he had landed on the northwest shores of the island of Reinøya.

Constable Rasch leaned over and said, "Are you okay?"

Without any conviction Hvoslef nodded and weakly said, "Yes."

The austere cliff-scraped landscape and the odd-shaped mountains and the thin and sporadic green plants and brush served as grim reminders to Hvoslef that this was indeed the Land of White Death and that he must return to town as soon as possible. Nearby clumps of spindly Downy Birch seemed ominous if not cruel hoaxes in comparison to the lush Scandinavian forests that grew south of the Arctic Circle. Shrieking seagulls added a dirge that promised death or madness.

Hvoslef's discomfort increased even more when he saw Leif Jørgensen the Third approach him.

"Chief Inspector," said the 68-year-old doctor, "what have we here?"

"Nine dead men. Shot execution-style in the back of the head."

Hvoslef went on to give the doctor a brief summary of the investigation thus far. He intensely disliked the medical examiner who had an imperial air of intellectual superiority.

Except for Hvoslef everyone in Tromsø felt that Jørgensen's arrogance was well-earned because the doctor was the third generation of Leif Jørgensens MDs who had served as highly-respected medical examiners of Troms County.

Hvoslef eyed the balding doctor and his angular bird-like features and giant beak of a nose and loathed him even more. This third version of Leif Jørgensens had also worked for decades as a professor of forensic pathology at the University of Tromsø's School of Medicine *and* at the University Hospital of North Norway and despite suicide being the leading cause of death in Troms County the good doctor like his father and grandfather always checked off the box marked ACCIDENT instead of the box marked SUICIDE for the sake of the surviving family and friends and the dead one's memory and that's why Troms natives adored the LeifJørgensens especially for the Jørgensens never having left Tromsø for Oslo as did most other educated or wealthy people in the forlorn land peopled with melancholy.

"Well now," declared Jørgensen, "I guess it's time to find out what really happened to these folks."

Hvoslef's face reddened at the stinging slight implied in the comment—that Jørgensen the medical doctor and medico-legal expert—and not Hvoslef the police detective—would discover what had really transpired at the crime scene. Hvoslef decided it was time to cut the doctor down a little. "Herr doktor . . . it's rather obvious that each of these nine men have been murdered with a gunshot wound to the head. Isn't it now?"

"No it's not obvious. . . . I won't know the cause of death until I fully examine the bodies. They may have other wounds somewhere in their bodies. . . . Those wounds may or may not be fatal . . . and those wounds may or may not be pre-existing to the cranial wounds. I won't know *that* until their clothes are removed and I determine the exact cause of death. Also . . . all or some of these individuals may have drowned or been poisoned first."

"Why would anyone shoot these nine men in the head if they were already dead?"

"Nine men? . . . You're wrong on that count Hvoslef . . . one of your nine men is a woman. The third from the right."

Waves of anger and nausea rolled inside Hvoslef. He almost threw up and he later wished that he had done so on the doctor's expensive and elegant clothes. "I think . . . I'm going to. . . ."

"What? . . . What are you going to do?"

Hvoslef's rage worsened with the sickening thought that he was forever stuck with the only expert in Tromsø and Troms County who was authorized to render forensic or medico-legal opinions on a person's cause of death by The Norwegian Commission of Forensic Medicine.

Soon after arriving at Tromsø to assume his new position Hvoslef had tried to fire Jørgensen and replace him with a younger and more pliable and less experienced candidate. The ploy failed. Under Norway's Criminal Procedure Act only the Commission of Forensic Medicine could choose the person who would testify as a forensic expert in criminal proceedings. The Commission was also the only government agency in charge of authorizing who could perform autopsies and write autopsy reports which had to be filed with the Commission.

"Hvoslef are you sick? . . . You're absolutely green. Let me get my stethoscope and bag."

~ ~ ~

Later that day the man came back to his cabin by the fjord. He dropped his enormous frame into the squealing sofa.

"The cops are out there in force . . . dozens and dozens of them . . . plus a bunch of scientist types in white smocks. They've got five big boats . . . and two helicopters."

"Did they see you?"

"Yes and no. I took the boat towards Ringvassøy . . . pretended I was fishing . . . I used the old binoculars."

"I hope you didn't go back into Hansnes."

"No," he lied.

"Someone in that stinking town is bound to put two

and two together."

"Bah. They're idiots."

"They have nothing else to do but gossip and spy on everyone."

"They won't."

"Who are you kidding? . . . They knew we were a couple long before your wife knew and she used to keep very close tabs on you."

He said nothing. No one ever won an argument with her. She was ten years older and acted too often like his boss. But she was smart and willing to live the hard outdoors life of the woman of a fisherman and a poacher and a thief and she ran his businesses well and exhausted him in the sack. He grunted and got up.

"Where are you going?"

He left the cabin and despite her harridan screams he felt very sure about himself and his decisions. He disappeared into the brush that surrounded the cabin and he checked the well-concealed tripwires that protected their rustic home. The nylon wires were tight and ready to trigger the deadly and silent missiles that would shoot out of the handmade crossbows that he had built several years ago for such an eventuality.

"Come back here! . . . You need to clean the boat's sump. I told you to clean it last week."

He gently picked up one of the crossbows and aimed it at her direction. She was standing by the front door—clueless to his aim. He wondered what she'd do if the steel-tipped bolt thudded deep into the wall next to her.

What if I instead shoot her in the head by accident with my crossbow?

Anything could happen out here in the wilderness. Anything.

5604059R00162

Printed in Great Britain
by Amazon.co.uk, Ltd.,
Marston Gate.